CW00381236

Sifting Sand

Caroline Meech

Sifting Sand

Copyright © 2018 Caroline Meech
All rights reserved.

Caroline Meech asserts the moral right to be identified as the author of this work.

This novel is entirely a work of fiction. The names, characters and incidents portrayed in it are the work of the author's imagination. Any resemblance to actual persons, living or dead, events or localities is entirely coincidental.

No parts of this publication may be reproduced, stored in a retrieval system, or transmitted in any form or by any means, electronic, mechanical, photocopying, recording, or otherwise, without the prior written permission of the copyright owner.

Cover Image by Jodi Davies
www.jodidaviesphotography.co.uk

For Mike,

and our Meechlets.

PART ONE
2002

CHAPTER ONE

*T*he evening had begun unremarkably enough. Summer was coming to an easy end; the evenings were still light, and the inevitable chill was yet to creep in. As Cara walked to her best friend's house, the sun radiated across her blushing cheeks. She enjoyed the moment. Finally, she was settled, she had what she'd always craved; a flat in her home town overlooking the historic village square with her boyfriend of three years and a steady, if uneventful and mostly boring, job. As she ambled along, her Nokia phone rang in her pocket. She answered it quickly.

"Hi Babe!" Her boyfriend's gruff voice sounded on the other end of the line.

"I won't be back tonight."

"OK!" she replied breezily. This wasn't a surprise, he often stayed at his brother's house on a Friday night. "Don't worry, I'm staying with Vix anyway."

"Alright then. See ya."

As usual, he didn't seem bothered and rang off before Cara could tell him she loved him. She was used to it, she often told herself he wasn't a great conversationalist, especially on the phone. Like most men, she assumed.

Vix's parents had lived in the beautiful medieval cottage not far from her own flat for the past 40 years. Cara would visit at least once a week for a catch up and a cup of tea, not out of obligation, but love and gratitude. The early evening sun shone through the leaves of the old oak tree and caught the highlights in Cara's hair as she passed. She crossed the quiet lane and with the smile firmly fixed on her face she lifted the cast iron knocker, Maggie yanked open the door and threw her arms wide and planted a sloppy kiss on her cheek before she had the chance to let it fall. Giggling, Cara was pulled inside.

"Victoria!" Shouted Maggie over her shoulder, "Someone here to see you!" Her attention turned back to Cara. "Where's your key you daft 'apeth? Forget your head if it wasn't screwed on, you would!"

Cara pulled off her jacket and hung it on the banister of the aged staircase, she kicked off her shoes and tucked them under the green Edwardian chair that had stood in the hallway for as long as she could remember.

"Drink love?" asked Maggie, "I've got a jug of Pimms on the go if I can tempt you?" She smiled a mischievous smile. She loved these girls, their youth, their hope for the future. She'd never been lucky enough to have another child, but Cara was more than she could have wished for as a sister for Victoria.

"Oh yes please Maggs, you know me so well!" Cara laughed as she ran up the stairs and headed towards Vix's room.

Victoria Margaret Ballantine was sat on her bedroom floor in front of her full-length mirror looking no different to the way she had when she was 16. She was surrounded by the paraphernalia she used to put her face on which included moisturiser, foundation, powder, bronzer, various eye shadows covering the entire spectrum, eyeliner, mascara, an eyebrow pencil and 14 lipsticks. What she didn't appreciate was the fact that she was naturally the most striking beauty. With her blemish free, almond coloured skin, round but perfectly formed cheeks, full lips and large chestnut eyes she didn't need an ounce of make-up and even though Cara repeatedly told her how beautiful she was but Vix just didn't believe it. The make-up ritual took 45 minutes every day, at least once a day, twice if she were going 'out out' in the evening; coupled with the straightening of her beautiful naturally wavy, dark auburn hair that tumbled over her shoulders it could then take another half an hour. What Cara couldn't understand is why Vix was making all this effort for a night in with her. She bent down to kiss her best friend on the cheek.

"Hello Vix, bit much for me isn't it?"

"Oh Car, it's the sun! It makes me want to dance! I know we said we'd have a girlie night in but I really, really want to go out. Say you don't mind, please!"

"Hey, I'm easy you know that, but I'm not sure I can wear this!" Cara waved her best jazz hands to demonstrate her less-than-glamorous outfit of grey jogging bottom and oversized pink T-shirt.

"Ah well now, it's a good job I got your birthday present early then isn't it!"

Vix spun around on the floor and jumped up.

Hugging her best friend on the way, she grabbed a bag from her rumpled bed, took out a beautifully hand wrapped package and handed it to Cara "I love you Car, you're the best sister a girl could have and as I don't get to see you much, now that you're loved up, I thought we should make the most of tonight."

"Thanks Vix! You shouldn't have," Cara was taken aback, she grinned widely, "... but I'm glad you did!"

She sat on the bed and admired the hand printed paper, running her hand across the purple filigree pattern. She knew Vix had made it herself, she always did. Not only was she beautiful and kind, she was creative too. She removed the ribbon slowly, enjoying the moment whilst Vix watched eagerly, clapping her hands like a five-year-old, she hoped Cara would love what she'd chosen for her.

Cara peeled back the paper to reveal a rich, crimson red fabric. She sat for a moment, her fingers lightly touching the material. Slowly, she held up the dress that had been so beautifully wrapped. It was the dress she'd admired in a copy of a glossy magazine last month, she couldn't believe it. Not only had Vix bought her the dress of her dreams, but she had got the right size and the right colour.

She threw her arms around her friend and hugged her tightly, "Thank you, thank you, thank you, thank you!" she screamed.

"Well put it on then." Vix chuckled.

She did as she was told, peeling off her joggers and squeezing her size 12 curves into the dress. Vix had always been the slimmer of the two of them, but she had always been envious of Cara's voluptuous figure and praised it at every opportunity.

Cara stood back to admire her reflection. She pulled her shoulder length strawberry blonde hair out of the messy ponytail she'd tied earlier and ran her hands through it, loosening her fine locks. The dress hugged in all the right places, she smoothed the vibrant red fabric across her hips and admired how it accentuated her ample, yet pert, bust. Turning on her tip toes, she noticed how the colour made her hazel eyes shine brighter than normal. Maggie knocked and poked her head around the door.

"Oh Cara, you look incredible, stunning! Quick take these glasses before I spill them." She passed the champagne flutes, full to the brim with Pimms and strawberries, to each of the girls. "There's something missing though, wait there!"

She ran out of the bedroom leaving Cara and Vix to exchange glances. They were used to Maggie's eccentricities and her random taste in jewellery and were unanimously dreading what ghastly set of baubles she was going suggest Cara wear when she burst back into the room with a crisp black, if slightly dusty, shoe box.

"Open it Cara, they'll go perfectly."

She took the box looking quizzically at Vix who in turn rolled her eyes and laughed as she wondered what monstrosity her Mum was forcing on her best friend. Cara opened the box and pulled back the tissue paper, when she saw what was inside, she threw her hand to her mouth.

"What?!" gasped Vix, "What's in there? How hideous are they exactly?" She grabbed the box from Cara and pulled the shoes out. "Louboutin's!!!! Mother! You own a pair of Christian Louboutin's! When have you worn these exactly? Oh my God! I can't believe I've inherited Dad's enormous feet! They're amazing!"

"Your Dad bought them for me a couple of years ago, he said I needed *Bedroom Shoes*," explained Maggie innocently, "I have no idea what he was talking about. The only shoes I need for the bedroom are slippers, these would ruin the oak floors!" Cara and Vix looked at each other and doubled up with laughter. "I tried them on but they're just too high for me. I'd rather someone get some use out of them, and that lovely red sole matches your dress exactly. Put them on love, give us the full picture."

Cara did as she was told, admiring the soft leather and blemish free soles, she slipped on the classic black heels and felt instantly sexier. The dress had half done the job, but with the shoes she felt complete.

"Wow, thanks Maggie! Are you sure? Do you know how much you could get for these on eBay?"

"Can't see the point in that, I don't need the money and to be honest I'd much rather you have them, you look so lovely." Maggie gave Cara a maternal peck on the cheek, "If you girls hurry up and get ready, I'll give you a lift into town."

Cara grabbed some mascara from Vix's sea of make-up and covered her lashes. "So, what's Harry doing tonight?"

Vix asked, not bothering to hide the disdain in her voice.

"Staying at his brother's, as per usual I expect. He knows I'll not be back anyway."

Vix rolled her eyes. She hated Harry, always had done. In her eyes, he wasn't good enough for Cara, a 'player' some would say. But Cara? She couldn't see it. No matter how many times Vix had tried to start the conversation, she was having none of it so her only choice was to hope the rumours were wrong.

"Phew, at least we won't get a rollicking for disturbing a legendary *Boys' Night*," she said sarcastically, "if he's not out we can't bump into him! Grab your bag, let's go."

Vix grabbed Cara by the hand and full of anticipation for a night full of dancing they made their way to their awaiting carriage.

The girls had managed to find a prime seat on the balcony overlooking the whole of the downstairs in the Orange Rooms, the liveliest bar in Southampton. Initially Cara felt a little self-conscious, it wasn't every day she went out in designer clothes but Vix had just returned to the table with their third cocktail and now she was almost past caring. As time ticked by Cara felt, and looked, more comfortable. The sweetness and warmth of the Strawberry Daquiri's did their job and soon the girls were chattering and giggling at the in-jokes they shared.

"He called it WHAT?" Cara exclaimed, tears streaming down her cheeks.

Vix shrieked, doubling over in her chair, she'd been telling Cara about her most recent dalliance with an older man she'd met at work when, from the corner of her eye, she spotted a familiar figure through the glass balustrade working his way through the crowd below. Her giggles subsided, a more serious expression unable to hold itself back. Reacting quickly, Cara turned to see what had caught her friend's attention. That familiar figure was none other than her boyfriend Harry.

"Oh look! He must've changed his plans." Cara commented innocently.

She stood and rose her hand to wave at her boyfriend, but it hesitated at mid-height when a second figure came into view; petite, stick thin and very much female. Harry was shoving his way through the crowds towards the front of the bar, one hand above his head waving a twenty-pound note, the other leading the girl behind him.

Leo had been in The Orange Rooms for an hour or two before Cara arrived. He and Keiran had ventured there straight from work and although he wasn't a big drinker, he enjoyed the atmosphere and the people watching. The lads had settled themselves into their regular cosy corner on one side of the balcony, from there they had a perfect view of the bar area and dancefloor below and the rest of the balcony on their level.

He couldn't help but notice Cara the minute she entered the bar. He'd been busily engrossed in conversation with Keiran about local DJs when she'd caught his eye, he continued to feign interest as Keiran rattled on and didn't let on that he'd seen her. His heart thumped in his chest and his hands became clammy as he drank in the image of her. This was a different Cara from the one he knew at work. At work she was quiet, slightly conservative in her dress sense, a little awkward even. Her hair was always tied back, and she wore a pair of black rimmed glasses that gave her the look of a mousy librarian – a look he had grown to have a bit of a soft spot for.

They'd struck up a casual friendship following Cara's numerous trips past his desk when answering the calls of their over-demanding boss. It had started with a roll of the eyes, then a smile and had slowly moved on to grabbing the odd coffee together with Keiran who'd known Cara since working on a project with her, it had never felt wrong or over familiar. He liked Cara, she was funny, kind and attractive in an unassuming way. They shared the same sense of humour, the same interests, and crucially, a mutual disdain for their boss.

Despite the flutter he felt whenever she smiled at him, Leo had never acted upon his feelings. As far as he was concerned, Cara was off-limits. She lived with a boyfriend she talked endlessly about and although he often had the inkling that Harry was taking her for a ride, he didn't want to interfere. It was the little things she threw into conversation that set alarm bells ringing for him such as Harry's second work phone that he was glued to every evening and his work trips that often took in a Friday night and saw Harry arriving home on the Saturday morning 'utterly exhausted and needing to sleep it off'. But he figured it wasn't his place to say anything. At least it hadn't been. Now, however, that reluctance to interfere subsided.

Leo had kept a discreet eye on Cara and her friend from the moment they'd sat down. He didn't want to be seen because he was fascinated by this other version of Cara. The thought of seeing her like this, without her seeing him excited him. Momentarily he had her all to himself; her shape, her smile, her laughter; his senses went into overload, her picture ingrained upon his memory forever.

The scene played out in front of him. As Cara stood to wave, he too looked down on the bar area below. A man he knew only from half-smiling photographs was doing his best to make himself the centre of attention. Leo's eyes flicked quickly between Cara and Harry, it wasn't hard to interpret the situation. Harry was enjoying making a show of himself and the girl he was with. Between shouting his order to the barman and shouting to his friends, who'd lagged behind certain in the knowledge that Harry would want to show off his wealth to his fling, he kissed the girl exaggeratedly with his eyes wide open. As his eyes flicked from the most beautiful woman in the room to her loser of a boyfriend, Leo realised just how much he really, *really* liked her.

He watched how, with complete composure, Cara took in the scene in front of her. Her boyfriend had walked into the bar with another girl, surrounded by a group of friends and had kissed her in full view of everyone. Clearly this girl was not someone he had just picked up, she was someone his friends knew, someone he wasn't scared of parading around town. As Cara surveyed the scene in the bar below, Leo noticed her expressions changing from happiness, to shock, to curiosity, to realisation and, finally, to acceptance.

Strange, he thought, he didn't notice anger. Leo would have at least expected Cara to have been upset to see her boyfriend canoodling with another beautiful woman, but she handled what she saw with absolute grace. Of course, this played in Leo's favour. He was already imagining their first date together. He'd take her to a First Class restaurant, have wine waiting on the table, he'd hold the door ajar and as she entered he'd put his hand in the small of her back, proudly telling the world *she's with me.*

Leo chose to sit back and watch for the rest of the evening. He wasn't going to let on to Keiran what he'd seen, he was still rattling on in Leo's right ear about where to go next and who would be playing. Leo found himself agreeing with Keiran without really hearing what he was saying. For now, he was entirely consumed with thoughts of Cara.

That was the moment it all fell into place. The late-night texts, the hushed phone calls taken in another room, the names of new friends used regularly in conversation. She hadn't wanted to admit it to herself, ignored it for as long as she could. She'd only ever wanted to meet someone and start a family, and she'd thought Harry was the one. But now, seeing him here in a new light, she realised, she had no idea who he was. His face, his posture, his clothes were familiar, but he didn't feel like a man she was head over heels in love with. She looked at Vix who stared back at her with wide eyes, not knowing what to say, then back at Harry. Shouldn't she be feeling something? Anger, hate? In fact, all she felt was relief.

The next morning Cara lay in the bath fully submerged, with the exception of her face, the water around her encouraging goosebumps. Her mind swam, as did her stomach. Although it wasn't so much the remainder of the previous evening's sambuca threatening to climb back up her throat that made her nauseous, more the thought of the impending argument. Above her, rain drummed against the skylight that was long overdue a clean, the grey skies beyond stared back at her, unrelenting. Harry thumped the door. She jumped but didn't respond. He tried the handle.

"What's going on Car? Let me in. Why have you locked the door?" He rattled the handle but Cara ignored him. "Hurry up, I need a piss." He shouted as he thumped the door again. "Stupid cow." she heard him mutter as he walked away.

She wondered why she hadn't noticed the way Harry

15

spoke to her before. She laughed to herself. She could have drowned in the bath, he didn't know any different, but as usual he thought only of himself. She lifted herself out of the tub and pulled the towel that had been warming on the towel rail around her shivering body. She couldn't hold back the overwhelming urge in her stomach and lifted the toilet lid as the bile rose in her throat.

Relieved that she'd kept her hair in a top knot, she wiped her mouth and stared at her reflection in the bathroom mirror. She remembered how in love her parents had been, that was what she craved. Not this. No more, she decided. Harry didn't deserve her. Pulling on her robe, she opened the door, Harry scuttled back along the hallway, holding himself like a desperate child. Cara stood in the doorway, purposefully blocking his way.

"Get out the way then." Harry huffed. Cara didn't move. Harry hopped from one foot to the other. "Urghhhh, what's wrong with you? Move!" He shouted, simultaneously pushing Cara to one side. She stood, her back against the door frame and watched. "Oi! Get lost, will you? What are you watching me for?" Harry asked, suddenly feeling self-conscious.

She laughed and headed towards the bedroom where she dragged a suitcase out from under the bed. She unzipped the lid and began throwing in items of underwear from the chest of drawers they shared.

"Going somewhere?" Harry asked as he returned to the bedroom and climbed back in to bed, rubbing his head. He eyed Cara suspiciously as she opened up the wardrobe. She unhooked a shirt from a hanger, folded it and put it in the case, followed by another, then another. "Hey!" Harry sat up, "they're mine!"

Cara smiled. "Yes, they are." she said as casually as she could muster, fighting the urge to scream in his face, "I just thought I'd give you a head start with your packing." Harry looked puzzled. "I messaged your girlfriend when you were asleep, she's expecting you at around 10, so you'd better get a move on."

His eye's widened. "Wha..? Bu....?"

"Oh, don't bother Harry. I saw you last night and to be honest I've got a bit of a headache." Grabbing an armful of clothes from the rail, she heaved them onto the open case. "I'll leave the rest to you, shall I?" Harry didn't even attempt to argue, which was a relief, he just sat there looking pathetic. "Excellent." Cara looked at her watch. "You've got just over an hour."

CHAPTER TWO

"Morning. Penny for them?" Leo leaned over the edge of Cara's desk partition, his dark curly hair flopping over his right eye. He'd been watching her for the past few seconds while she stared blankly at her screen.

"Oh. Hi Leo, sorry I was miles away. Bit of a weekend, ya know?" She replied.

"I do actually. "Leo said "Come on, I'll treat you to a coffee."

Cara felt drawn to Leo, it didn't even occur to her to turn down his offer. He had a relaxed way about him that made her feel comfortable, perhaps it was his Italian heritage that gave him that demeanour. She smiled wearily, pulled herself out of her chair and found herself at his side, heading towards the coffee lounge. Their arms touched, and they looked at each other. Leo smiled, Cara found herself blushing.

"Where's Keiran?" She asked, masking her feelings.

"In a meeting." Leo breezed. Cara felt her heartbeat quicken.

It didn't take long to satisfy their orders and within a few minutes the two of them were sat at the farthest table of the canteen by a window overlooking the duck pond outside. It had been beautifully adorned with an upturned rusty shopping trolley for as long as anyone could remember. With her hands seeking comfort in the warmth of the eco-friendly cardboard coffee cup, Cara smiled thankfully at Leo.

"I appreciate this Leo, I've not had the best of weekends." She raised her eyes with a sad smile.

"I was there." Leo said gently "I saw everything. Are you alright?" His hand reached across the table and touched the back of hers.

"Sorry?" she felt suddenly uncomfortable and a little confused, "What? Where were you? You saw...what exactly?" Panic rose within her.

Leo snatched his hand back self-consciously. "In the bar. I saw, who I can only assume is supposed to be your boyfriend, with his hands all over someone else. I'm sorry you had to see that, you don't deserve to be treated that way."

She blushed and sunk back into her chair. Being humiliated in front of Vix she could deal with but *other* people? She hadn't seen him that night. In fact, after the spectacle she'd witnessed, she and Vix had proceeded to get exceedingly drunk and the night ended with them both dancing on a table in a club before stumbling out of a cab and landing on the pavement in a heap. She winced at the hazy memory. She suddenly felt embarrassed and vulnerable.

"What? Where were you then? I don't remember seeing you out." Cara replied in a *trying-to-be-relaxed-but-failing* kind of way.

Leo let out a quiet laugh. Cara noticed how plump and inviting his lips were.

"Don't worry! You didn't embarrass yourself. Far

from it in fact. I don't think I've seen anyone handle a situation like that with as much composure and grace as you did." Cara listened. Her cheeks reddened. She stared at her coffee. "I have got to say though, Cara, the bloke must be insane. I mean, what on earth is he doing, that girl he was pawing was not a patch on you."

Leo became louder and more animated the more he talked. Cara looked over her shoulder self-consciously.

"Seriously though, there you were looking, well, breath-taking, and it didn't even occur to him that you're *the* woman that men want to be seen with. I just don't get it. What is *wrong* with him!?" Those last five words were shouted, rather loudly.

She stared open mouthed as Leo looked back at her, wide-eyed and exasperated, he didn't seem in the slightest bit embarrassed by the outburst. She, on the other hand, was torn between being embarrassed by her *getting-sexier-by-the-minute* mate shouting about her weekend in public and realizing that he might *actually* seem to like her.

Cara allowed Leo, who was taking a cautious sip of his espresso, a few seconds to relax. He looked at her earnestly. She tried hard to regain her composure.

"Thanks, I think, Leo. That's all very...flattering. Although having said that, if you'd seen me a few hours later you might not be thinking of me as such a great catch!" She smirked.

"Turn out to be a big night did it?" He asked. She let out a sigh of relief. He hadn't seen her making a drunken fool of herself.

"You could say that. And to top it off I had the headache from hell on Saturday morning." She fiddled with her cup some more while Leo watched.

"Don't feel bad. He doesn't deserve you."

"Didn't." Cara corrected. "I packed his case for him. He's not even bothered texting me since."

"So, that's it then?" Leo's stomach fizzed, "Over and done with? No more Harry?" He tried not to smile.

She shrugged "I think it's safe to say that's true. I was kidding myself that he was the one. He just happened to be the one I clung to at college. I was geeky and boring, no-one ever fancied me. When he asked me out I couldn't believe my luck, to be honest. I just ignored the signs that he didn't really love me. I was just a convenience. If you think about it, he fell on his feet when he moved into my flat. I was just going along with the 'norm'."

"What do you mean?"

"Oh, you know. Find a boyfriend, move in with him, wait for him to propose, get married, have kids...etc."

"If you want my honest opinion, I don't think Harry is the marrying type!" He raised his eyes.

"And you are?" Cara quipped, more sarcastically than she had intended.

"One day." Leo replied earnestly. "I just want to live my life a little first."

Tears pricked Cara's eyes, realising the enormity of losing what she thought she'd had. "Sorry!"

She sniffed, feeling stupid that she felt any kind of

emotion towards Harry. Leo pushed his chair back and walked around the table. He pulled out the chair beside Cara and sitting down, he put his arm around her shoulder and pulled her close. Her pulse raced.

"You've got nothing to be sorry for. He treated you terribly. Just be glad you're rid of him." He soothed sympathetically.

She felt the warmth of his breath in her hair and smelt the freshness of his recently showered skin, the sensual aroma of his aftershave. Her mind began to drift. Feeling his bicep against her shoulder, she imagined peeling away his shirt, exposing his naturally tanned and sculpted torso, his taut stomach, her eyes tracing the line of hair from his belly button down below his...she shook herself back to reality, feeling somewhat inappropriate.

"Perhaps we should get back? Mr Baker will be after us if we're not careful." She muttered, somewhat reluctantly, the thought crossed her mind that she shouldn't encourage him but she couldn't help the unmistakable lust she felt for him.

Leo relaxed his arm and stroked her tear stained cheek. "You're right. But first promise me something?"

"What?" Cara asked, her breath shallow, the room around her disappearing.

"Don't cry any more tears over him. He really isn't worth it. OK?" His face was serious.

She smiled. "Deal. No more tears. Definitely not over him."

She had felt it too, he was sure. Leo didn't want to seem like a creep taking advantage of a broken heart, it certainly wasn't his intention, it just felt right at the time. He couldn't watch a woman cry and not comfort her. Putting his arm around her was instinctive and now he couldn't forget how her head felt against his shoulder, the smell of her hair, the softness of her cheek as he wiped away the tear. He tried not to think about what this could all mean. Was it just lust, or was it something more? He dismissed the thought. It wasn't what he was looking for right now, he had plans, but maybe there wasn't anything wrong with getting to know her better. Was there? After all he enjoyed her company, she made him smile, he looked forward to going to work every day and he was damn sure that wasn't because of the job!

The feeling of being alone wasn't unfamiliar to Cara, in her thoughts at least, but she always tried to be around other people. When Vix's parents had fostered her, she and Vix shared a room for several years. When she asked Harry to move into her flat it wasn't because she was madly in love, although that was what she told herself; it was really because Vix had left to go to university. So, for the first time in years she was at home on her own. After her coffee with Leo, Cara had spent much of the day trying to dismiss the thoughts that continually crept into her head. Keiran had joined them for lunch, which she was quietly grateful for. Every time Leo passed her desk her palms become clammy, so having Keiran with them was a welcome distraction.

As the week progressed, she made plans with Vix but by Wednesday she told herself she needed to try and enjoy her own company. She snuggled up on the sofa alone with a glass of wine and flicked through the TV channels unable to find anything to watch. Harry had insisted on getting the satellite channels, but she realised that she never actually watched them. She'd cancel the subscription first thing in the morning.

Five minutes after sitting down she still hadn't found anything remotely intelligent to watch. She was still trying to find something when her mobile phone rang.

"Hi Leo! How are you?" She answered.

"I was just calling to see how you're feeling this evening." He sounded genuinely concerned.

Cara grinned, it seemed it was only Harry that wasn't capable of normal conversations on the phone. "I'm much better now thanks. Must have been the coffee" She flirted.

"That's good. I hope you're not feeling lonely all on your own in that flat of yours?"

"Well, I was, but now I've got someone to chat to, which is nice." She giggled.

"I'm glad I could be of assistance." Leo's voice was warm and comforting. "I'll chat to you all night if it makes you feel better."

"Sounds good to me!" It was nice for a guy to pay her

some attention at last. "Seriously though, sorry about the crying bit the other day. It was nice to have someone give me a sympathetic shoulder. I wasn't crying because I miss Harry, you know, it was because I felt like such an idiot! I feel *so* stupid! It's like everyone else knew what he was doing, but me!"

Leo sensed the sadness in her voice. "It's OK, I get it. He was a knob. Time to move on. Don't you think?"

"I totally think. Perhaps you can help with that?" She laughed.

"I'd be happy to. Why don't we start with a drink?" Leo asked, tentatively.

"I see you for a drink every day!"

"I mean a proper drink...after work?" Leo worried that he was sounding a little too keen and putting Cara off.

"Ahhhh, I see. I hope you don't want to get me drunk, Mr Dolce." Cara teased.

Leo was relieved, it seemed she might be feeling the same way. "Never. But it might be nice to have something other than coffee?"

She hesitated. Was she being too flirty? Would Leo think she was on the rebound?

"Sounds nice. How about Friday? I'm seeing Vix tomorrow for our aerobics class." She didn't want Leo to think she was *too* available.

"Perfect. Although I may still have to take you for coffees until then...if that's ok, of course?"

"I think I can cope with that." It seemed he liked her too.

"See you tomorrow then. Sleep tight!"

"Night Leo, thanks for calling. It was really thoughtful of you."

"Night." And he blew her a kiss down the phone.

Cara sipped her wine with a smile on her face. She wasn't entirely sure what would happen but figured that, if nothing else, she was entitled to a little fun - something that had been severely lacking in her relationship with Harry.

The rest of the week passed in a flirtatious blur. Coffee's, lunches, and a plethora of texts passed between the couple. By the time Friday came Cara was functioning purely on nervous energy. Vix was both pleased and amused in equal measure. Truth be told, it was a relief to see her best friend getting some positive attention for a change. She was yet to meet the infamous Leo but knew anyone was better than Harry.

"Top up?" Vix offered as she watched Cara look at her reflection for the umpteenth time.

"Obviously. Surprised you had to ask." Cara replied distractedly. "So, this?" she asked, turning to face her friend. She had been shopping to find a dress that said *not trying too hard to be sexy.* She'd picked a green, body-hugging, short-sleeved knitted number and had accessorised it with a wide black belt that pulled in her waist and accentuated her hourglass figure. She'd paired it with silver hoops and a thick silver bangle. Now she was trying to decide if heels were too much.

"Gorgeous. And with the nude courts. They give you height without them being too dressy."

"Not the wedges?" Cara double checked.

"Nope, they're a bit too casual. It is Friday night after all. You never know where the evening may end." She winked, knowingly.

"I'll have you know that I am *not* that kind of girl." Cara raised her nose in the air.

"Well, I hope you're wearing matching underwear, just in case." Vix winked.

Cara giggled as she took a sip of her drink. "No, no. There'll be no funny business tonight." She concluded.

"Don't be such a prude, the best thing you can do is go for it. You've spent the past three years having boring sex with a man-child who was far more interested in pleasing himself than you. In fact, I think I even pity the woman he's ended up with! In my opinion you should see how the evening goes and be open to anything that may or may not happen." Vix advised.

"Anything?" Cara laughed.

"Anything. Well within reason. Nothing too kinky...at least not on a first date!" Vix smiled as she rummaged through Cara's underwear drawer. Selecting a rather racy black lace bra and lace shorts, she noticed the labels were still intact. She held them up for Cara to see. "Perhaps you were planning ahead after all!" She quipped before throwing them at her best friend.

Cara ducked, her face flushed. "Maybe!" She cringed

at the thought of her best friend encouraging her to be naughty.

Vix laughed and hugged Cara. "Don't be daft. It's good to see you with a smile on your face at last! Just remember, it's a bit of fun."

"To a bit of fun!" Cara chimed and raised her glass in the air, secretly hoping that it might end up being slightly more.

Leo had purposefully chosen The Chesil Rectory, a nice restaurant in Winchester which was housed in a Tudor building. He hadn't wanted to venture into Southampton and risk the two of them bumping into anyone Cara knew. Having lived in the city for a few years, he knew it well. Most of the time he and Keiran frequented the bars but he knew which restaurant would be the right one to impress Cara. He'd never been with a woman who he'd wanted to wine and dine until now. No-one seemed special enough yet at the same time he felt he had to remind himself that it was just a bit of fun. Of that, they had both been clear. When he'd booked he had requested the most secluded table and ordered a bottle of wine, requesting that it be chilled and waiting on the table. He'd bought himself a new shirt and had his hair cut straight after work before showering and tidying his flat. Not so much out of expectation, more out of trying to expunge the nervous energy he felt. He checked his watch, keen not to be late, and with an hour to go started on the

20-minute walk to the restaurant. He'd offered to pick Cara up, but she'd insisted upon meeting him there.

He waited outside nervously, unable to keep his hands still. One minute he had them in his pockets, the next they were by his side. He didn't want to give off the wrong impression. He was looking nervously at his feet, willing them to stay still when Vix's car pulled up alongside the kerb. Vix practically pushed her best friend out of the car, shouting something about it being 'double yellows!' before waving mischievously and driving off. Cara tumbled onto the pavement in front of Leo, who chuckled, before standing upright and straightening her dress. The wind caught her hair and swept it gently off her face, her eyes sparkled in the last of the evening sun, she bit nervously on her bottom lip. Leo caught his breath and he realised how lucky he was that she had agreed to a date. Feigning confidence, he held out his hand, Cara reached out her fingers and interlaced them with Leo's telling him all he needed to know.

He acted every part the gentleman, cool and calm, at least outwardly. On the inside, he wanted to stand on the table and shout that he was finally alone with Cara, that he found her stunningly beautiful and her eyes reminded him of toffee. That every time he looked at her he felt himself melting from within. Cara felt as though she was having an out of body experience. She couldn't quite believe that he had brought her to *this* restaurant. Leo was charming, polite and, despite having lunch with him every day for the past week, she still felt nervous. She stared at the menu, not knowing what to order. She didn't want to choose soup and spill it on her dress or anything garlicky that might taint her breath later. Sensing her discomfort, Leo gestured to a waiter.

"Excuse me, what would you recommend? We're having a little difficulty choosing."

The waiter smiled. "Personally, to start, my favourites are the Venison Carpaccio or Crab Capellini, and for the mains I would recommend the Trout and the Blackmoor Wood Pigeon, Sir." He nodded as he finished his sentence.

"Then perhaps we'll go with your recommendations, what do you think Car?" He asked. Taken aback by this first use of her nickname, it signalled the start of a new familiarity between them.

"Sounds perfect." She agreed.

The evening continued perfectly. The food was delectable, the wine flowed easily and the conversation never ceased. When Leo excused himself for a comfort break, Cara had the chance to reflect. Harry had never taken her anywhere like this, not in three years. Three years! The most impressive place he could bring himself to take her to was Pizza Hut *and* she'd had to pay. With Harry she was always the one making the effort whilst she forced conversation from him. With him she felt like an inconvenience. With Leo, she couldn't have felt more different. She felt... grown up. She couldn't pin-point exactly what it was that she liked so much about Leo, but she felt valued. He was interested in her and her feelings.

He made her feel special. He made her feel sexy.

She'd promised herself this wouldn't happen, but the evening had been so relaxed that the taxi ride seemed the most natural next step. It didn't take long. They rode in silence, hand in hand. Now and again Leo turned away from the window and smiled at Cara. Oh, how she wished she could bottle that moment. The warmth, the electricity, the desire they were feeling, knowing that the minute this car ride was over their relationship would be changed forever and there would be no turning back. Unwittingly she'd fallen for Leo. She hadn't intended to, having had such a bad experience with Harry, but it was a feeling she couldn't control. At work, whenever she was near him she felt her heartbeat quicken and her palms become clammy. She only had to see his desk a few steps in front of her and she felt her face flush. She felt silly yet exhilarated at the same time. She didn't know what the future would hold for them both, but she couldn't resist, she was entranced.

The taxi slowed as Leo pointed out his flat to the driver. He leaned across to pay the fare and Cara looked out at the street. It was dark now, the street lights shone brightly against the star-studded night sky. The street was lined with age old horse chestnuts standing guard to the Victorian semis, each emanating a soft glow behind the ground floor windows. Cara knew where she'd be spending the rest of her evening.

"Come on, stop day dreaming." Leo instructed as he held the car door open.

"Nice pad!" Cara exclaimed as she stepped onto the pavement in front of possibly the largest house on the street.

"Ha!" Leo laughed "Sorry to disappoint but my place is this way."

Instinctively Cara reached out for his hand, and as their fingers entwined she told herself he could live in a cave and she couldn't be any happier.

As it turned out, Leo lived in a 1970s low level block of apartments that had ill-advisedly been given planning permission by Winchester Council to replace the Edwardian 4 bed detached house that had once stood in its place.

"Not quite the Victorian Semi I'm afraid and I only have this flat, not even a whole floor. Sorry if it's not what you were expecting." Leo teased.

"Nice pad!" Cara repeated, giggling as she caught his eye.

"I like it." He smiled as he turned his key in the lock and pushed the door open.

Stepping inside he turned on the light and walked to the end of the hall, throwing his jacket on the sofa in the lounge he turned right into the open-plan kitchen. Opening the very dated melamine cupboards, he grabbed two mugs.

"Coffee?" He asked.

"Don't be such a cliché!" Cara laughed, "A G&T will do just fine."

After touching up her lipstick in the bathroom, Cara returned to find Leo sat on the sofa with the drinks in front of him. She sat beside him and reached across for her drink. His closeness made her tremble slightly, she felt the electricity pass between them. Leo rested his warm hand upon her thigh, she lifted her eyes to meet his.

Slowly, she eased herself forward until their lips met. She felt her heart quicken and his breath upon hers. Leo kissed her with the lightest of kisses then pulled back ever so slightly. Cara waited, holding her breath, every single molecule in her body willing him to grab her and kiss her passionately. Steadily, Leo traced Cara's lips with his tongue, before his lips joined hers once again. The kisses became stronger, but still slow, passionate, lustful. Leo moved his hands up her back and he drew the tips of his fingers along the curve of her spine. Cara gasped, every nerve in her body tingling. She had never known such a small touch could cause so much ecstasy.

Leo kissed her full on the lips and she pulled her body closer to his, desperate to feel his flesh against hers. Easing herself from his grasp, she stood up. Reaching down, she pulled the hem of her dress up and over her head, for a moment she stood in her new lace underwear feeling every bit the woman she was about to become as Leo's eyes ran the length of her body.

Reaching up, Leo traced his hands down either side of her body, his eyes drinking in her perfect, pale pink flesh. He eased her body closer to his until she stood directly in front of him, his face just a breath away from her skin.

His fingers gently stroked her belly, it caught Cara's breath. Smiling, Leo leant forward and traced the spot with his tongue, across the soft flesh and down towards the black lace. Cara doubled over with pleasure. Holding her with both hands, Leo gently pulled Cara back onto the sofa, whispering to her to lay on her front. She did as she was told, not knowing quite what to expect but aching with every inch of her body for more.

As she lay out in front of him Leo straddled her. Removing his shirt, he leant forward. Brushing her blonde hair to one side he marvelled at how soft it was. He leaned down and planted the lightest of kisses around the nape of her neck. He worked his way down and across every inch of her back, stopping only to unlatch her bra strap. She silently thanked Vix for making her wear her new underwear before letting out a sigh.

Leo paused, "Are you OK?' he whispered in her ear.

"I never knew it could feel like this." Cara replied as she turned over and looked Leo in the eyes.

"Are you sure about this?" He asked, the excitement surging out of every one of his pores, given the closeness of their bodies. Cara couldn't mistake that he was sure about this.

"I'm sure" She breathed. She lay back and allowed Leo to continue tracing the rest of her body with those wondrously luscious lips of his.

"Things will change," He muttered, "between us."

"I have never been so sure of anything in my life." she whispered in return.

She awoke to the gentle sound of a train slowing down as it approached the station, she didn't open her eyes; she savoured the moment. She could sense the closeness of Leo's body as he lay beside her breathing softly, feel the warmth of his skin. She listened to the world outside, it was probably a freight train from the slow trundle of the carriages. One by one the morning chorus began, bird after bird, as though they were calling to her 'Wake up! Wake up! It's a beautiful day. It's real, this feeling, it's real!'

She opened her eyes gingerly, the digital clock blinked at her. 06:29. She was lying on her left side, on the left side of the bed. She thought about how strange it was that they lay like this all night as though they had done so for their entire lives, yet with Harry she always felt as though she was sleeping next to a stranger. Leo's arm was resting gently around her waist, it didn't feel heavy or uncomfortable, but as though it belonged there. Cara moved her right hand so that it lay over Leo's, she entwined her fingers within his, feeling the softness of his hands. Sensitive to Cara beside him, Leo responded with a soft squeeze and she gently wriggled herself back so their bodies were touching. Feeling Leo respond beneath the covers, Cara edged back a little more. Leo moved his hand away from hers, put it under the duvet and stroked the length of her spine, stopping in the small of her back. He kissed the nape of her neck once more and moved her hips with a firm but tender movement, pulling her towards him until there was no doubting what would happen next.

Cara finally left Leo's at 4pm that afternoon. She had to drag herself away. They embraced on the doorstep, Leo kissing her again like it was the first time, and despite wanting to stay, she knew she'd have to leave at some point. There seemed to be no end to his power. Leo had begun the night before by making love to Cara, the experience was deep, sensual, exciting and fulfilling. Cara had allowed herself to be guided by Leo and when they finally fell into Leo's bed it was 5am.

The past 14 hours had been a revelation to Cara, she was finally shedding the chrysalis that had ensconced her. She felt she was at the beginning of a journey of discovery with Leo and she wanted to give herself freely, both emotionally and physically but she worried about what it may mean. She swore she wasn't on the rebound and she knew that already she knew more about Leo than she ever had Harry. She wondered if Leo felt the same.

Leo stood at the door for a few moments watching Cara as she shimmied along the corridor and down the stairs. As she turned and waved, he felt his heart jump. He smiled and carefully closed the door. Pushing the door until he heard the latch, Leo dragged his hand slowly away and turned, leaning back against it. He stood for a while, breathing calmly, listening to his heart thump in his chest, waiting for it to slow.

He couldn't quite get his head around the past week. They had gone from work mates to lovers in such a short space of time and here he was now feeling exhilarated and happy after the night they'd spent together. It wasn't supposed to happen this quickly, was it? He looked at the crumpled bed sheets as he made his way past the bedroom and down into the kitchen where they'd begun. As he stood filling the kettle with water he couldn't settle the excitement he felt deep within. He pushed the button on the kettle then set about neatening the paperwork on the table, he hesitated, his eyes wandering over the red and blue logo of a letter addressed to him. He pulled the paper out and skim-read its contents. In the background the kettle boiled, steam filling the corner of the room. Telling himself it didn't really matter and that he had plenty of time to deal with it, he put the letter to the bottom of the pile, and with it any doubts to the back of his mind.

CHAPTER THREE

*I*t was a little strange going back to work on Monday morning. Despite spending a very hot and personal night with Leo, Cara was nervous about seeing him again. He'd called the night before and he still seemed to be into her, but still she worried that perhaps she'd imagined everything that had happened between them. Perhaps it was too good to be true. After checking her inbox for the fifteenth time and pretending she was *very* busy, Cara continued her game of Solitaire.

"May I have a word in my office Cara, now." Boomed a voice behind her, she jumped and closed the window on her screen as quickly as she could. She spun around in her chair and leapt to her feet. Her head shot up, her eyes met Leo's chest. Laughing, he put his hand on her shoulder. "Ha, ha, ha, sorry Car but I just couldn't resist. You look so guilty!" He kissed her quickly but tenderly on the cheek.

"Jeez Leo! I nearly wet myself then! I thought I was in serious trouble!" Cara breathed deeply, calming herself sufficiently to cover how cross she really felt.

"It's OK, we all need to better our score!" Leo smirked with a twinkle in his eye. Cara's mood immediately dispersed, and she smiled. "Come on, let me buy you a drink, we could even treat ourselves to a muffin, what d'ya think?"

The first couple of weeks were great. Cara flipped between feeling ecstatic and worrying about what people might think, but she decided to throw caution to the wind and enjoy the moment. And it seemed like Leo was doing that too. After introducing Vix and Keiran, most evenings the four of them would head into Winchester for a drink after work. They all got on brilliantly and evening after evening the conversation, and wine, would flow.

"Whose round is it? My glass is looking decidedly empty." Vix teased, staring at Keiran with a smile. It was the end of a particularly stressful week for each of them and they were letting off steam in the Slug and Lettuce pub, which was buzzing.

"Alright! Alright! Give me a chance, I may as well get a bottle this time hadn't I?" Keiran mocked. Cara noticed the glint in Vix's eye as Keiran stood up and brushed her cheek with is hand. Shocked she glanced at Leo who was looking a little distant, "I think Keiran needs a hand Leo, *don't you?*" she nudged him and he quickly jumped up and followed his friend to the bar.

"OH MY GOD!" Cara screeched "Why the hell didn't you tell me?"

"Tell you what?" Vix teased.

"You know what!" Cara exclaimed, half excitedly, half offended.

"There's not *that* much to tell you, Car," Vix smirked, blushing, "honestly, there isn't!"

"Well, I know that look Victoria, why didn't you tell

me?" Cara asked earnestly.

"Did you want an announcement? I like Keiran, Cara, he's funny, he makes me laugh, and I think he might like me too."

"He's a great bloke, Vix, I just didn't realise you felt *that* way about him!"

"Why would you?" asked Vix, "You're head over heels in love with Leo. Don't take this the wrong way, because I'm not knocking you, but you do only talk about him. Despite telling me that you're going to take things slowly, that you're not going to fall in love this time, that it's just a bit of fun, it's clear that you've fallen for him."

Cara didn't know what to say. She couldn't argue with Vix, she was absolutely right, as she normally was. She twisted her empty wine glass between her fingers.

"Sorry if I've offended you, Car. I promise I'm not being mean." Cara glanced across at the bar where Keiran and Leo were chatting animatedly and laughing, they continued chatting as they made their way back to the table. Vix continued, "Leo is a really lovely guy, he seems totally genuine. He's quite good looking too, I suppose, if you like that kind of thing. Personally, I go more for the tall, blonde, surf dude look." She gazed longingly at Keiran, "I do think he likes you too by the way. As in properly *likes* you." Cara continued watching, absorbing what Vix was saying as Keiran grabbed the tray of drinks from the bar, "I just don't want you to be hurting when he gets on that flight."

She opened her mouth to speak just as Keiran and Leo

reached the table. Her mind registering what Vix had just said.

"Alright babe? What's with the mouth?" Leo laughed stroking Cara's cheek, "Careful, you'll be catching flies!"

She slammed her jaws shut. Had she heard right? What flight? Where was he going?

"Excuse me, lipstick run." She mumbled as she pushed her chair back and grabbed her silver clutch bag.

After making a hasty retreat down the stairs to the loos, she dashed into the nearest cubicle and slammed the door shut. Closing the toilet seat, she sat on the lid, trying to process what she'd just heard. She didn't understand it. Was Leo leaving? Why hadn't he told her? Her instant reaction was to blame herself. Tears stung her eyes, she wiped them away furiously, angry with herself for letting her guard down. For letting herself feel the way she did. She kicked the cubicle door in frustration. It was her fault, she'd been too full on. They'd never made any kind of commitment to each other of course and now she felt silly. Perhaps she'd jumped the gun and Leo didn't feel the same way at all. She scolded herself, she didn't want to be the kind of woman to hold someone back, no matter how she felt about them. She wouldn't tell Leo how she felt, she couldn't.

After a while she unlocked the cubicle door. Thankfully it was still early so the loos were still empty. She splashed her face with a bit of water and touched up her make up. As she stared at her reflection, she smiled. To the world beyond the toilet door she was still the same girl, but if they looked very closely, they'd have seen the sparkle dull as she contemplated life alone once more.

It had been a thoroughly pleasant evening, Leo thought, as they passed the statue of the man on the horse. His arm draped around Cara's shoulder, he hugged her closer as he felt her gently shiver. There was a substantial chill in the air, two more weeks and the streets would be bustling with families watching the famous bonfire night procession, but tonight it was decidedly quiet. As they walked, their pace fell into a comfortable rhythm. Leo enjoyed this feeling of protection, the softness of her form against his. They walked in silence, Leo watching their breath as it formed clouds in front of them. Cara felt comfortable and safe with him, but she felt her temper grow as she considered how unfair he was being.

"They make a good couple, don't you think?"

"Am I the only one who didn't know?" She snapped.

"What do you mean you didn't know? Wasn't it obvious?" Leo responded, surprised.

"Seriously, I had no idea! I feel like a complete idiot... and a crap friend."

"A crap friend? Why do you feel like a crap friend?" Leo was genuinely surprised, he sniggered.

"Don't laugh at me!" Cara shouted. "I was so wrapped up in you, that I no idea what was going on in front of me!" Stopping in her tracks she wished she could take it back. "Oh God! Sorry!" She quickened her pace.

"Hey! Car! Stop!" Leo called running up behind her, he grabbed her hand and gently pulled her around to face him. Her cheeks were flushed, her hair was damp from the cold air, curls forming around her forehead, her hands freezing cold. She looked so pretty, it caught his breath. He cupped her soft cheeks with his hands, stroking the end of her button nose with is thumb he looked into her eyes. Her heart fluttered. As he brought his lips to meet hers Cara thought her knees would give way. There was no doubt, all it took was a look and a touch and she was lost. Every intention of not falling for him was long gone. It was him, and she knew in that moment it would always be him.

Leo couldn't deny the wrench he felt inside his chest when he kissed her. Everything about her made him smile. Even when she was vulnerable she was beautiful. Was this what he liked? Her vulnerability? He knew she'd fallen in love with him, and he loved her, but he couldn't tell her. He told himself he was protecting her, yet in truth he knew it was about self-preservation. He admired her, wanted to protect her, he found her beautiful. He loved the way her hair flopped in front of her right eye when she got animated; he loved the way she dressed, in just the right way that her curves were accentuated, nothing tarty, but in every way flattering. He hoped she wasn't going to tell him she loved him, because if she did he didn't know what he'd say in return and life would become even more complicated.

It would have been easy to forget what Vix had said in the pub, especially given how much wine they'd eventually consumed. The familiar sound of the 06:02 to London Waterloo as it pulled into Winchester station was normally a comfort, but that feeling was absent today. They hadn't made love when they returned from the pub, Cara's heart wasn't in it and all she could think about was Leo leaving her. She didn't sleep much. Feeling a little groggy given the early hour of the morning, she decided to make herself a cup of tea to clear the headache that was beginning to fog her brain.

Easing back the covers, she was careful not to wake Leo who was snoring quietly on the right-hand side of the bed. She pulled on his dressing gown and headed for the kitchen, being careful to close the door as quietly as possible. The laminate floor was cold under foot and Cara cursed herself for not remembering to put on his slippers aswell. She adjusted the thermostat as she passed it in the hallway and, checking the kettle was full, flicked on the switch.

She opened the fridge and looked inside, trying to decide if she was hungry or not. She knew she needed to eat, but everything she considered seemed to turn her stomach. Closing the door, she reached up to the cupboard above the toaster and with each hand simultaneously grabbed a mug and a tea bag. After plonking the mug on the Formica worktop with the tea bag inside it, Cara turned to face the lounge while she waited for the kettle to boil. She sat at the kitchen table and rifled through the various free newspapers looking for something to read. The kettle clicked behind her and she pushed herself up from the table. She poured the boiling water into the mug and twisted the egg timer to 2 minutes, she was fussy about having her tea just right.

She wanted to read something, do something, anything that would take her mind off Leo's mysterious impending departure. Again, she picked up the old newspapers. Holding them in the crook of her left arm, she selected them one at a time with her right hand and checked the date. With her right foot on the pedal of the recycling bin she dropped the papers one by one, silently praising herself for being useful despite the way she was feeling, she continued until the egg timer buzzed. Throwing the remainder of the pile on the table she turned, twisted the top of the egg until the buzzing stopped, lifted the bag out of the mug and placed it in the bin under the sink. As she waited for the tea to cool she turned back to the pile. After dumping the final two papers Cara returned the rest to the table and neatened them, along with the pile of post laying there. Inadvertently her eyes flicked across first of line of the letter which now lay atop the pile.

> *Dear Mr Leonardo Dolce,*
> *Re: Round-the-World Flight Itinerary'*

Holding her breath, she read on:

> 'We have the pleasure of confirming the itinerary for your Round-the-World Flight booking. Please ensure the dates and times are correct, if they are not please contact as soon as possible to make any necessary amendments.
>
> Yours sincerely,
>
> A Turner
>
> British Airways Customer Services Representative'

She continued to stare, unseeing, at the letter in front of her trying to process what she had just read. She didn't hear Leo behind her.

"Morning Gorgeous, what's happening? Your tea's getting cold."

She sat, motionless as Leo leaned towards her and kissed her hair. On autopilot, he felt the kettle, pushed the button on, picked up the blue mug of tea and placed it in front of Cara. Their routine had begun to take shape already, the ease of dancing around each other in the kitchen, filling each other's space, just so.

Sitting across the kitchen table, Leo absent-mindedly ran his hand through his dark curls which fell back down across the left side of his face, his bicep bulging as he did so. Cara raised her eyes. Watching his arms, his chest, his stomach tighten and pull around his small appendix scar, all at once she felt she knew everything, yet nothing about him at all.

"Cara?" Leo asked, touching her hand. She flinched. "Cara?" his eyes questioned.

"Why didn't you tell me?" Cara answered quietly, "You should have told me."

Leo's eyes scoured the table. The newspapers were gone and in its place his letter stared back at him. "I, I.... oh God, sorry Cara." He didn't know what to say, he knew he should have told her, but he wasn't sure he would be going. In fact, he wasn't sure of so many things.

Moving her hand across the table Cara wiped away the small puddle that had formed in front of her. Hoping Leo hadn't seen, she stood and made her way to the bathroom. "Excuse me," she muttered quietly, "I need a shower."

The long, hot shower gave Cara a chance to think before she finally composed herself. What *was* she thinking? She'd only been seeing Leo for a few weeks, yet she thought she loved him. She chided herself. The last thing she wanted to be was a possessive, bunny-boiler girlfriend. Leo had clearly made plans, the letter had been dated two months previously, and the last thing she had the right to do was to spoil them for him. She switched the water off and stepped out of the cubicle. She reached for the window, opening it to let the steam escape. Too impatient to wait for the mirror to clear, she rubbed it with her towel. She wiped her face, smiled at her reflection and faked happiness as best she could. Flicking her hair so that it hung in loose, wet strands around her shoulders, she wrapped the towel loosely around her chest and taking a deep breath, she unlocked the bathroom door.

Leo had spent much of the past twenty-five minutes pacing the hallway. He was kicking himself. He knew he should have told Cara weeks ago. The trip had been booked for a while, since he'd received his Nonna's inheritance. He'd been single, not particularly enjoying his job and thought that if he didn't do it now, he never would. Now, though, things were different. He was so fond of Cara, a feeling he was unfamiliar with, he thought it might be love but had no real way of knowing.

That first night, when they'd been together properly, getting to know each other at the restaurant, and after, what he felt was new. It wasn't about a conquest or having a laugh. This time, he knew Nonna would approve. It wasn't that they'd slept together, it was that they had connected on the most intense emotional level he had ever experienced. When they talked he revealed more to her about himself and his feelings than he ever had before with anyone else. It felt as though they'd been connected in another life. With her he could see a future, the love-making had been incredible but on an intellectual level he felt as though he'd met his match. He didn't know if he could tell her that yet and he certainly wasn't ready to make any promises. He didn't want to tell her that he loved her only to disappear for six months. That wouldn't be fair on either of them. Hearing the door to the bathroom open, he busied himself with making the bed.

"There's nothing that turns me on more than a man doing the housework." Cara purred seductively.

Surprised by the tone, He turned around just as her towel dropped to the floor.

CHAPTER FOUR

*I*t wasn't the reaction Leo had expected, but he'd enjoyed it nevertheless. Sitting at his desk on Monday morning he thought about the weekend's activities. It was as if Cara had never seen the letter. They'd spent Saturday, wrapped in winter coats, scarves and gloves, walking along the water meadows. They'd stopped at The Bishop on the Bridge for lunch, accompanied by a warming bottle of Malbec. Cara had asked Leo about his plans, where he was planning to travel and what he was wanting to see. She had the uncanny ability of making him feel comfortable, he thought he'd feel awkward discussing his plans with her, but he didn't.

He explained that after his great-grandmother, or Nonna as he had affectionately known her, had passed away she had left £15000 in her will to each of her grandchildren, but more to Leo who was the only great-grandchild. As a child he had visited Nonna in her small stone-built house in the Sicilian medieval village of Erice where she'd told him countless stories about wonderful cities, and fantastic little known historical sites such as Huacachina, the hidden oasis in Peru, the Marble Caves in Chile, The Tanah Lot island temple in Bali and the remote island of Masirah in Oman. They'd spent many a hot summer evening imagining their travels together when he grew up, but time and life took over. The wonderfully imagined travels never happened because as Leo got older so, inevitably, did Nonna. Or at least her body did. Nonna was cruelly let down by the failing of the most vital arteries of her body. At the age of 83 she suffered a catastrophic stroke and heart attack but not before writing in her will the conditions of Leo's inheritance which went something like this:

I leave equal shares of £15000 to each of my grandchildren, except Leonardo Guzeppi Dolce, my only great-grandchild to whom I leave £20,000 with the following conditions. Upon receipt of this sum, Leonardo must book a 'Round the World' air ticket of his choosing. If he should fail to do so, the amount will be reduced to £5000 with the remainder being left to a charity of my Executor's choosing.

The booking of the air ticket had therefore not actually been initiated by Leo himself, and he wasn't doing it to ensure he got his share of his inheritance. He was doing it because he would be honouring the woman who, for all of his life, had meant the world to him.

Cara listened intently as Leo told her his story. How could she possibly feel any bitterness towards a man who was fulfilling an old woman's wishes? Of course she didn't, but it didn't slow the rate at which she felt her heart crack with each detail he divulged, for she knew in two weeks' time it would be but a pile of broken china inside the cavity of her chest.

"That's amazing, Leo. What a wonderful woman your Nonna was!"

"She really was, Car." She loved Leo for using her

nickname but hated him at the same time because she knew that the moment he left her, she would never allow any other man to call her that again. "She would do anything for anyone. Her cooking was amazing, and she loved my Grandfather, Nonno. No-one else ever really knew her true story, though."

"What was her story?" Cara asked, genuinely intrigued. "She was born right at the end of the First World War. In 1937, at the age of 19, she left Sicily. Her farming family were pretty much distanced from the fascist onslaught that was headed their way, but Rosetta knew in her heart their views were wrong. The family were seen as small and insignificant, tending to their orange grove and, for that time, her parents were uncharacteristically relaxed about her leaving. They figured that if they let her find her own way in life she'd come back fulfilled and happy. They were right. After finding her way to London she was befriended by a young woman called Rose Coventry, kind of an English version of herself. She'd recently been vetted by the Foreign Office who needed Italian speakers at the now famous Bletchley Park to help with some intelligence work. They enrolled together and spent the next 7 years cracking codes and translating radio signals."

"Wow, Leo! Can you imagine? You are related to an actual real-life heroine! Someone who helped end the Second World War. What an incredible woman! Tell me more."

"Well, she was good friends with Rose, and another woman called Vera, in fact I now know there was more than friendship between them. Nonna always spoke very fondly about Vera, she told me that they'd met after Nonna's third year at Bletchley. Vera was an excellent code breaker from what I can tell, she didn't have a huge circle of friends and from the pictures I have seen she seems to have been quite bookish to look at, in fact quite the opposite to Nonna, who was actually very glamorous and outgoing."

"Why would you think there was more than friendship? I mean, the 1940s was a very different time to now. Men were referred to as 'happy and gay' and women slept in the same beds all the time, it didn't mean they were having same sex relationships!"

"I know that Car, but before she died last year, I had the chance to see Nonna one last time. Her health wasn't great, but her mind was all there. I think she knew it would be the last time we'd see each other. She told me that she'd loved Nonno for the 50 years they were together but that the only one who'd loved her soul, and she in return, was Vera. She told me that Vera had been killed the day Victory was declared in Europe, 8th May 1945. They'd heard the news officially over the wireless and following a bit of a raucous party with their friends at Bletchley, Nonna and Vera had snuck out quietly hoping to spend a bit of time together before the inevitability of change hit home for good. The music was loud in the village hall behind them and because street lamps had still not been switched back on, it was dark. Feeling a little risqué and sensing a major change ahead of them they took a risk and embraced under the cover of darkness. Nonna described the kiss as 'one that she still felt on her lips'. Feeling the excitement of the moment and the electricity of everyone in the village, Vera grabbed Nonna's hand and pulled her towards the road. Nonna held back to pick up her handbag as Vera ran backwards towards the road laughing and shouting 'Come on Rosetta, live in the moment!' As Nonna bent down to pick up her bag she heard a bang and the screeching of brakes. She said that everything went silent before she heard the screams. At first she thought it was Vera's screams but later realised it was her own."

"Oh my God, Leo, your poor Grandmother! The woman she loved, killed in front of her! I can't imagine how horrendous that would have been."

"Nonna didn't say much more than that, except to tell me that I had to live in the moment and to enjoy what fate put in front of me. She said that when she and Nonno, a fellow Italian, got together she was still grieving for Vera and that he understood. Attitudes after the war were less progressive than wartime and she was expected to go back to her homeland and raise a family. That happened eventually when she and Nonno took over her family's orange grove, but not before she and my Grandfather travelled a bit with his work for the Intelligence Services, which is how she was able to tell me stories about the wonderful places I should visit. She told me that she had loved Nonno dearly and wanted nothing more than the life he had given her, but she never forgot

Vera."

"So, she still lived a happy life then? Do you think she had regrets?"

"She said she lived a very full life. It was something she was determined to do after losing Vera, she said, and she was clearly very happy whenever we visited. She made the best of what she had. Perhaps if she had been our age, in our time, her life would have been different, but I guess I learnt from her that there is more to life than meets the eye and that if you've known real love like that at least once in your life then it can be enough. I told her that I didn't think I'd been in love, not properly and she told me that when it happened I would just know.'

"Do you think she loved Nonno?"

"Yes, I don't doubt that. She said that living half a life just wasn't acceptable."

Cara sensed something stirring deep inside of Leo but was afraid to ask. She knew she couldn't tell him she loved him. If he loved her back then she'd never forgive herself for holding him back, and if he didn't respond in kind she'd look, and feel, irrecoverably stupid. She did, however, understand that he had to use the ticket he had bought, and no matter what she felt about him, it would make no difference to his feelings towards her. She decided that whatever it was that neither of them wanted to say, it would remain unsaid.

CHAPTER FIVE
2 Weeks to Departure

It was Friday morning. Cara was just finalising her monthly events report that was due at 5pm. She'd only just started it but far from being stressed, she'd concluded long ago that she worked best under pressure and knew she could pull it together in less than a couple of hours. She was concentrating hard on her attendance figures when a shadow covered her screen.

"I think we should have a weekend away. You know, make the most of our time together before I leave for a while." Leo whispered in her ear.

"You'll be coming back then?" Cara teased as she spun her chair around.

Leo considered his response carefully before replying, "You know I'm coming back Car, I just don't really know when. It's an open-ended ticket. I could be 4 months, I could be 12. Either way I will be coming back, but I won't ask you to wait."

Cara felt elated that Leo was suggesting a weekend away together, but at the same time she felt another crack in her heart as she tried to dismiss his last few words. This man she'd fallen deeply and overwhelmingly in love with would be leaving her in two weeks' time. She was happy that he wanted to spend the time he had left with her rather than with his family, that must mean something, surely?

"OK, Mr Dolce, this weekend it is. Where are you taking me?"

"I was thinking somewhere near the sea. I know it's pretty cold now so if you've got a valid passport we could nip away somewhere a little warmer? You can fly to Palermo from Gatwick pretty inexpensively on a Saturday…"

"Palermo? As in Sicily?" Cara asked, surprised.

"Yep. The weather is quite pleasant for this time of year. It's hardly beach weather but it's certainly nice for sightseeing. If we can both get Monday, Tuesday and maybe Wednesday off work I'll hire a car and drive you round the island. There's so much to see. Mount Etna, the Greek temples at Segesta and Agrigento, Siracusa - which as an amateur historian you will love - Monti Nebrodi… the list is endless. We won't see it all, but we can at least make a start."

She could tell, the travel bug had already bitten him. This was the island of his childhood, somewhere he'd spent many long weeks each summer and was encouraged to explore by his great grandparents. "I'd love to, I really would. Give me another hour to get this report finished and I can go present it to The Ogre and sweet talk him at the same time."

Twenty-four hours later Cara and Leo were sat on the A3 having taken the scenic route. As a child, Cara's parents despised the Motorway and would do whatever they could to avoid it. Cara was convinced this meant she spent at least an hour more than she needed to in the car on each day trip but, on this occasion, she didn't mind. The drive was arguably prettier and definitely less congested than the M3, and if it did take them longer at least it meant that she got to spend that extra time with Leo. They talked animatedly about their plans for the next few days. Cara had even managed to nip out on Saturday morning to grab a 'Lonely Planet: Sicily' guide. She knew she wouldn't really need it, but she liked to read about the sites before she visited to get a bit of historical context. As she read out facts and figures from the book Leo grinned and nodded, playing along dutifully. She knew he was humouring her and she loved him even more for it.

For the next four days Cara wanted to spend the precious time they had left together pretending it would last forever. Since she'd found out about his upcoming trip and they'd talked about why he was going and what it meant to him, Leo had both visibly and audibly relaxed. She'd realised in the past week how good an actress she could be. Leo was high on life and Cara didn't want to spoil that by showing her true feelings. Leo did all the right things, taking her case, opening doors, even buying her a glass of bubbly at the bar in the airport. In the departure lounge he held her hand and gazed into her eyes before kissing her lightly on the end of her nose. The only things missing were the words she longed to hear him say.

Once they reached Palermo, retrieved their cases from the baggage carousel and taken possession of their car keys, Leo drove them expertly along the northern coastal road. The couple had reached the point in their, what was it? A relationship? Friendship? where they were comfortable in silence. Leo concentrated on avoiding the death-defyingly erratic drivers approaching him on the impossibly small lanes ahead as they overtook each other at pace. Meanwhile, Cara looked out of the window and imagined the breath-taking views across the Tyrrhenian Sea which was currently swathed in darkness, backlit only by a full moon peeking curiously from behind the wisps of noctilucent clouds.

After an hour in the tiny Smart Car, Cara's stomach began to churn. This was partly from being a passenger in a car the size of a tin can, but mostly because she realised she'd be meeting Leo's parents, who had returned to sort out his Nonna's affairs and not left after the funeral. Cara looked out of the front windscreen and saw a sign signalling Erice at the next exit. They passed the exit.

"I thought...?" Cara began

"Patience young grasshopper." Leo answered with a smirk.

A while later Leo indicated and took the turnoff for a 'Trapani', Cara quickly picked up her guide book and flicked through looking for their destination. Leo reached across and put his hand on the book.

"I want to surprise you il mio amore." He smiled, his eyes bright with excitement.

Cara threw the book in her handbag. "Surprise away then Sir, surprise away."

They followed the dim street lights around the tightly packed streets of the old town. Each time they turned a tight bend they both took a sharp breath in and silently thanked the rental company for giving them the smallest, and now most practical, car known to mankind. Leo pulled up outside of 'Ai Lumi', a sign advertised it as a 'Bed and Breakfast' but just looking at the great stone arch entrance overlooked by a gargoylian looking cherub and into the romantic stone courtyard beyond, Cara knew Leo had put some thought into this.

"Leonardo! È meraviglioso vedere! E questa deve essere la bella Miss Cara."

Leo was welcomed by a large, greying man with a face mapping out a very happy existence. Giovanni hugged Leo closely, kissing him on both cheeks.

"Buona sera Zio Giovanni, e' bella, ed è così bello vedere molto più felice." Leo replied, quickly reverting to English as he realised his cheeks were colouring. "Thank you for having us at such short notice."

"Eet ees no a problemo, Leonardo. Come, I show your room, eet ees ze best room 'ere!" Giovanni turned to Cara and bear hugged here in a similar fashion, then followed with a kiss on either cheek. "Bella, come!" He exclaimed as he took her far-too-big-for-just-3-nights suitcase.

"Uncle Giovanni is a good family friend and *this*," Leo whispered as he gestured to the building around him, "is one of the oldest hotel's in the region. It is also the most beautiful."

Cara gazed appreciatively at the old building with its stone walls, huge wooden doors and trailing flowers growing across the internal balconies which surrounded the courtyard she'd seen from the front door. The ancient stairs led them up three floors. She was beginning to realise how unfit she was as she panted her way up and was feeling incredibly guilty about how large and heavy her case was as she could see Giovanni was beginning to struggle slightly.

"Uncle, please let me take that," Leo said as he slid his hand onto the handle of the case, "please, go ahead and show Cara the room."

Cara smiled to herself at this small but thoughtful gesture. The old man looked pleased for the excuse to stop carrying the case.

The key was in his right pocket; it looked to Cara like something a monk would use to lock a monastery door. The old man deftly turned the key and pushed open the door to reveal not just a room, but a small suite. Cara stood, open mouthed.

Giovanni whispered across to her conspiratorially "Zis ees, what you call, zee 'oneymoon zuite." Her cheeks flushed as he winked and handed Leo the key. Striding back down the staircase he cheerfully shouted over his shoulder ""Elp yourself to zee vino, Maria will bring zee breakfast to you by nine. Sleep well!"

Leo stepped into the room then locked the door. Cara moved slowly across the floor, tracing her fingertips across the tops of the antique furniture which gave it a rustic and romantic feel. Making her way across to the window she pulled open the shutters and peered out of the window. She stood for a moment taking in the smell of the night air, she could taste the sea, and the odd hint of garlic and rosemary from the restaurant below.

Leo laid the key on the dressing table and quietly sidled up behind Cara. Slipping down one shoulder of the loose linen shirt she wore, he kissed her neck. She closed her eyes as he slowly unbuttoned her shirt.

They woke the following morning to a light tapping on the bedroom door. Cara covered herself as Leo got up to open it, stopping quickly to grab a towel to cover his modesty. He opened the door to find a tray with pastries, fresh coffee and flowers had been left on a chair outside of the room. Looking like a model in a photo shoot, he carried it inside. As the door swung shut behind him his towel became loose and with both hands full Cara was quite glad he was unable to save it.

Smiling in the cheeky way he did whenever he was naked Cara giggled, "Hmmm, just how I like my breakfast served!"

Leo put the tray on the bed and climbed back under the crisp white sheets. He poured the coffee. Cara wished this would never end.

"So, how about we take a little walk around town this morning and then head up to Erice for lunch. Mum and

Dad are looking forward to meeting you."

"That sounds lovely." She hoped she didn't sound nervous. "It'll just be your parents won't it?"

Leo tore a pastry and put some in his mouth, "Yeah, well apart from Maria the housekeeper, she's like, ancient, I think she's about 104, you'll love her. I can't imagine anyone else will be there though."

She sighed. If only things could be different, this would be so perfect.

They arrived in Erice just before midday, it was a medieval city built high up into the hillside with the traces of generations of its inhabitants evident everywhere. Two-hundred-year-old graffiti chiselled into the walls of the tiny gift shop, green mosses growing between the ancient stones in the cities archways fed by the sweet, pure rainwater that had trickled down the mortar for centuries, and trees that seemed to whisper stories of lives passed as they walked by. She could see why this was the perfect place for a couple of ex-wartime spies to hide away and be anonymous.

"This way." Leo smiled as he gently pulled Cara across the street toward an ancient oak door with a large black cast iron knocker. With a clunk, the door opened just as Leo reached out to lift the knocker. An old lady, doubled over and no taller than four-foot-eight stood to one side. She and Leo embraced in silence.

"Il mio piccolo Leonardo, è cosi bello vederti!" The old lady whispered in a gruff voice.

"E tu Maria, e tu." Leo replied softly. He gestured to

Cara, "Come, I'll introduce to you to...." Leo's voice was suddenly drowned out as a crowd of people called his name from the room beyond. "Leonardo!"

The couple entered a grand looking lounge with stone floors and a large fireplace, housing a roaring fire.

Leo looked at Cara, his eyes wide with shock, "Oh God! Sorry!" He whispered in her ear, "It's a Sicilian thing!"

Two middle aged ladies manhandled him and Cara into the middle of the room, smothering them both with bear hugs and kisses whilst simultaneously shoving glasses of orange liquor into their hands. At the back of the crowd an attractive couple waited for the hubbub to cease and then stepped forward. Leo freed himself from the clutches of a sprightly, elderly lady and gestured for her to join him.

"Mum, Dad, this is Cara."

"I'm very pleased to meet you Mr and Mrs Dolce." Cara held out her trembling hand.

"So, this is her! At last we meet you Cara, please don't be so formal. Eleanora and Tony." Leo's Mum reached out and embraced Cara warmly, kissing her on both cheeks. Addressing Leo, his mother spoke mischievously, "She is so beautiful Leo." Then pulled her son towards her and bear hugged him, as did his father.

Where some people would find the whole family introduction thing a little much, Cara found it endearing. It seemed that far from being able to surprise his parents, 'Uncle' Giovanni had told Leo's father who had told the neighbours, who had told the shopkeeper, who had told the restaurateur who had told all of his customers who had turned up. There were aunts, uncles, cousins, second cousins and children galore, it was the family Cara had secretly yearned for.Absorbing the atmosphere, she took a sip from her glass, the sweet, strong liqueur. It warmed her throat as it made its way down through her body, it seemed to reach to the tip of every nerve and make it tingle. She held the glass up for a closer look and watched the orange nectar glisten in the firelight, glowing like the evening sun. Raising her glass in Leo's direction, she momentarily forgot.

As he lay there in the dark, light from the moon punctuating the silence, Leo silently wept. He knew she was the one. He knew with certainty that the beautiful, thoughtful, kind, clever woman who lay beside him was the one and only person who would ever make him feel this way. He'd watched her throughout the evening and caught a glimpse of what their life could be. He wanted it so much. She'd navigated the conversations with ease, not understanding a word but smiling at the right people at the right time. She'd endeared herself to everyone he held dear. Every elderly aunt who'd played with her hair, remarking upon how light and soft it was, every Uncle who had touched the freckles upon her cheeks, every child who'd hugged her legs, not wanting to let go.

But he also knew that he had to go. He'd promised

Nonna. She'd accepted his complexities, his inquisitive mind that at times his mother found frustrating as he asked question after question. Nonna had put no boundaries on his learning. Every question was greeted with an answer. He had loved Rosetta beyond compare and was devastated when she'd passed. This trip was about more than just fulfilling a promise. He knew that Nonna had wanted to satisfy his thirst for life before he settled down with a wife and family. She understood, as he now did, that if he didn't do it before he committed to a woman, to Cara, he could not commit himself entirely to what life had to offer without any ties. He remembered Nonna's words *'Viva una vita piena il mio ragazzo!'* Live a full life.

He lay next to the woman he knew would always hold his heart and felt forlorn. He wouldn't ask her to wait for him, that wouldn't be fair. He knew that she'd been tied to a man before, albeit a man who didn't appreciate her and love her the way he'd come to love her. He looked at the curve of her body that seemed to glow in the moonlight and her hair which fell like gossamer threads across her shoulders and across the nape of her neck. Reaching across to touch her hair he stopped himself and lay a gentle kiss on her cheek as he whispered in her ear, "I want this too, my love, but I have to go. I have to." He couldn't see another way.

The following morning Cara awoke from the best nights'

sleep she'd ever had. Ensconced by crisp, fresh white sheets it felt like a romantic dream. She moved her eyes to the right just to check that Leo was there. She couldn't quite remember how she got to bed and she wanted to make sure Leo had got there too. Seeing his mop of curly dark hair out of the corner of her eye she let out a sigh of relief. His eyes were still shut, his beautiful plump lips parted slightly. Slowly turning onto her right side her eyes followed the outline of his body, down to his chest where she watched it gently rise and fall with each breath.

Hazy memories came slowly back to her from the night before. She remembered the feeling of his arms around her as he'd scooped her up and lay her gently on the bed. Sleepy from the numerous glasses of that wonderful orange elixir she'd been handed throughout the evening, she'd had a warm, fuzzy feeling.

Every person she was introduced to welcomed her as though she was one of the family, his future wife perhaps? Did they know something she didn't? She smiled at the thought. Hoped. As he'd placed her on the bed he'd gently unbuttoned her dress and slipped it out from underneath her. He'd left her underwear in place and pulled the sheets and blankets around her. Delicately he slipped in behind her, his arms embracing her, protecting her. Remembering, she began to cry, large tears slid across her face and onto the pillow. Those words, she hadn't imagined them. He was in love with her too.

CHAPTER SIX

*O*ver the next couple of days they explored the island, dipped their toes in the turquoise sea that tickled the shore, walked along clifftops and admired the views. They began ticking off the list of sights visiting Mount Etna on the east of the island and the Greek temple at Segesta to the west. The guide books could do neither justice. The sun hovered overhead as Cara stood at the base of the temple exploring the unfinished columns, so strong, a beautiful beginning, lovingly crafted with the intention of having it linger upon the landscape forever, yet never completed.

"Wondering what happened to the rest?" Leo appeared behind, wrapping his arms around Cara's waist he pushed her hair aside and kissed her on the cheek.

"Something like that." She replied, not wanting to give away her true thoughts. Turning, she slid her hands across his chest and around his neck, pulling him closer, she kissed him. There was a change. The passion was still there, but the kiss was slow, their true feelings expressing themselves as time stood still. Cara opened her eyes, meeting Leo's. Breathing each other in, Leo traced Cara's cheek with his fingertips, their lips close, almost touching. Cara closed her eyes, submitting herself to his touch, she was in no doubt. He loved her. No matter what the future held, they'd always have this memory.

The following day they woke early, it was still dark as

Cara pulled the zip closed on her case. Checking his watch Leo put his finger to his lips as he beckoned Cara across the room. She pulled on her jacket and tiptoed across the dark oak floorboards. Opening their bedroom door slowly, Leo peered out. Checking the coast was clear he took Cara's hand and led her up the ancient staircase to a large oak door. Pulling up the heavy iron latch with both hands he pushed it open. He pulled her by the hand up the remaining stairs and through the door onto the roof terrace, where he led her to the edge. Slipping his arm around her and pulling her closer he kissed her on the top of her head.

"Stunning!" Cara whispered as she watched the sun rise over the ocean in the distance. "I..."

"Shhhh." Whispered Leo, "This is for us Cara, only us." He pulled her closer. Her heart ached. In just over a week she would lose him, and she wasn't sure she'd ever get him back.

She knew she should be thankful for the time they'd spent together, for feeling unmistakably loved, for finding the one person she believed could make her happy for the rest of her life. She absorbed every detail. The sound of the tide breathing in the distance; the smell of the air, fresh and cool; the unforgettable smell of Leo, a mix of fresh sheets and cologne; the grey stone wall surrounding the terrace, the terracotta tiles beneath their feet; the evergreen clematis punctuated with cerise pink flowers trailing and overhanging the walls. Leo's arms enveloping her, his chest warm against her back, his heartbeat almost reaching through her skin to connect with hers. And as the sun rose higher, the sky in the distance with its amber hues graduating into pink and then purple beneath the altocumulus clouds settling in patches across the horizon.

By 9am they were at the airport. After checking their cases in, they made their way to a cafe for breakfast. Sitting across from each other they ate pastries and drank orange juice as they made small talk about the past few days.

"It's been amazing Leo, thank you."

"Thank *you*, Cara! Without you I wouldn't have got to see every single person who lives in Erice in one go!" Leo smirked.

"Ah well, in that case you're welcome. I can not only vouch for the nosiness of the inhabitants of said picture perfect town, but also their kindness and generosity."

"Ha ha! You're right there Car, nosy they are because we both know they were only there to see the only woman I have ever taken home, and not my rugged, handsome face."

"Seriously Leo, I couldn't understand a word, but I had the *best* evening ever, although the more of that orange drink they forced down my throat, the better my Sicilian became!" She giggled at the recollection of her attempt to speak a foreign language she had no previous knowledge of.

"And your ability to encourage a load of octogenarians

to dance on the table was *quite* remarkable!"

"WHAT?! I didn't, did I? Oh God, please say I didn't do that!" Cara exclaimed in astonishment.

Leo laughed even harder.

"You ARE joking, aren't you? Please tell me you're joking Leo! LEO!"

"I'm sorry Car, I couldn't resist it," He wiped the tears from his eyes, "had you actually done that I am sure they would have still loved you."

She reached across the table in an attempt to thump Leo on the arm. "Seriously Leo, you're SO mean! I could've sworn I didn't do that but I *did* have quite a lot of that drink, what was it called? *Soffio?*"

"Solerno, or at least my family's version. It's intoxicating isn't it. The Dolces have been producing it since they settled after the war. The entire town loves the stuff, perhaps it's the reason everyone is so happy!"

"Well, I can't disagree, but I will say that it's only *one* of the reasons I'm so happy." Cara flashed a flirty smile at Leo, to which he replied with a blush. "Just make me one promise,"

"What?" Leo asked.

"Next time we visit, we stay longer?" Cara pleaded.

Leo held up three fingers in a cub salute, "Agreed! I promise that next time we visit it will be for more than a weekend."

Cara laughed at the sight of a grown man giving the salute of a nine-year-old boy to seal his promise.

'This is the last and final call for Easyjet flight EZY5244 to Gatwick. Would passengers Dolce and Morris please make their way to departure gate 3, this is your final call.'

Letting out a synchronised screech they jumped up from their seats. Holding out his hand to Cara she reached for her new leather handbag, pulling the seat over as she did. Laughing aloud, they ran as fast as they could to the departure gate. Slamming their boarding passes on the departure desk Leo was the epitome of charm.

"Mi dispiace signora, io ero così ipnotizzato dalla bellezza della mia ragazza ho dimenticato di guardare gli schermi di partenza! Per favore rimetti a noi." Finishing with a smile he leant over and kissed Cara on the cheek.

Replying in a smooth Italian accent the stewardess replied. "You are indeed a lucky man Senore Dolce," she smiled at Cara, "on both counts. Welcome aboard."

CHAPTER SEVEN

*L*eo was leaving in two days. Cara kept herself busy at work, Leo had left at the end of the previous week and had been busy tying up loose ends and saying goodbye to various friends and family. Keiran was moving into his flat to look after it while Leo was away, and Cara was sure Vix wouldn't be far behind. They'd spent a couple of nights together just enjoying each other's company, their love making slow, sensuous and full of tenderness. Every minute played out with the purpose of leaving a permanent imprint on their memories. Now, as she sat at her desk watching the seconds tick by on her screensaver Cara recalled their parting conversation that morning.

They'd eaten breakfast together in virtual silence, dancing around each other as they buttered toast, made tea and watched the news. Trying her best to fake a smile, Cara headed for the door. As she picked up her car keys and opened the front door Leo reached over her shoulder and gently pushed it to.

"At least kiss me goodbye Car."

"I can't," she replied, refusing to meet his eye, wishing she'd not stayed over. Leo turned her shoulders so that she was facing him. Lifting her chin with his right index finger so that he could look into her eyes, he spoke, his voice soft.

"Why not?"

"Because I hate goodbyes, they make me cry, and I

don't want you to see me cry." She raised her eyes to meet his.

"All I see is a beautiful woman in front of me. A woman who in the past couple of months has set my world alight. Losing Nonna left me feeling so blue but being with you gave me back my spark, my love for life. But you see, that's why I *have* to go, why I *have* to say goodbye. You made me realise that life is precious and that when an opportunity is given to you, you make the most of it. We've made the most of the time we've had together, my world is richer because you're in it. It's a bittersweet irony that if I hadn't met you I'd have seen the trip as an obligation, honouring an old lady's wishes. But now? I know it's an opportunity. It's an opportunity to grow, for us both to grow. You need some time without me around, you need some time to just be...you. The time isn't right for us now, but I will come back and the time will be right, we will be right." He brushed the tear from her cheek and kissed the trail it had left.

"I'll wait." She whispered.

"Don't wait, Car. Just give me the chance to go, be happy for me and I'll find you again."

Before she could reply he kissed her tenderly, then held her close. Oh, how she would miss his touch. She inhaled his scent. "I love you." she whispered before instantly regretting it.

"I know."

"I'll be late." she mumbled as she pushed herself away. Not wanting Leo to hear her sobs, she hurried out to the street.

"Bye Car. I'll write," He called after her, "I promise!" but before she heard his final words she was gone. "I will," he said to himself, "I will."

"Another?" Vix waved her wine glass at Cara as she pushed herself off the sofa.

"Absolutely, fill me up and bring the bottle. Nothing's going to make me feel better tonight so I may as well make the most of the horrendous hangover I'm going to have in the morning."

Even though she still had her flat, Cara had spent most evenings at Leo's since they'd started seeing each other, so being back at her own place seemed a little strange. Not wanting to be lonely she'd invited herself round Vix's.

"God! I am *such* an idiot!" Cara thumped the sofa in frustration. "I can't believe I told him I love him!"

"To be fair Car it's not the *most* stupid thing you've ever done. Putting up with Harry was the *most* stupid thing you've done. Why is this so bad?"

"Because of his reply!"

"Which was?" Vix asked as she tipped the bottle of Prosecco and refilled Cara's glass.

"I know." Cara replied

"I know you know, what was his reply Car?"

"I know! That was his reply. I told him I loved him and he said *I know!* For Christ's sake, I feel like a complete knob!" She raised her voice. "I mean, who replies, I KNOW!?" She was exasperated, "He could have said, I love you too, or I like you, or you mean a lot to me...but no. He said...I know!"

"Well, what did you expect him to say?" Came a voice from the door. Keiran approached the sofa and leant forward, kissing Vix on the head, angering Cara.

"What's *that* supposed to mean?" she asked, angry tears stinging her eyes.

"What did you want him to do? Express his undying love for you just as he was about to leave the country? I'm sorry Cara but it was never going to happen."

"Hang on a minute," Vix interjected, suddenly protective of her best friend, "how do you know?"

"Think about it Vix. If he loved Cara, he wouldn't have gone. I mean, if he felt about Cara the way I feel about you there is absolutely no way in the world he would have left."

"He's not Harry!" Cara bit back. She didn't want to believe him, but the doubts started to fill her head.

"God, you're such a bloke, so bloody insensitive Keiran." Vix put her arm around her friend's shoulder.

"What did *I* do?" Keiran asked, surrendering his hands, "I was just giving you a bloke's perspective on the situation."

"Kinda' sweet, but insensitive. Now bog off and leave us to it." she waved Keiran out of the lounge as she continued to console Cara.

Keiran shrugged before heading to the kitchen. "Fine!" He shouted from the corridor, "I'll put the kettle on then."

"It, it makes sense now," Cara sobbed. "He told me that he didn't want me to go to the airport. He said it was because his family were going to see him off. He thought it would be better if we parted a couple of days beforehand. To be honest I was a bit gutted when he suggested it, but I just thought he was right. I couldn't bring myself to say goodbye, it seemed so...final." She gulped back some fizz.

"To be honest Car, I think he's a bit of a dick. I mean, he knew all along he was going to leave but he still strung you along, made you think he liked you."

"He *did* like me! I mean, does. He *does* like me. I know he does." Cara whispered. "He's not Harry." She was convincing herself as much as Vix. "He's not Harry."

She didn't sleep easily that night, or for a few nights after. The only thing she saw when she closed her eyes was his face. Her thoughts were so vivid that when she did fall asleep she'd wake with a start, thinking he'd be there when she opened her eyes. What she felt for Leo was so intense, so unexpected, that it magnified the hurt a hundred times over. Had she really been taken in by him? Did everything mean nothing to him? Did he touch other women in the same way, kiss them in a way that made them feel the moment would last forever? Was she only ever destined to be with one type of man? After Harry, Leo had made her have faith in men again. He'd convinced her that not all men were bastards, but now Keiran had done an outstanding job of undoing all of that good work. She just didn't know what to believe.

Leo stepped out of the taxi at Heathrow's Terminal five. He'd said goodbye to his family that morning in Bromley with the tearful farewell that only Sicilian families specialise in. He'd told them that Keiran was driving him but the truth was he needed to be alone. When Cara had told him she loved him it took every bone in his body to resist, to not tell her how much he adored her. But he couldn't do it to her. He had every intention of coming back to her but he wanted Cara to be a young woman who could enjoy life without the tie of a man who didn't know when he could commit to her. He didn't want her to live half a life. He told himself he was setting her free.

CHAPTER EIGHT

*T*o begin with Leo was true to his word and did keep in touch, but he didn't email, he sent postcards. Initially Cara found it romantic, it made her feel special, but in the back of her head was Keiran's voice reminding her that Leo couldn't possibly be in love with her. She decided that Leo was probably just humouring her, letting her down gently. Surely it would have been easy for him to find an internet cafe and to send her a quick email. Wouldn't it? And it was impossible for her to write back. Leo never gave a return address, she knew that he had planned to stay in remote places and to move from place to place as and when the mood took him, something he wouldn't have been able to do if he felt tied or had to wait for post. Cara did find it frustrating. She couldn't tell him how she felt, she couldn't tell him she missed him.

The weekend in Sicily, the night with his family, watching that beautiful sunrise, his touch, his kiss. Everything in her gut told her that he loved her too, but Keiran was his best friend so he knew better than she did. Didn't he?

As the weeks passed Cara and Vix rode an emotional rollercoaster. When Cara was sad, Vix was sadder; when Cara was angry, Vix was angrier. For Vix it was infuriating seeing her best friend being treated badly by a man who wasn't even on home soil. The last thing she wanted for Cara was another Harry, but she was acutely aware that Keiran had completely put his foot in it and had to juggle the two relationships very carefully. She wanted to spend time with them both but at times it could be exhausting. As weeks turned into months Vix saw less and less of Cara. Vix had all but moved in with Keiran whilst Cara spent almost all of her spare time at work and at the weekends threw herself into the gym. As hard as she tried, she felt their closeness slipping and she couldn't help but blame Leo for that.

Every three or four weeks Cara would seem to have got over Leo when a postcard arrived and it set her back emotionally, but she kept it to herself. She guessed that he was probably romancing girls at each location, she found him irresistible so it was logical that others would too. She liked to think that Leo wouldn't act on any advances but Keiran's little nagging voice kept telling her otherwise. Cara found spending time with Vix and Keiran difficult. She didn't *want* to feel jealous of her best friend, but she couldn't help it. She knew that Vix deserved to be happy, she'd been single long enough, but Cara couldn't help wishing it were *her* living in Leo's flat...with Leo.

Eight months after he'd left Cara finally felt like she was moving on. Work was going well and she'd been put forward for promotion, something she knew wouldn't have happened had she been concentrating on Leo rather than her job. The last postcard from Leo was two months ago and she'd gotten over it and moved on, almost forgetting about it. She'd just completed her performance review with her boss, who'd been in an unusually good mood, and received the highest rating possible. She closed the door of his office, leaving with a smile on her face, safe in the knowledge that she was '*An exceptional employee who regularly goes over and above what is expected to achieve results for the benefit of both her team and the company.*' And on top of that she had bagged herself a £3000 bonus for pulling off the planning and organisation of an event that had seen the company sign a multi-million-pound deal with a client!

Feeling *exceptional* Cara looked across at Leo's old desk, for the first time without pining for him. Over the past couple of weeks, the pain had lessened and had become more of a numbness. As she stared at the young male intern sat in Leo's chair, typing away at his screen, she smiled to herself. He wasn't Leo, and she didn't mind so much. Maybe she'd be able to move on after all. Swivelling on her chair, she turned to face her screen. Casually, she opened her Hotmail account, she thought she'd let Vix know her good news, maybe they could celebrate tonight.

Leo sat in front of the PC in the lobby of the hotel in Male. The Maldives were one of the places Nonna had wanted him to visit but after 8 months pining for Cara he decided that this would be the place he would bring her on their honeymoon. He didn't want to stay in an idyllic waterfront chalet surrounded by other couples without the love of his life, so he had stayed on the main island, in the city, instead. He had meant it when he'd told Cara not to wait for him, he had tried not to make promises that he wasn't sure he could keep and had decided to send her only occasional postcards. If anything, he was wary of saying too much and interrupting her life. They'd got together so quickly after she'd split with Harry and he had to be sure that he wasn't her rebound relationship. He needed to know that she loved him as much as he had grown to love her. He wished he'd told her how he felt before he'd left, at least then they could have maintained a deeper connection whilst he was gone. He should have been honest but he'd thought that was selfish. He knew better now. He could have spent longer travelling, but he decided that he wanted to head home and put the plans he'd been making into action It was time to tell Cara how he felt.

With her finger hovering over the left mouse button Cara didn't know if she should open the email. Nothing for two months and then this. She told herself, with a little uncertainty, that she didn't care and being a stronger, more independent woman, she could read his words without becoming emotional. It was dated the week before. She opened his message:

Hi Car, how are you? I'm so sorry I've not been in touch, there's a long and a short story about why I've not written but I'll just give you the short one. I've been a bit poorly. I picked up a nasty bug in Sri Lanka and had to wait until I recovered before moving on. It was nothing major but I had no internet access in the hospital, so it was virtually impossible to contact anyone.

Anyway, I hope you are well, I can't wait to hear what's been going on with you. I'm heading home soon so if you're free I'd love to catch up. I know you're probably busy so when I've unpacked I'll give you a call and if you'll let me, I'd like to take you out to dinner?

I've missed you.

L xxx

She stared at the screen feeling awful about herself. Here she was feeling pissed off about not getting a postcard, and Leo had been ill, really ill, ill enough to be in hospital! Her heart leapt as she re-read the last paragraph. She looked at her watch, 4.53pm, not quite clocking off time but she figured she'd earnt enough brownie points to leave a few minutes early. She shut down her PC pulled her phone out of her bag, as she walked to her car she called Vix.

"Hi Car!" Vix answered, "Where've you been? Haven't you been sucked into a work vortex that you couldn't escape? It must be urgent?!"

"Shut up, idiot," Cara laughed "I need to see you, tonight. Now!"

"No problem Car, come on over, the spare key is in the usual place. Let yourself in and wait for me, I won't be long. Keiran might be there already so knock just in case, you don't want to catch him dancing around in the nude or something equally bizarre!"

Keiran had moved jobs, much to Cara's relief. The last thing she wanted was to see him every day at work. She couldn't quite remember if she had congratulated him or not so stopped at the off licence en-route and grabbed a nice bottle of red wine for them to share. It was a pleasant drive to Leo's flat. It was now June, the evenings were long and warm, the trees lining his street were a vivid green and children were playing in the street. Cara felt good about life, for the first time in quite a while, her heart raced, her stomach fizzed, and her mind played through a range of scenarios of her greeting Leo.

Just as she held her hand out to knock, the door opened. "Bloody hell Cara, where did you disappear too!" Keiran hugged Cara awkwardly and stepped back to let her pass.

"I've just been busy working, that's all. Here, this is for you, congrats on the new job, and... the whole flat thing." She replied thrusting the wine in his hands, kicking off her sandals and walking nervously down the hall to the lounge at the end.

Scanning the room she noticed how un-Leo-y it was. Vix had done a great job of adding a female touch with cushions, a mink coloured rug and thick cream curtains. She was impressed. Then she noticed the boxes. Some packed and sealed, some half packed, strewn across the floor.

"Car!" Vix exclaimed, throwing her bag on the hallway floor and running towards her friend, hands outstretched.

Cara turned and stood stiff, feeling suddenly awkward. Vix bear hugged Cara and kissed her on the cheek dramatically. "Where have you been! We've missed you!"

Cara half-smiled. "How long have you known?"

"Known what?" Vix replied innocently, releasing Cara from her grip.

"About Leo coming home." Cara said quietly.

"Oh!" Vix replied awkwardly "That. Not long, honestly! A week maybe?" She looked at Keiran, who confirmed with a nod.

"Long enough to start packing though, hey? Long enough to get a load of boxes, pack and seal some of them and, by the looks of the coffee table, start looking at flats." Cara was hurt. Hurt firstly that her best friend had kept the news from her, and secondly because it seemed she was the last to know that Leo was coming home. She lowered herself onto the sofa.

"Look what Cara brought Vix! How about I open it? Yes, I'll open the wine," Keiran offered, "Want some?"

"Yes. I really do. Please."

Vix pushed the cushion mountain aside, the smaller cushions scattering across the floor, and plonked herself down beside Cara. She put her arm around her shoulders. "Sorry Cara, it's not what you think. Honestly."

"Really?" Cara asked, "And what is it that I *think*?"

Vix looked guilty. Her eyebrows raised, Cara glanced at them both in turn. "Come on, please tell me what it is that I am not supposed to know." Anger simmered within her.

Vix and Keiran exchanged glances. "You'll have to tell her." Vix pleaded with Keiran. Looking at the floor, Cara tried hard not to show how angry she really felt.

"Oh, fine," Keiran huffed, "just don't blame me when you're annoyed. Leo wants to surprise you."

Cara's heart leapt "What?" she asked. The mood in the room instantly lifted.

"He wanted to just turn up and surprise you." Keiran repeated.

"But how can that be true when he has no *feelings* for me?" Cara asked sarcastically, head tilting to one side.

"I'm sorry, it seems I was wrong. I shouldn't have said what I said," Keiran replied sheepishly, Vix nudged him "and I should have apologised sooner. Forgive me?" he looked at Cara with puppy dog eyes and pouty lips.

The anger subsided. She knew she should have trusted her gut, trusted what she'd felt. "You're such a plonker Keiran. Yes, I forgive you." She reached out to smack him playfully, "So, when does he actually arrive? You have to tell me now you know."

"Ummm, in about four hours I think." Keiran replied casually, glancing at his watch before placing two glasses of wine on the coffee table.

"FOUR HOURS!!!" Cara shouted. "He lands in FOUR HOURS! You're kidding, right?"

"No, I think I've learned not to mess you about any more, dear Cara."

"Are you picking him up?" she quizzed, jumping to her feet.

"Not me, no, he's going home to his sister's first. He lands at Heathrow, T5 I believe. Knowing his luck BA will have upgraded him." Keiran looked up from his glass to see Cara dashing down the hall, pulling on her sandals as she went.

"Thanks, I'll see you later!" She called as the front door slammed behind her.

Cara sat in her car in the street and waited on hold for BA customer services to tell her which flight arrivals due that evening, then without a second thought made her way onto the M3. She was beyond excited. She *knew* he loved her, she should have trusted her instincts rather than listening to Keiran. Cara turned the radio up and sang along at the top of her voice, something she hadn't done in exactly eight months.

She was lucky, the traffic was free-flowing and she was making good time. In fact, her excitement to get to the airport as quickly as possible meant she was very early. Ahead of her she could see the sign for Fleet services and thought it might be a good idea to pull over and have a bite to eat, as long as it was something without onions, or garlic.

The car parked, Cara headed into the ugly building which housed various fast food outlets, shops and the world's smallest gambling arcade. She felt proud of herself as she passed the chocolate aisle without even stopping to look. This was not a day that needed chocolate. As she peered at the sandwiches, she heard a voice behind her

"Please could you send another taxi, I desperately need to get to Heathrow." The voice spoke politely into her phone. "Yes, your driver has been wonderful but unfortunately he just can't fix it. I'd ring a local firm but I have no idea who to contact...If you could that would be great, thank you... Yes, my flight is at 8pm... T3...I'll wait to hear, thanks again." She hung up.

"Er, excuse me?" Cara touched the lady on her shoulder.   She was smartly dressed and immaculately made-up but looked a little tired.

"Oh, hello, yes? How can I help?" the lady replied.

"Well, I think I might be able to help you actually. Did I hear you say that you need to get to Heathrow?" Cara asked.

"Yes I *really* do. I'm heading home and my taxi broke down. Poor chap was very apologetic and I'm trying to get another car, but I think I might actually miss my flight at this rate. I wouldn't normally be that worried by my daughter is in a school performance tomorrow so I really need to get home tonight so that I am there when she wakes up in the morning."

"Well then in that case let me give you a lift. I'm meeting... someone... at the airport so if you're happy accepting a lift from an over-excited weirdo who is proud she hasn't bought herself a Curly Wurly because today is a GOOD day, then I can take you." Cara realised as she finished speaking that she probably sounded a bit strange, speaking to strangers is just not the done thing.

"Really? Wow, that would be amazing, you're an

absolute lifesaver!" The lady held out her hand "I'm Rebekah by the way, VERY pleased to meet you."

"Cara-May Morris at your service." she grinned, returning the handshake. She waited for Rebekah to pay before leading her to the car, thanking God that she'd vacuumed it only yesterday.

"So, Cara, tell me about you. What do you do?"

"Oh, well, I've just been put forward for a promotion at work actually. I am an administrator at an Insurance firm, but I've recently been pushing myself, volunteering for things that I normally wouldn't. I've just organised a big event and realised that I'd love to do more of that. The promotion is for a more senior position, which is great and I am really thankful for the opportunity, but it's more of the same really and I think I might like to change direction." Cara realised she was talking quickly and felt a little self-conscious. "God, sorry, I'm babbling aren't I?" She blushed.

"That's great! Congratulations on clearly doing a great job. Not everyone gets put forward for promotion. You must have really impressed someone and I can see why."

"I'm sorry I shouldn't talk about myself like that, it's a bit vulgar, isn't it?"

Rebekah laughed. "Far from it Cara. In my opinion, everyone should be talking about their successes. There're far too many people ready to moan about their jobs these days. If you've done well you should tell people. You never know where it may take you."

Cara was about to ask Rebekah what it was she did

when she spoke "What, or who, is taking you to Heathrow?" Rebekah smiled as she reapplied her make up in the passenger seat.

"Well, it's a long story but basically I think he's The One."

"The One, eh? What makes you think that? Where has he been?" Rebekah enquired, genuinely interested.

"Well, I just *know*. You know? We spent a lot of time together before he left and neither of us told the other how we felt, we just knew. He's been travelling for 8 months and I'm going to surprise him by meeting him at the airport." Cara went on to explain their complicated relationship, finally allowing herself to feel a little bit smug.

Rebekah listened then responded, "Surprise him hey? Well good luck with that. I really hope it works out for you."

For the rest of the journey the women made small talk, Rebekah talking about her daughter, Cara about Leo before pulling into the terminal drop-off area. She got out of the car and took the case out of the boot as Rebekah gathered her handbag inside the car. Her passenger stepped out and approached Cara

"Hey! You didn't have to do that! You shouldn't be waiting on me!" She put her arms around Cara and pulled her close, hugging her. "Thank you so much Miss Cara-May Morris. Today you have been my guardian angel. Because of you I will now see my daughter's face when she wakes up and I'll be able to wish her luck. Something I wouldn't have been able to do if it weren't for your kindness." She placed her business card in Cara's hand. "If there is *anything* I can do for you please call me. You never know what lies ahead, or who you might meet. There will be many things in life that will test you and you may be unsure of which path to take but please don't change for anyone. Be yourself and be confident. Good Luck with Leo."

Smiling, Rebekah extended the handle on her case, which Cara now realised was Louis Vuitton, and made her way towards the terminal doors. Cara fiddled with the card in her hand, then held it up in front of her. On one side, it read:

Rebekah Carter
CEO
Moon Shine Events, Dubai

She turned it over and saw a handwritten note:

You're amazing, every company needs a Cara-May Morris. If you ever need a job, call me, there will be one waiting for you in Dubai. X

Cara looked up to see Rebekah Carter in the distance entering the terminal and heading towards First Class check-in. Cara felt bad that she hadn't found out more about Rebekah whilst she was in the car, but she'd kept asking questions and Cara had kept answering. Every time she'd tried to ask a question Rebekah had diverted the attention back to Cara. She smiled as she slipped the card into her back pocket and got back in the car. Looking down at the gear stick she saw a Curly Wurly on the passenger seat and laughed. All she had to do now was find Terminal 5!

Waiting in the arrivals hall Cara looked for the best place to stand. She wore her new wide-brimmed hat, using it to hide behind. She positioned herself to one side of a pillar so that she had a good view of the automatic doors and thought about getting a Coffee but reconsidered as she was worried it would induce a weak bladder. She had already gone to the loo twice as soon as she'd got in to the terminal and worried she'd get bad breath if she drank anything other than water.

Bad breath! She hadn't brushed her teeth after an entire day at work! She rummaged around in her handbag looking for her chewing gum. She knew it was there somewhere underneath sunglasses, tissues, lipsticks, random pieces of paper and three pens that she had failed to find earlier in the day when she was trying to locate just one. Finding the almost finished packet she breathed a sigh of relief and put the final piece it in her mouth. As she did so she looked up to see the arrivals doors open.

Her heart pounded, she held her breath as people began streaming through. She stared, nervously, clenching and unclenching her fists. Time seemed to pass endlessly until at last, she saw him. He looked even more delicious than she'd remembered. He'd lost weight which accentuated his cheek bones and his hair had grown, dark curls now fell around the sides of his face. A pair of Oakley sunglasses sat nestled in amongst the curls on the top of his head. He wore a pair of navy patterned shorts and a white grandad style t-shirt with the sleeves rolled up and the buttons undone revealing his chest. She'd forgotten how erotic she'd found his hairy chest. Taking a moment to compose herself, she repositioned her hat, brushing her fringe to one side beneath the brim. She rubbed her lips together, took a deep breath and stepped forward.

A tall, slim young woman with long, dark curly hair nudged past her, skipping quickly under the barrier and threw her arms around Leo. Dropping his bags, he embraced her, lifting her off the floor and spinning her round. Cara pulled the brim of her hat down to hide her face. Was this why he wanted to 'surprise' her rather than asking her to pick him up? She looked again to see Leo's arm draped around the girls' shoulders as they laughed. "Bastard." She muttered under her breath. She didn't hang around to see any more. Subtly, she passed the couple and made for the exit. Reaching into her pocket she felt Rebekah's card. In that instant, her mind was made up. She took her phone from her bag and dialled.

CHAPTER NINE

*S*he found it an easy decision in the end. With no real ties to worry about, Cara was free to do as she pleased. She'd managed to get through to Rebekah who was sitting in the Emirates' First Class Lounge waiting for her flight. Rebekah had genuinely been very pleased to take her call and had been intuitive enough not to ask any questions. They arranged a call for 48 hours later. On her way home from the airport, a tearful Cara called Vix and asked her best friend to meet as soon as she got back. Despite it getting late, Vix was worried at the tone in Cara's voice and agreed without hesitation.

The two friends sat up most of the night discussing what had happened. Cara came to the conclusion that Leo had not wanted her to meet him because he had met the very tall, dark, indescribably beautiful girl on his travels and had wanted a last fling before settling down. Vix couldn't disagree, she and Kieran hadn't heard anything from Leo that evening and so the obvious conclusion seemed to be that he was guilty of something and that he didn't care much for Cara. A lot of tears were shed, by both girls. Cara because she was heartbroken, and Vix because she knew Cara had to move on with her life and if that meant her best friend relocating to another country to start again, then so be it. The early morning sun peeped through the curtains; lying in bed like they had as teenagers, the friends reminisced about their friendship, their lives and their loves.

"What are you hoping to get out of this 'chat' Car? I mean, don't you think it's a little weird that a woman you've literally just met yesterday would offer you a job?"

"Not really, Vix. They say that as one door closes, another opens. Rebekah is my open door."

"Well I suppose if you put it like that then you can't let the opportunity of moving abroad pass, it would be like JK Rowling deciding to be a waitress instead of an author, or Kylie not auditioning for Neighbours! You just don't know what's out there waiting for you."

"Really?" laughed Cara, "Your analogy is to compare me to JK Rowling, the best author this country has ever seen, or Kylie Minogue, who is admittedly gorgeous, but she is *the* pint-sized actress who stole Jason Donovan's heart?"

Vix playfully hit Cara on the arm, "Shut up, you know what I mean! You have so much potential, but you've been holding yourself back. First with Harry, you wanted marriage and children, all in your early twenties and then when he let you down you fall in love again with a man who made you no promises and put his happiness before yours..." Cara opened her mouth to argue and Vix held up her hand, "he made you no *concrete* promises, Car. He may have given you the *impression* that he loved you, he may have given you the *impression* that he cared for you, from what I can tell he was great in bed, but he never told you he loved you." She knew Vix was right but it hurt to hear it out loud. "What you should be doing, is thanking him. While he's been away it has given you the chance to concentrate on your career and because of that you have an amazing opportunity right in front of you."

Cara wiped the tears that had welled in her eyes and were now sliding down to pool in her ears. "You're right." She said quietly. "I know you're right. It's hard to hear, but this could be the first day of the rest of my life."

"Could be? It *is* the first day of the rest of your life, so come on, think positively. Everything else will fall into place."

"OK, but can you do me a favour, please?"

"Anything to ensure my best friend's freedom is not scuppered" Vix replied dramatically.

"Don't tell Keiran anything about this. If I am offered a job, and I do leave, I don't want Leo knowing where I am. The last thing I need is for my plans to be confused by him. I have to accept that he moved on whilst he was away and that the feelings I had for him were all in my imagination. He took me for a fool and I don't want that to happen again."

"Can I at least tell him that you saw Leo?" Vix asked anxiously. "I don't really want to lie to him."

"OK, but not yet. If Leo really is planning to contact me when he's back then I'll make sure I'm unavailable. When I am on a plane, *then* you can tell Kieran. I know you two are going to have your happy ever after, so I don't want to be responsible for any arguments over trust or whatever, so just blame me."

"Fine Car, but only because you are the only one who

can corroborate Kieran's story that I snore." Vix giggled as she nudged her best friend.

"I can also confirm that you fart in your sleep, but he may not have discovered that one yet!" Cara laughed as she leapt out of bed and headed for the shower.

Three days later, ridiculously early for work and Cara was stood outside of her boss's office with a coffee in her hand, pacing back and forth reciting her resignation speech under her breath. Anyone who saw her might think she'd been stealing more than biros. Her call had gone well and, true to her word, Rebekah said she had the perfect role for Cara, the wheels were set in motion and so now all she had to do was tie up the loose ends at home before the end of the week.

"Good Morning Miss Morris." her boss approached his office, key in hand, "Waiting for me by any chance?"

"This is for you Mr Baker." Her shaking hand offered the coffee. Her greying, slightly overweight boss took the cup and sipped it quizzically.

"Ever-so-slightly-warm coffee, you really shouldn't have! Come in. I am thinking perhaps I am not going to like what you have to say."

Cara followed her boss into his glass box and sat down in the chair opposite him. She looked around the room and thought, for the first time, of him as an actual person. He had books, interesting looking books with scruffy spines, covering every inch of the shelves behind his desk.

There were photographs of him shaking hands with various important looking business men in suits. Small football trophies all awarded to a Thomas Baker, sat next to some ageing photographs of a young boy whom Cara supposed was Thomas. There were ten photographs, one of a newborn baby with two happy, smiling parents and then the following nine taken, Cara guessed, on each of the boy's birthday.

"He was ten."

"P...pardon?" Cara asked, embarrassed that she'd been caught looking at Mr Baker's personal photographs.

"When he died. He was ten." Mr Baker picked up the last photo. "We hadn't got around to taking his birthday photo when it happened. He'd been playing with his new puppy in the garden when he slipped and fell, knocking his head. He never regained consciousness." He smiled as he stroked the photo in his hands.

"That's why there's no more photos." Cara stated quietly. "I'm sorry Mr Baker, I never realised."

The middle-aged man in front of her visibly softened, his shoulders relaxing as he smiled at her. "Why would you my dear, it was twelve years ago. We've never sat down and had a proper chat, there's no reason why you would know about my personal life. I suspect I know a little more about yours, though."

"Really?" Cara replied, surprised.

"Well, first of all, I know you are seeing our very own Leonardo Dolce, are you not?"

"No. Not any more I'm not."

"Oh!" Mr Baker was confused. "I thought you were waiting for his return. At least that's what the postcards dotted around your booth have been telling me."

"Well I was, but as it turns out, he wasn't as keen to see me as I was to see him, Mr Baker."

"Oh, now that is quite disappointing, I thought you made quite the lovely couple. By the way, please call me Paul." Cara's cheeks pinked. "So, what can I do for you now Cara?" he smiled.

Cara now saw the human side of the man she'd always assumed was a work robot. She realised why he worked as hard as he did. The office was his escape.

"I want to leave." She whispered, embarrassed. The excitement of her job offer quickly diminishing.

"And why would you want to do that? I've only just put you forward for promotion. You've excelled yourself these past few months!" Paul wasn't angry, as Cara had expected, but genuinely intrigued.

Cara proceeded to tell her boss what had happened with Leo, how she thought he was The One and how she had realised that without him around she didn't have a distraction, and without the distraction she realised that she had really enjoyed the events coordination and that she wanted her life to move in that direction. She was completely open with her boss and told him about Rebekah and about the promise of a job and a new life and Dubai. After placing a box of tissues in front of her, which disappeared rapidly, Paul sat back and listened patiently. Blowing her nose for a final time Cara sat back in her chair and said: "So, what I am asking now, although I realise it's not great for you, is if I can please take the remainder of my holiday and give you my notice as soon as possible. Oh, and if you'd also give me a reference that would be great too. Please?"

There was a long pause, Paul looked at his hands as he rubbed them together. His eyes shifted from his hands to the picture of his beloved son which he'd placed next to his left hand. He picked it up.

"Tom would have been about your age Cara. I often wonder what he would have been like as a young man. What he would be doing, would he have a girlfriend? A flat? A decent job? We have so many hopes and dreams for them and map out their future. When our child is born we want to comfort them when they cry, then we yearn for them to sleep all night so that we can too, then we wish they'd eat all of their dinner without arguing, then we worry about the friends they'll make at school, then we worry about how well they're doing and what they'll be when they grow up. Now all I wish for is that I had cherished the cuddles we shared, that I'd lain with him all night when he couldn't sleep, that I'd said 'It's fine, leave the peas' whenever he didn't want them, that I'd asked him about every one of his school friends and at the end of every day asked him how school had been. But I didn't. I was too fixated with the tomorrow. But it never came." Cara sniffed. "Cara, I know you lost your parents when you were a child, and I've never asked what happened to them, but I can assure you they would have wanted you to take every opportunity that presented itself to you. I am not going to stand in your way, in fact I insist that you leave at the end of the day. With a full month's pay, a reference and my very, very best wishes."

Cara was stunned. "Really?" she asked. Wiping the tears that were now streaming down her cheeks, "but how will you cope?"

Paul laughed. "We all think we are indispensable my dear, but the truth is, the only people we are indispensable to are ourselves, and those we love. Never make the mistake of putting work first. Work may pay the bills, but it won't hold you at night when you're sad or lonely and it can't celebrate with you when you're happy. Work to live, Cara, and live well." Paul walked around the desk and gave her a fatherly hug. Cara was grateful for the comfort she felt. "Go for it Cara, but please promise me something."

"OK," Cara replied rather sheepishly.

"Choose to be happy."

"I will. I do." Cara smiled at her boss, "Thank you Paul."

CHAPTER TEN

"**J**ust wait here one moment please Miss Morris." The stewardess at the check-in desk smiled politely as she got up and approached her supervisor. As if she wasn't nervous enough, Cara now worried that it had all been a mistake, a con. Maybe there was no ticket after all! She did have her suspicions when she'd read 'Business Class' on the email sent supposedly by Rebekah's PA. She looked at her watch and then at the check-in staff. The supervisor was looking at Cara and back at her passport, frowning. She tried her hardest not to look guilty. She looked down at her attire. In the few days she'd had to prepare she had done a considerable amount of shopping to update her wardrobe and today she'd dressed as smartly as she could, thinking that Rebekah would appreciate a more polished Cara than she had previously met. Now she couldn't help but feel a bit silly. The supervisor approached Cara.

"Good morning Miss Morris, how are you today?"

"I'm fine thanks, is there a problem?" asked Cara, on the verge of tears. The past few days had been very emotional for her but she'd thought her head was finally empty of water!

"May I ask the nature of your trip today? Business or pleasure?" The supervisor enquired.

"Um, business. No. Pleasure... well both really! I'm starting a new job you see. My new boss Rebekah Carter booked the seat for me. Perhaps there has been some mistake?"

At the mention of Rebekah's name, the supervisor and her clerk exchanged glances. "Well, that sounds wonderful and rest assured there has been no mistake. Unfortunately, today's flight is overbooked, and we have no seats in Business Class..."

"Oh no!" her face flushed red as she looked around to see the Business Class check-in queue growing. "Shall I move over?"

"Absolutely not Miss Morris. In fact, we would like to offer you a complimentary upgrade to First Class if that's acceptable?"

Cara laughed, "Ha! What? This is a joke, right?" She looked around expecting Vix to jump out and shout 'Got you!'

The supervisor smiled and reached her hand across the check-in desk, she gestured for Cara to move closer so that she could speak more quietly. "This isn't a joke Miss Morris, I promise. Please don't be nervous, we'll make sure your flight is as pleasant as possible." She let go of Cara's hand before handing her back her ticket and passport. Returning to her normal tone she said, "Thank you for travelling with Emirates today Miss Morris, if you'd like to follow my colleague here, he will direct you to our First Class security gate and Lounge. Have a wonderful flight."

Stunned, Cara took her boarding card and stared at it. *First Class!* She couldn't quite believe her luck.

After having been shown to her rather fancy, fully reclining seat at the front of the plane in First Class, Cara felt like a child travelling for the first time. She didn't quite know what the etiquette was for travelling First Class. She sat on her seat and fiddled with various buttons and switches as other passengers boarded. Having been priority boarded, Cara had a good half an hour to work out what the various instruments did. As a smiling air stewardess stopped at her seat and smiled, Cara guiltily snatched her fingers away from one of the buttons she'd been fiddling with, catching her in a half reclined, half not-reclined position. Cara grinned awkwardly.

"Welcome aboard Miss Morris, my name is Naomi and I will be looking after you today. May I offer you some Champagne?" She smiled warmly, proffering a chilled bottle of Veuve Cliquot.

"How much is that?" Cara whispered conspiratorially.

Naomi leaned closer to Cara. "It's complimentary." she whispered back.

"Oh! Sorry, I've never flown Business Class let alone First Class!" Cara giggled quietly, trying not to embarrass herself further.

"In that case, I'll make sure your glass is never empty." Naomi winked as she placed the glass in the conveniently placed holder next to Cara's seat then pressed the button to sit her upright.

Now, with a drink in her hand, she had time to reflect. She couldn't believe the rollercoaster she'd ridden in the past couple of weeks. Her emotions had shifted from excitement to heartbreak and back to excitement again, but only now, after making the monumental decision to leave the UK, did she feel free. This opportunity had come about because of a good deed she'd done, and because not having Leo around allowed her to concentrate on herself and her career. She felt so grateful to her boss who had sent her off with his blessing, *and* a bonus to get her started. Vix had waved a tearful goodbye, and with the promise of not letting on where Cara had gone, Cara left knowing that she could just get on with starting her new life and her new job without the worry of any distractions. Time for her to grow up and become the woman her parents would be proud of. No more stupid boys to get in the way, no more talk of having kids, for a while at least, and no more missed opportunities. Her only choice was to look like she belonged and to just get on with it.

"Hello."

She'd just finished her glass when she noticed a tall, dark but slightly greying man, who may have been extremely handsome had the old Cara been checking, standing next to her paired seat. Cara was surprised to see the man was addressing her. She reminded herself that although handsome, she no longer needed a man to make her happy. She was an independent, smart woman. Then she noticed his eyes.

"Miles." He extended his hand. "Miles Granger."

"Hi Miles Granger, I'm Cara-May."

"Lovely to meet you. Thought I would introduce myself as we're going to be plane buddies!"

Cara shook his hand politely. She didn't want to give off any signals of encouragement, despite Miles Granger being one of the most handsome men she had ever seen of the more mature variety.

"Cara-May...?" he asked as he tucked his bag into the overhead locker.

"Morris." Cara smiled politely.

"So, what line of business are you in Cara-May?" he asked smoothly.

Miles took Cara by surprise with his direct manner

"I'm a...a...an events manager," and with increasing confidence "I'm relocating to Dubai. What about you? What line of business are you in?" Their conversation continued for the next hour. Cara gave away as little information as she could whilst enjoying being the centre of Miles' attention. She didn't flirt and did her best to exude the aura of a professional woman, finally relaxing into the new persona she was creating for herself.

Miles was keen to share that worked in a five-star hotel in Dubai and often dealt with high profile clients and told Cara keenly that he would be happy to help her out, as a newbie to the country, he assured her. Cara couldn't help but feel flattered. As her dinner was served, she thanked Miles and politely asked if he would mind if she watched a film.

The rest of the flight passed blissfully with Cara being fed two delicious meals and free-flowing drinks. Cara and Miles exchanged pleasantries, but she purposefully didn't give too much away. On more than one occasion she found her mind wandering. What would her future in Dubai hold? What did she actually want from her new-found freedom? She took her new notebook out of her new Marc Jacobs handbag that had been a treat to herself, and made a list:

1. Impress Rebekah
2. Work hard, play hard
3. Make a few, good friends (must be real and trustworthy, no fakes)
4. Save, save, save
5. Be the best at whatever job I do
6. <u>DO NOT fall in love.</u>

She underlined point number six several times, it was *absolutely* the most important. She then took each of her points and expanded them. She felt like a little kid on her first day at secondary school, writing with her new pen in her new notebook about what she wanted her friends to be like and how she'd impress the teacher.

She'd been warned by a girl who worked with Vix that people who lived in Dubai could be fake and that it might be hard to find like-minded, nice people to trust. Cara had always thought that her willingness to trust was a weakness because it had led to her being betrayed, but her reasoning was to trust people unless they proved otherwise. With this new chapter beginning, however, she realised she might need to re-evaluate. She knew she needed to trust her gut and be a little more guarded than she had been before when it came to her affections.

She looked at the flight information screen and realised that very soon her new life would begin. She packed her notebook away and took out her washbag and hairbrush. She knew that whatever lay ahead, she needed to at least *look* the part, even if she didn't feel it just yet!

PART TWO
DUBAI

CHAPTER ELEVEN
A Fresh Start

Cara was met at the airport by a chauffeur. She'd hoped Rebekah would meet her personally, more than anything to steady her nerves, but it was dawning on her that her boss was probably way more busy and important than she'd initially realised. She was being driven in a black Lexus to an unknown destination. By the time she'd landed it was dark and twinkling lights shone across the Dubai skyline. She gazed out of the window and was in awe of the juxtaposition of sand and skyscrapers. It was obviously a work in progress, but she couldn't help but be impressed.

"This place is amazing!" She exclaimed, addressing the driver.

"Yes Ma'am." Came the reply.

"Oh Cara, please call me Cara." She said feeling uncomfortable at being treated so formally.

"Yes Ma'am." The driver answered again.

"What's your name, can I ask?" Cara enquired.

"My name is Aatif, Ma'am."

"Nice to meet you Aatif."

She was a little puzzled by the formality but supposed this was what was expected of a chauffeur. She sat back in her seat and gazed out of the window absorbing what she could. This was her new beginning and she wanted to embed this first memory deep in her brain so that she'd never forget how fortunate she was. The car approached an area approximately 45 minutes from the airport. Aatif indicated and turned left.

"Where are we going?" Cara asked.

"To a new area Ma'am. It is called Dubai Marina."

"Am I meeting Rebekah there?"

"Not this evening Ma'am, Ms Rebekah sends her apologies for this evening. She will meet you in a few days after you have rested."

"I don't understand, why am I here? I mean, it's lovely and all, but it's a bit late for sightseeing, isn't it?"

"You are staying here Ma'am." And with that Aatif swung the car in front of the main entrance of a tall skyscraper, one of the most exclusive addresses in Dubai.

"Good evening Ma'am."

The doorman opened the passenger door, beckoning Cara out into the oppressive heat. By the time she'd hauled herself and her handbag out of the car, her luggage was already on a gold luggage trolley being wheeled into reception.

Cara turned to thank Aatif who handed her a business card and wished her a pleasant evening before returning to the car and driving off across the grey marble cobbles.

"This way Ma'am."

The doorman motioned towards the large, spotlessly clean glass doors which led to the reception desk. The stark contrast between the oppressive humidity outside and freshness of the air conditioning inside was immense.

"Good Evening Ma'am, I hope you had a pleasant

journey. May I have your passport please?" The reception clerk with her perfect alabaster skin and long dark hair scraped into a low ponytail smiled professionally, revealing her perfect teeth.

Cara felt self-conscious. She touched her own hair, smoothing down the frizz that had started to rear its ugly head. She handed over her passport. There was a short pause as the clerk looked at the passport and typed Cara's details into the computer in front of her. Mesmerised by the sheer glamour and cleanliness, she hoped she was in the right place. Naively she'd boarded the plane knowing her country of arrival and the name of her new employer but absolutely nothing else! What if the driver hadn't been meant for her, or if he'd brought her to the wrong hotel! This was very modern and much more luxurious than anywhere else she had been in her life before. So much for finding more out about people before putting her trust in them!

"Thank you, Miss Morris. If you would like to follow the porter he will take you to your room on the 9th floor. You have a sea view and breakfast will be served between 6 and 10am. Have a pleasant stay."

Cara smiled. Taking her passport, she walked towards the lifts. Stopping suddenly, she ran back to the receptionist. "Erm, can I just check please," squinting at the receptionist's name badge "Annie. How many nights do you have confirmed for me?"

"Three nights Miss Morris. Is there anything else I can do for you?" Annie replied with a genuine smile, seemingly pleased that Cara had thought to use her name.

"Three nights, wow! Great! Thank you, Annie!" Cara had to stop herself from skipping. Reminding herself that she was now a proper grown up she composed herself and joined the porter in the elevator. Wanting desperately to pinch herself she found it hard to contain her excitement. What a place! What a city! She'd never imagined it would be so, so...Dubai! She did have to remind herself that she was seeing the very best of what was on offer and that living in Dubai was unlikely to be like this every day but nevertheless she was going to enjoy it while it lasted.

"It's very posh isn't it!" She whispered excitedly to the porter, he smiled in return. "I'll let you into a secret," she began, "I've never stayed anywhere like this in my life! I'm not important, or rich, just lucky! In fact, I'm sure I must be dreaming! Maybe you should pinch me."

The porter leaned in closely and behind his hand whispered in return, "Don't worry, neither have I. Enjoy yourself."

She blushed as she realised how privileged she was. Stopping on the 9th floor, the porter led her along the corridor and to her room where he opened her bedroom door and showed her in. She opened her purse to find a note to hand him as a tip. He thanked her with a large smile and a nod of his head and closed the door behind him, leaving Cara to contemplate at her new future. Opening the full-length aubergine curtains she revealed a breath-taking view of the Persian Gulf.

A phone rang interrupting her thoughts, she searched

the room for anything remotely resembling a telephone. Following the sound, she found a piece of black plastic on a side table in the lounge, which could have easily passed as a TV remote, and pressed the red button before holding it to her ear with a shaky hand.

"Cara, are you there?" the voice sounded familiar, Cara pushed the receiver closer to her head.

"Yes." She answered quizzically.

"You've settled in then. How's the room? Sorry I couldn't be there to meet you in person, I had to take a quick trip to Abu Dhabi to scout some locations for a client."

"Rebekah!" The penny dropped, "It's great, thank you. Your chauffeur was lovely. This place is amazing!"

Rebekah laughed, "*Your* chauffeur. Mr Aatif is now at your full disposal. Please feel free to use him as you wish over the new few days. I won't be back until the day after tomorrow. It is hot though, I didn't think to warn you. The humidity can be suffocating this time of year, so your sightseeing will probably be limited to the mall but do make the most of it. I'll give you a call when I land, and we'll catch up then. You won't have far to go though; our offices are in the adjoining tower."

Our offices Rebekah had said, a fuzzy, warm feeling grew inside Cara as she began to realise that she may well now be part of something special.

"I don't quite know what to say Rebekah, except thank you! It's hard to keep saying and not sound like I'm grovelling but.... thank you." She was grinning from ear to ear.

"Ha, ha, ha. One good turn deserves another Cara. You'll find your work mobile on your bed along with a company credit card. Please use the next couple of days to get some clothes suitable for meeting our exclusive clients, and suitable for our arctic air condition. Helena, my personal shopper will meet you in the foyer of the hotel at 10am tomorrow." All of this was said good humouredly and without a hint of being patronising, ringing off before Cara had a chance to thank her again. "I'll see you in a couple of days. Bye!"

The line went dead. Cara replaced the receiver and made her way into the bedroom excitedly. True to her word, Cara's new mobile phone and credit card were on the bed. Pushing them to one side, she threw herself back onto the impossibly large bed. As she sank into the feather duvet ensconced in crisp white sheets she felt at peace for the first time in months.

CHAPTER TWELVE

"Cara, it's so good to see you, at last!" Rebekah embraced Cara tightly who'd be waiting nervously in the restaurant, she felt instantly at ease.

"It's good to see you too Rebekah." She smiled as she sat back in her seat.

"You look incredible Cara; did you find it helpful meeting Helena?"

"Yes, thanks. She's a bit like a magician. She looked at me, turned me round a few times and within minutes she and her team had selected me a whole collection of outfits, each one fitting perfectly!"

"Wonderful, I see also she took you to see Marco at the Saloon! So now you look the part, how do you feel?"

"Why's it called a Saloon?" Cara asked, "What an odd name for a hairdressers'! I felt like I should have donned a waistcoat and Stetson for the occasion!"

"Funny you should notice that, it's a bit of an in-joke here. It was misprinted on the first ever hair salon sign and they've been printing *Saloon* ever since! Hilarious isn't it?"

"Well, I'd be lying if I said I wasn't nervous, but I have to say that looking the part helps! Even if I did have my hair done in the wild west," She giggled, "I feel like a completely different person - someone who is ready for a new start."

"I'm sorry you've had a couple of days on your own,

missing a meeting with this new client wasn't an option I'm afraid. You'll know what I mean when you meet him!" Rebekah raised her eyebrows and took a sip of the ice-cold wine which had miraculously appeared on the table a millisecond after she'd appeared at the door.

"When I meet him?" Cara was surprised, she didn't think she'd get to meet clients so quickly.

"Absolutely. I'm handing him over to you once we've done the usual introductions. He can be a tough cookie but as long as you impress him, which you will, he'll never use anyone else. He is exceptionally loyal." She took another sip of her wine and placed the glass down on the table with purpose. Smiling at her new sidekick, she continued. "But let's not worry about that for now. This is our first proper chance to catch up after our very serendipitous meeting. How are you? Have you acquainted yourself with Dubai yet?"

"Kind of," Cara replied "it's a wonderful place. So vibrant, so friendly, so... Dubai!"

Rebekah laughed, "That's a great description! I've lived here for so long I guess I've become a bit immune to it. Everything is constantly changing. Buildings spring up out of the ground like geysers, desert tracks which were there a week ago have been replaced by completely new roads with diversions that send you around the moon and back, it's crazy! But Dubai's motto seems to be: if it can be done, Dubai will do it! I love it! I really couldn't live anywhere else."

"Have you lived here your whole life?" Cara asked as

she relaxed a little more, sipping her wine.

"Pretty much. My Father moved here just after the Emirates were born in 1971. He worked in the British Embassy and had a pivotal role in ensuring relations between the UK and the Emirates was healthy. He met my mother here, she was the daughter of an Arab colleague. Back then it was unheard of for a western man to marry an Arabian lady but because he was so highly thought of, my mother, Faiza, was granted permission to marry him so long as they remained in the country. After a managed courtship where her parents met with my paternal grandparents and my father's agreement to be respectful of my mother's religion, permission was granted. It was all very romantic by all accounts and after a traditional Arabian wedding I came along at the end of 1972." Rebekah smiled, "It was a very different place back then. There were no roads, just sand tracks and only the old town by the creek. If you planned on driving anywhere you had to tell several people, take plenty of water and a compass and hope that a Shamal didn't kick in before you got back."

"A Camal?" Cara puzzled.

"A Shamal! A sandstorm. If you were caught in a sandstorm you'd almost certainly find yourself disorientated. The environment was particularly harsh back then. I can't imagine the pressure it put my mother under. Father travelled a lot between the Emirates and although Mother had plenty of help at home she must have really missed my Father, Bapi. She never complained though and although they could never express it outside of the house they were very much in love until the end." Rebekah sighed as she gazed at her glass.

"Oh, I'm sorry, what happened?" Cara enquired, sensitively.

"Nothing spectacular really. Bapi, died of a heart attack ten years ago and my poor Ummi was so lonely without him she passed too before the week was out."

"Oh, how sad, and awful for you." Cara sympathised.

"The most extraordinary funeral procession was organised for him, he was honoured for the work he'd done in the Emirates, there was even a day of mourning for him. Ummi just couldn't live without him I suppose; she was left heartbroken. It was the archetypal love story."

"Imagine being that in love that you can't live without someone." Cara pondered sadly.

"Hang on Cara, I seem to remember that a couple of weeks ago you were deep in the middle of your very own love story..."

"I was in love with the *idea* of my very own love story." Cara replied quietly, taking a gulp of her drink, "It didn't quite end as I'd hoped."

"So? What happened?" Rebekah asked gently. "I guessed that things hadn't gone as you'd planned when you called me so soon after we parted at the airport."

"Let's just say he'd arranged his own lift home which I guess was the reason he hadn't told me when he was arriving. They didn't see me though so rather than confront him or make a scene I thought it was better if I left quietly. What is it they say? If you love someone, set them free? Well, he looked ecstatic with the greeting he got so I thought setting him free was the fairest thing I could do. When he left to go on his travels I was devastated, don't get me wrong. I was, still am if I'm honest, head over heels in love with him but whilst he was away I got a chance to find out who I really am, and who I have the potential to be. I don't need a man to define me."

Rebekah smiled, "You're so young Cara, how did you get to be so wise?"

"I don't think I am, but I do think, for any faults I might find in Leo, he gave me the opportunity to grow. I met him after a rather horrible break up with my serially unfaithful ex. We just kind of fell into a... relationship, if you could call it that. I mean, for all intents and purposes we were a couple. We were dating, we confided in one another and could talk about anything, we went on holiday and I met his family in Sicily, who all told me we were perfect for each other by the way. I guess the only thing we didn't do was tell each other how we really felt. While I was with him I could have sworn he felt the same way I did. He was my world. Not only was the sex amazing, we connected on an emotional and intellectual level...or so I thought. I assumed that he never told me he loved me because he didn't want to feel a commitment whilst he was keeping a promise to his Grandmother."

"Do you still think that?" Rebekah asked.

"I don't know what to think about it now." Cara

reflected. "Looking back, I think that maybe he could have been my rebound after Harry, and maybe I wasn't in love with him after all? Perhaps it was just me wanting to not be alone again. I must be honest though, he never made me any promises. He did keep in touch with the odd postcard but after seeing him with that girl I am more convinced than ever that it wasn't *me* he wanted."

"That's a very mature way to look at it, most women I know would be spitting feathers." Rebekah interjected, raising her eyebrows.

"Yes, but he's done me a favour."

"Expand please..."

"Well, I was with Harry for three years and we were young, we moved in together pretty much straight after college. I got any old job to pay the bills because I wanted the security of being with someone I loved. Ironically, I had the security, but Harry didn't love me, he loved that he had someone to come home to. In those three years my eyes didn't wander, and even when I became friends with Leo it was a genuine friendship. But he gave me so much more with his friendship than Harry ever did, so when I found out about Harry being unfaithful I'd already realised that I was ready to move on."

"Leo sounds like a nice guy."

"He is. Really nice but perhaps I was more in to him than he was me. When he left I had the chance to concentrate on myself and my career. Perhaps it was something I should have done immediately after Harry. My heart broke when Leo left but I really did think we would get back together when he got back. I think that's why I wasn't waiting for his next postcard to arrive. I was happy and sure that he would come back to me."

Cara's eyes stung with tears, Rebekah passed a tissue across the table and rested her hand on Cara's.

"It sounds to me like he just moved on." Rebekah spoke softly, maternally. "Perhaps if you'd stopped around to speak to him you'd have found that out properly."

"I couldn't face him," Cara sniffed "I didn't want him to see how much I cared about him."

"Why? Maybe you've got it wrong, maybe he really does care about you too."

"Maybe I *am* wrong, but I wasn't about to stick around and be humiliated *again*. Imagine that. Him stood there with his arms around a beautiful girl, so stunning that if the modelling world hasn't snapped her up yet they're mad, and I turn up in a stupid hat, trying to be all *don't worry I'm cool with the whole 'free-love' concept* and awkwardly ask if they both want a lift home!" Cara laughed at the thought. "No. That's just not me. They both looked so happy, so handsome together that I had to let him be happy and walk away."

An easy silence fell between the two women. Looking out through the large windows of the restaurant across the Arabian Gulf, Cara felt at peace with her decision. She knew she would always love Leo and nothing could change the special time they'd shared in Sicily, but she knew she *had* to put the past behind her and move on.

"You'll find someone else. You're still young."

Rebekah reassured Cara. She was impressed with Cara's maturity. She was so kind-hearted and was prepared to put her own happiness to one side to ensure Leo was happy with his new love. A waiter broke the silence with the delivery of a large platter of seafood. A large slab of ice was decorated with a whole lobster, its black eyes staring endlessly at the ceiling, fresh oysters, large succulent crayfish, baby squid and pink caviar.

"Your starter Miss Rebekah, may I offer you some Ruinard Blanc de Blancs?"

"Thank you, Marcel, that would be lovely."

Cara had never heard of the fancy wine, which turned out to be an expensive but delicious Champagne, and the only place she'd ever seen a Lobster was at the Sea Life Centre in Portsmouth... very much alive and swimming. She looked at the platter nervously as another waiter approached the table and began serving the seafood. Cara smiled at the waiter as he moved away from the table and made a small nod-bow, leaving Rebekah and Cara to enjoy their food. Cara moved to pick up her knife and fork but was stumped when she looked at a pair of nutcrackers and a contraption which resembled a skinny spoon attached to a double ended toothpick.

Rebekah smiled, leaned across the table and whispered with a smile "Just copy me."

Cara laughed with relief, "Thank you!"

The women talked whilst Rebekah navigated the cutlery puzzle with ease and Cara copied. Onlookers could easily be fooled that this was an intimate dinner between sisters.

"So how was your daughter's show?" Cara inquired.

"It was lovely Cara, thank you for remembering. Azizah was thrilled to see me. To some people it wouldn't have been important. Most people wouldn't have offered to help, certainly from living out here I notice that people like to just get on with their own lives. What made you offer?"

"Well, I could see you needed help." Cara replied, a little puzzled by the question.

"And that was it?" Rebekah asked, surprised.

"Yes. My parents always taught me that if someone looks like they need something, you offer to help. If they don't want your help they'll say no and you'll have lost nothing. If I hadn't offered then you wouldn't have been back for Azizah and, to a child, having her mother there to share something special can't be measured."

"I think your parents brought you up exceptionally well Cara, I'd love to meet them."

Cara swallowed a mouthful of lobster and took a moment to compose herself. She didn't normally get upset by the subject, but Rebekah had taken her by surprise. She took a deep breath. "My parents were wonderful, I still remember them. Mum's smell, Dad's moustache and glasses. Mum loved anything floral, her favourite flowers were poppies, every skirt she owned resembled a garden." Cara smiled at the memory. "Dad used to wear this navy blue knitted jumper, he never took it off. It had a little hole where the left cuff met the arm and I'd sit on the sofa and cuddle up to him with my little finger hooked through that hole so that he couldn't escape. He'd stroke my fingernail with his right hand as he watched TV. He never missed the 6 o'clock news."

"How old were you?" Rebekah asked tentatively.

"I'd just turned eleven. I was staying with my best friend Vix for a sleepover and Mum and Dad had gone out for a meal to celebrate their anniversary. We'd had a great time, we'd watched Grease for the umpteenth time and I remember we were leaping across the lounge with hairbrushes pretending we were Pink Ladies." Rebekah smiled at the thought. "I went to bed happy but when I woke up my world changed forever. Mum and Dad had been driving back from their meal when they were hit by another car. No-one survived."

"That's terrible, Cara, I'm so sorry." Rebekah reached across and placed her hand upon Cara's for a second time.

"It is, isn't it? I often think how much my parents missed out on. How much life they still had to live. They were only in their mid-30s. I was so lucky that Vix's parents were able to foster and, eventually, adopt me. I stayed with a family I knew loved me and they never missed any of my assemblies or parent's evenings. I will be forever grateful to them, but it wasn't the same. I never felt I could cuddle up on the sofa with John, but they treated me like I was their real daughter. If it weren't for them, goodness knows what would have happened to me!" Cara shook off the sadness she could feel might ruin the evening. "Let's make a toast to our parents!" She raised her glass and as she did, the waiter comically sprinted across the restaurant to top it up.

"To wonderful parents, and equally wonderful daughters!" Rebekah raised her glass with a cheer and the women's glasses clinked in mid-air. "You're going to get on just fine Cara-May Morris." Rebekah humoured.

"Do you know what?" Cara replied, "I think you might be right!"

"Please, tell me where she is!" Leo pleaded with Vix.

"No." Vix replied frostily, "I won't."

"Don't be so silly!" Keiran interjected, "He only wants to know where she is. It's not like he's going to go storming over there... are you?" he asked directing the question at Leo.

"Well, I was going to give her a call, but her phone is permanently off. I don't know what's going on." There was a hint of desperation in his already sad voice.

"Well perhaps you might have a bit of sympathy for her now that you're getting a taste of your own medicine." Vix couldn't help herself. She wondered if perhaps she'd said too much but the sanctity of the sisterhood kicked in and she knew she had to fight for Cara.

"Taste of my own medicine? I don't understand." Leo seemed genuinely perplexed.

"Oh, for Goodness sake!" Vix was starting to lose her temper now. "How can you *not* know what you've done! Urgh! Men!" Shen threw her hands in the air leaving Leo on the doorstep of the new flat as she flounced back up the hallway.

Keiran and Leo exchanged glances, Leo pleading with his eyes, still clueless as to what he could have done wrong, Keiran trying to tell his mate that his loyalties were well and truly split and that he didn't know what the problem was either. The two men followed Vix, almost tiptoeing into the kitchen behind her. Vix made her current mood known. She filled the kettle, slamming on the lid and hitting the switch. She opened the mug cupboard, chose her favourite mug and slammed the door shut again, not offering to make anyone else a drink. As the kettle boiled an uneasy silence fell across the kitchen, Vix drummed her fingernails on the kitchen work surface. As the boiling reached a crescendo and steam filled the room, Keiran and Leo felt like two boys who'd been chastised by their mum. They stood in silence, hands in their pockets, staring at the floor.

Vix made herself a drink and pushed past them, towards the lounge. The men quickly stood back against either side of the door frame, breathing in. Instinct told them to move fast because Vix was in no mood to be polite. Exchanging nervous glances, they followed her into the lounge. Keiran sat, diplomatically, on the sofa next to Vix and nodded to Leo to sit on the armchair to their right. Vix picked up the TV remote and began flicking through the channels.

Keiran plucked up the courage to speak to his girlfriend. "Perhaps you should fill Leo in?" he spoke nervously but smiled at Vix to try and ease the atmosphere that hung heavy in the room. Vix shot Keiran a look.

"I honestly don't know what you're talking about Vix, please help me out." Leo implored.

Vix took a sip from her coffee and with her eyes firmly fixed on the TV spoke, without hiding the irritation in her voice. "What bit *don't* you understand Leo? You made Cara fall in love with you, *despite* knowing that you weren't going to be sticking around. You left her distraught and didn't even bother to keep in contact, other than the odd postcard. When you do finally return, you don't bother telling her when you're getting back and when she'll see you!" Vix was now staring at Leo, her eyes burning into his skull. "When exactly *were* you going to tell her you were dumping her?"

Leo was genuinely shocked. He was sure he'd left Cara knowing the situation. He had never professed his love for her, even though love her he did, very much, and he didn't make her any promises. He thought he had left Cara free to get on with her life without feeling she had to wait for him.

"I never told her I loved her." he said quietly.

"You didn't have to," Vix spat back. "Couldn't you tell? She had just had her heart trampled on by that loser Harry, you stood by her, you were there to pick up the pieces...or was that the plan all along?" she spat.

"No!" Leo replied incredulously.

"Whatever, Leo. If I had known you were going to just bugger off and leave her on her own, again, I would have told her to back off. Cara has had enough heartbreak to last ALL of us a lifetime!"

"I, I didn't realise."

"And what about..." Vix stopped herself before she said anything else she might regret. Cara had sworn her to secrecy about what she'd seen at the airport.

"What about what?" Leo asked.

"Oh nothing. I'm sorry Leo but I won't tell you anything else. Cara is better off without you." And with that Vix turned back to the TV, put her feet up on one of the half-empty boxes littering the lounge, and turned up the volume.

Keiran looked at Leo apologetically. "Sorry mate, I, er, think you'd better leave." He stood and made his way to the front door. As Leo approached, Keiran leant across and whispered conspiratorially "I'll give you a call later, just let me make peace here first."

Crestfallen, Leo nodded and headed outside. It was a short walk to his flat, Keiran and Vix had managed to find a maisonette one street away from him. He stood on the doorstep in his T-shirt feeling crestfallen. Slowly he put one foot in front of the other and crossed the front lawn which was bordered by lilac rhododendrons in full bloom.

For the first time in months Leo took the time to think about someone other than himself. Suddenly the thought of heading home to his empty flat no longer appealed. After staying with his Mum for the past week he'd got back to his place earlier that day. He'd desperately wanted to reach Cara several times in the past few days but thought that it was unfair on his family to disappear off to see his girlfriend. After all, he'd been gone for almost nine months, a few more days wasn't going to make much difference! Now though, he couldn't believe what a fool he had been. What was he thinking? He felt crushed, but why? Then the lightning bolt hit him. She was The One.

Stupidly, Leo had told himself that he was setting Cara free, that he was doing the right thing. He couldn't believe how naïve he'd been. He *had* to do what Nonna had asked but why on earth had he not invited Cara to go with him? Did he honestly think she was going to wait for him? Before he'd left, he'd told himself that he could live without her, but who was he kidding? The truth was he'd missed her the minute he'd set foot in Peru. At every destination all he could think about was how much Cara would love it. It was the chance of a lifetime, but he had no-one to share the memories with. Leo had sent Cara postcards now and again, he made a point of being uncontactable. He'd wanted an 'authentic experience'. What a load of bullshit! He'd had no idea what that even meant! Now he realised, it meant sharing it with someone.

As he stood at the end of the path he caught his reflection in the window of Keiran's car. He felt like an idiot as he ran his hands through his longer, curlier hair. He brushed his hands down his linen shirt and felt like a fraud. The experience had been great, he couldn't dispute that, but the truth of the matter was that it should have been amazing.

The trip to Sicily with Cara had topped every moment of his travels, purely because she'd been there with him. He wished that he'd told her how he felt before he left, rather than make the decision for her. Nonna had told him to embrace love when he found it, but he hadn't been brave enough. He didn't know what he'd been afraid of but in hindsight he couldn't have been crueller. He'd fallen in love with a woman who had been orphaned in her teens, he'd looked after her after her break up then he'd shown her his roots and introduced her to his family, all the time comfortable in the knowledge that he was going to leave her high and dry for almost a year. And to top it all off he realised that he *had* expected her to wait for him. Leo was gutted, but for once he knew he had to do the right thing. He had to find Cara and tell her what she meant to him, no matter how long it took.

CHAPTER THIRTEEN

"*O*K, the lighting rig is secure, can we test the spots please? And then run through the sequences for each track. Over." Cara spoke into the mouthpiece of her headset. Six months into the job and she was already running large scale events. This event in particular was for the client Rebekah had been visiting when Cara had first arrived. Rebekah had alluded to the fact that the client may have been important, but Cara had no idea just *how* important.

Rebekah had spent just under a month training Cara and was very clever about it. She had full confidence in Cara's ability and pushed Cara beyond her comfort zone. This boosted Cara's confidence and gave her the courage to get on with whatever needed doing, and to do it well. Rebekah invested her time in Cara and in return Cara was loyal and hard-working. She was introduced to Rebekah's team which consisted of thirty permanent staff who organised events across the Emirates for a whole range of large and influential clients, and it was clear that Rebekah had hand-picked each and every member of staff. It fast became evident that Rebekah was hugely successful, her staff were all not only highly professional and hard-working, but also courteous and considerate, which was something Cara had found to be lacking in Dubai. Because of the large mix of nationalities and huge amount of wealth Cara was finding that too many people thought the way to get things done was to be rude. Rebekah and her team did not agree with this approach and as such it meant that they gained more respect and, as a consequence, more work from the most influential people in the Emirates.

This client had turned out to be from one of the most influential Emirati families. He was very pleasant, as were his wife and children, but he was exacting in his demands. This birthday party, for one of his daughters, seemed perfectly doable within the timeframe, however she soon came to realise that it was in fact a small pop concert! Her client told her which stars he wanted to see and in which order. He wanted a full stage with lighting rigs, Arabic and European catering for two thousand people and additional entertainment which would run throughout the day. He made it clear that there would be a mix of family, friends and business associates in attendance, plus there would be a number of children needing assistance whom he had invited from two special schools, of which he was a patron.

"Yes of course Sir, I will take care of this for you."

"Thank you. You will also have use of my personal jet if any artists need it."

"Shukran, thank you, that is very kind." Cara replied sincerely, desperately trying not to give away how excited and nervous she was.

"Now, I will leave you with my wife to discuss the finer details. Please make her happy. Ms Rebekah has assured me you are her best employee, if this proves to be correct then it will be most beneficial for you."

They rose together, shaking hands.

"Shukran, Ma btendam."

He laughed, "Shukran Miss Cara-May, I'm sure I will not regret it." and with that he left the room.

As the women waited in silence for the gentleman to exit with his male entourage, Cara had the chance to absorb her surroundings. The opulence was outstanding. The room was positively huge, and one of many, Cara supposed. The ceilings were high, the walls painted in a neutral colour, an enormous crystal chandelier hung from the centre of the ceiling. The floor to ceiling glass doors were dressed with luxurious deep red and gold drapes. There was a large patterned rug inlaid into the marble floor tiles upon which rested the three antique Queen Anne style sofas covered in a yellow silk fabric, in the middle of which stood an antique mahogany table. A large box of expensive looking cigars sat in the middle.

Her client's wife nodded and a Filipino maid appeared within seconds to replenish the Arabic coffee on the table and left. She smiled at Cara in an attempt to put her at ease.

"OK, now the men have gone we can really get down to business," She said excitedly, "first things first, enough of the formality, please call me Aiya." She smiled a warm smile and removed her head scarf.

Aiya's beauty took Cara's breath away. Her skin was incredibly pale creating the most exquisite contrast against her dark titian hair that was pulled back in to a neat chignon. Her eyes, just a hint of a shade darker than her hair were framed by highly defined eyebrows. The perfectly applied eyeshadow was a shimmering emerald green, her black eyeliner sweeping outwards to create a sultry and striking look.

Cara was incredibly grateful to Rebekah for insisting she learn Arabic. With Leo she hadn't wanted to learn Italian because she thought it made him more mysterious and sexy, but this was different. This was going to make the difference between staying in Dubai and putting all of her energy into her career and pining for Leo. Dubai emptied as the summer heat soured and Rebekah took the opportunity to hire Cara a tutor for six weeks of intensive Arabic lessons. At times Cara had found the language so hard to grasp that she'd wanted to get on a plane and fly home, but Rebekah insisted she continue, and knowing that Rebekah was investing in Cara's future she knew she owed it to her to give it her best shot. And give it her best shot she did. The 14-hour days paid off and to her surprise, Cara found it earned her a huge amount of respect and opened doors that would have remained locked shut otherwise. This client was a case in point. Aiya addressed Cara in Arabic, Cara knew this was a test, she listened hard and considered her answers carefully.

"Do you really think you can get all of the people my husband wants here for the party?" Aiya asked eagerly. "Our daughter is very excited."

Cara was amused. "I am going to do my very, very best Aiya. Is there anything, or anyone else you would particularly like to be there?"

Aiya clapped her hands together as if she were five again. "We would like the grounds filled with inflatable slides. There must also be children's entertainers, clowns and such like. Catering must be Arabic and Western. I would like the show to take place in the evening, but the party will begin at 2pm." Cara was busy scribbling notes, translating the Arabic in her head and writing her notes in English. Aiya noticed and respectfully switched to English. "If there is anyone else you think might be suitable then please do feel free to book them too. The jet will be available for anybody who needs transport. This includes you Cara-May."

Cara blushed "Really?" She was buzzing inside. "That is very generous Aiya, thank you. Oh, and please call me Cara, just Cara."

"And they even offered me use of their private jet!" Cara squealed as she paced the office gesticulating furiously. Rebekah sat back in her leather chair and grinned. She paused in the middle of the room, arms in the air, beaming from ear to ear.

Rebekah laughed. "Finished?"

"Yup!" Cara replied happily and skipped back to her desk.

"I knew it." Rebekah exclaimed.

"What?" Cara asked, "What did you know?"

"I knew they'd like you. You're just the kind of person that people fall in love with the minute they meet you.

You put people at ease with your trustworthy demeanour," Cara blushed, "you really have made an impression Cara, not only did they give full access to one of their jets for their entertainers, but to you too! That doesn't happen very often at all."

"Really?" Cara was surprised. She really had supposed that this was the done thing. "Oh, that's quite good then. I have to say Aiya was really nice and she knows what she wants.

Rebekah raised her eyebrows disapprovingly. "Did Mrs Thawadalia give you permission to use her first name?"

"Oh yes, as soon as Mr Thawadalia left the room with his entourage she removed her head scarf and before long we were chatting like old friends."

"That's incredible, Cara. You're incredible. Now I *know* I've made the right decision."

"Yeah, I was nervous, but I think it will be OK." Cara smiled as she looked at her notepad, not noticing the sadness that lay behind Rebekah's eyes.

"Come on, we should celebrate. Grab your bag Cara, I'm taking you out."

"Oooh, I love it when you say that! You know all the best places! What shall I wear?"

"You know what I say Cara, go sparkly, you can't go wrong in sparkles!"

Cara laughed, "Sparkles it is! At least I don't have far to go to change!"

When she'd first arrived in Dubai and after her initial three nights at her hotel Cara had packed her bags ready to leave. Rebekah had told her that she'd organised a serviced apartment for her, and that it came with the job, *in addition* to her salary. Cara couldn't believe her luck. She'd innocently believed Rebekah when she'd been told she'd be looked after and that she'd have a good salary. She hadn't really thought to ask what that would be, her very British reluctance not enabling her to ask awkward questions.

The same porter, David, who had delivered Cara's bags when she'd arrived, knocked the door to her room. She was genuinely pleased to see him and as she followed him and her bags to the elevator, she told him of her excitement at moving somewhere else but being nervous about not knowing where! He smiled at her but kept quiet, she could have sworn she saw a mischievous glint in his eye. The door to the elevator opened in the lobby, David gestured to Cara who stepped out first, thanking him as she left, she turned right towards the reception desk. He coughed discreetly to catch her attention. She turned to see him nodding his head in the opposite direction. Puzzled she quickly turned, deciding to follow rather than lead. As far as she could work out she was following her bags across the lobby to a *different* elevator.

As they approached the other elevator the doors opened and a tall handsome man in a very expensive dark blue suit stepped out, speaking into his phone. His face seemed familiar and Cara watched him as he spoke animatedly. Suddenly realising who he was, she hid behind the porter's trolley. The man smiled and nodded at David. Cara blushed and assumed Miles hadn't noticed her as she looked at the floor. "David?" She asked quietly "I have two questions."

"Yes Miss Cara-May?" he replied.

"Well, one, where are we going? And two, who was that man?"

David took a black master keycard out of his pocket and held it against a small black panel and pressed the '30' button. He waited for the doors to close.

"The first answer is: to your apartment in our Residences." Cara raised her eyebrows, "and the second answer is Mr Miles Granger. He is our Customer Services manager."

She wondered what the chances were of their paths crossing again. "What's he like?" she asked before she could stop herself.

"He is very nice Miss Cara-May. He is a kind man. He ensures we are looked after."

Cara smiled. At last! A nice guy. She hastily shook away any further thoughts of Miles just as the elevator dinged and the doors opened. She followed David to Room 3004 where he opened the door and gestured for her to enter before him. After placing her bags in the lounge, he gave her a tour of the two-bedroom apartment before explaining that 'serviced' meant a team of housekeepers would clean and tidy her room *every* day, including her washing up, laundry and ironing. She reached into her handbag extracting 50 dirhams which she gave to him, thanking him wholeheartedly before closing the door behind him and conducting a celebratory lap of her new home.

After opening every single cupboard and trying out both beds, she stood at the window and admired the view out across the ocean. The apartment was decorated in a sleek contemporary style with the white, black and silver fabrics and lush cream rugs throughout. She sat at the black gloss table and opened the A4 white envelope with her name on it. Pulling the contents out Cara realised this was her official contract and salary in writing.

Initially, she skim-read the paperwork looking for the numbers. She found them and re-read them multiple times, even turning the paper over in disbelief. Half an hour later Cara was still reading her contract in detail, and after triple-checking, she found that the apartment came as part of the package, as did full use of Aatif the lovely driver of the Lexus, a full expense package with no exclusions and a monthly tax-free salary of £20,000 with a bonus package of 30% for each event, based upon client feedback.

Feeling utterly dumbfounded Cara rang Vix, not to gloat, in fact she wouldn't be telling anyone what her package was, but to keep herself grounded.

"He's been round again Car..." Vix started.

"I don't want to know!" Cara interrupted her best friend before she could properly broach the subject.

"Just hear me out, Car, please." Vix pleaded. Cara fell silent. She didn't want to hear it. She was, moving on. She'd not been out of the country for more than a week and Leo was trying to smooth talk his way out of his betrayal. She didn't want to give the subject any airtime while she did her best to move on. Vix took the silence as permission to speak. "He says he doesn't know what he's done wrong and he just wants to talk to you. You should give him a chance."

This made Cara angry. Vix knew how heartbroken she was. Vix knew the whole story. How Cara had pined for Leo whilst he was away and her excitement at realising he was back. Vix *knew* that Cara had seen Leo at the airport with another woman and she just couldn't understand why her best friend would be taking his side. "He told you who that other woman was did he?" Cara asked, knowing full well that if Vix had asked Leo then she was giving away a confidence

"Well I couldn't ask him that could I? If I'd asked him then he'd have known you were at the airport. You know me better than that, Car."

She was relieved, at least she knew she could trust Vix. "I'm not giving him a chance Vix. Leo knew about Harry's betrayal and even if I was a bit naïve thinking that he would come back to me, he should have at least told me he was seeing someone else. Or maybe he wanted to keep two of us on the go just like Harry did. I'm sorry Vix, I can't allow him to think that he can make it up to me when the truth is, he can't." She sighed. "I need to move on. I need to make a new life for myself out here without having to worry about him."

"Message received loud and clear. I promise not to mention him again, well not to you anyway. It is a bit difficult this end given that he is Keiran's best mate though..." Cara didn't want to put Vix in a difficult position. "Can we make a deal?" Vix asked.

"Well, I think you have proven your trustworthiness so yes, OK." Cara replied with a hint of a smile.

"I promise not to talk to you about Leo, but I can't *not* see him myself. Whether you, or I, like it he will be at our place all the time. I will tell him that I won't talk about you, and I won't tell him where you are. OK?"

"Fine, deal. Now can we please move on from this? Tell me about the new flat."

"Oh it's lovely. It is literally just around the corner from...er...the old place."

Cara laughed. "It's OK, you're not banned from using his name! So, it's around the corner from Leo's flat, yeah?"

Vix giggled with relief. "Yes, it's actually the bottom floor maisonette of a Victorian Semi. It's really nice, and the bonus is that we get the back garden too!"

"Sounds lovely Vix, I'm sorry I didn't get a chance to see it before I left, I just didn't want to bump into Leo, and I wanted to spend some time with John and Maggs."

"Don't worry about it, I'll email you some pictures. Now tell me about this fabulous job."

Cara didn't want to boast so she spent the next few

minutes giving Vix the low-down about her experience so far. She told her about her upgrade on the flight and where she was staying, and that she'd had a good chat with Rebekah but that was about it. She realised that she still didn't have any real idea of what she was going to be doing. If only she'd known!

CHAPTER FOURTEEN

Cara was stood backstage applauding the performer who had the audience in the palm of his hands. Peering out from the wings she could see the family watching from the front row, clapping enthusiastically. She didn't know how she'd managed to wangle this final surprise, and to keep it just that. She looked at her phone as it vibrated with an incoming text message.

'How's it going?'

Cara was surprised that Rebekah had decided not to join her, but then she supposed these events soon lost their sparkle if you were doing them all the time.

Cara replied. 'It's going great I think. Lots of clapping and cheering so I am guessing that's a good thing. The special package is about to be delivered.'

And with that she turned to the woman behind her.

"Ready?" Cara asked.

"It's the girl at the front in the red, isn't it?" the woman asked as she peered around out of the wings. The private jet had just about got her here in time.

"Yes, that's her. Jumana." Cara replied. From the stage Cara could hear the performer introducing his special guest. "Thank you! You've been a great crowd. I'd like to wish the special birthday girl, Jumana a very happy thirteenth birthday." The crowd cheered. "And if I may, could I ask you to join me up on stage?" Jumana grinned from ear to ear and shyly headed up on stage. The singer bowed slightly as Jumana looked apprehensively out to the crowd. "Please don't worry, we have a special surprise for you. I asked a special friend of mine if she was free tonight..." The crowd gasped, Jumana threw her hands across her mouth. "...and luckily she was!" The woman stepped out of the wings and onto the stage.

The crowd, particularly the teenage girls, went wild. Jumana was jumping up and down, screaming. Cara smiled. She'd actually pulled it off! For a thirteen-year old's birthday party this really had been something special. She'd managed to deliver everything that the family had requested, and more. Never in a million years had she thought that Jonty Taylor and Stacey Louise, the world's biggest stars, would have agreed to this but when they found out that the party wasn't about showing off and that Jumana herself had requested that the children from the special schools be invited, they *insisted* on being there. Half an hour later the two singers made their way off stage, laughing and smiling. Cara handed them each a bottle of water.

"Thank you so much guys, that was amazing. I think you have made a little girl very happy!"

As the backstage crew busied themselves clearing instruments from the stage making it ready for the DJ who was taking over, the three of them continued to chat. Cara knew that they were to wait for the family to make their way backstage and before too long they appeared. The superstars asked the birthday girl if she had enjoyed the show.

"You were very entertaining, Mr Jonty, Miss Stacey, thank you very much for joining me for my party." Jumana commented politely in impeccable English laced with a beautiful Arabic accent. "Please may I have my photo taken with you both?"

While the girls took pictures, Mr Thawadalia turned to Cara who was doing her best to remain professional, despite her elation. "I have not always been a fan of this kind of music, it's for the young kids I think, but you have changed my mind. I am now a big fan!" He reached out taking Cara's hand and shook it furiously. Cara stifled a giggle. "Please stay as long as you wish and help yourself to refreshments." He turned to leave then paused, he addressed Jonty. "My wife, she would like some autographs."

Aiya laughed. "It is for our daughter." Aiya smiled, nervously.

"No, it is for you." He smiled back. Joining his bodyguards, he left. Leaving a slightly embarrassed Aiya with Cara.

"You were great," Cara did her best to save Aiya's blushes, "and being able to spring that final surprise, you have surpassed yourself. Jumana is clearly very happy. I think you may have earned me a few brownie points there! Wouldn't agree Mrs Thawadalia?" Aiya nodded gratefully.

"No worries, Cara, it was good fun. The place was kicking!" Jonty smirked, Stacey Louise nodding enthusiastically in agreement.

Aiya laughed. "Ah, that is something you should know

about the Emirati's, when we party, we do it properly."

One of the backing singers disappeared for a moment behind a curtain, reappearing with a bag which he handed to Aiya, it was full of signed merchandise from the performers. Her eyes lit up.

"Thank you so much, Jumana will be thrilled!" She turned to Cara, "Thank you Miss Cara, I'll leave you to see to our guests."

"Of course, Shukran." Cara replied then turned to thank the performers again for their professionalism.

As a DJ started playing songs from on stage, she showed them out to where the children from the two schools had gathered. Unlike everywhere else they performed, they were greeted politely by the guests and then were left to enjoy the rest of the evening before being transported to their accommodation.

By 6am Cara had made it back to her room in the extensive villa grounds. Aiya had insisted that she stay on site in one of the guest villas to ensure everything ran smoothly. The room was as grand as Cara had expected but she had been so busy and she hadn't really had the chance to notice.

Crawling under the feather duvet without even removing her clothes, she took a final look at her phone. The last message she read before closing her eyes was from Rebekah.

'I knew you'd do it Cara. I am so proud of you. Well done. Call me when you're on your way back. We need to talk. Xxx'

When she returned to the office the next day there was a mini-celebration. Rebekah had got caterers in and decorated the place with balloons. Cara opened the door to a thunderous applause and much whooping. Rebekah, looking tired Cara noticed, shoved a champagne flute in her hand.

"What's all this?" Cara exclaimed.

"We've had a bit of good news!" Rebekah replied.

Cara took a sip from her glass. "Oooh, sounds exciting!"

"First of all we all want to say a massive congratulations to you for pulling off the birthday party of the year! How you managed to get everyone there? That was some kind of mastery at such short notice."

Cara smiled, "I aim to please Madam." She raised her glass. Her colleagues cheered and raised theirs back in celebration.

"Shhh" Rebekah hushed them good naturedly. "Secondly, you impressed Mr Thawadalia so much that he called me this morning and asked me to fax him a FIVE-YEAR CONTRACT!" The office once again erupted in cheers and screams. Rebekah threw her arms around Cara, spilling her Champagne. "And YOU are to be their exclusive agent, Cara."

She couldn't believe what Rebekah was telling her. She'd only done her job. Rebekah, with her arm around her shoulder, guided her over to the window. "You understand what this means, don't you Cara?" she asked.

"That Jumana enjoyed her birthday party?" Cara answered.

Rebekah laughed, coughed a little then sipped her wine to settle her throat. "It means a bit more than that my love. It means that you *have* to stay here for *at least* five years. It means that we will probably become the busiest events agency in the UAE and that expansion is highly likely."

The realisation slowly dawned on her. She wouldn't be able to move back to England. In terms of the weather she was more than happy with the arrangement. Her life here was incredible. Like many of the people she had met during the past seven months she only really missed the people at home. She only had her adopted family at home... and Leo. Oh, how she'd missed Leo. Often when she was out with her new friends she would see couples smiling and laughing with each other and her heart would physically ache for him. But at the same time, she knew he'd betrayed her. She knew that if she went back home he would find her and she would be coerced back into a relationship with him.

She raised her now almost empty glass to Rebekah. "Rebekah, yes, I know it means I have to stay here, but this is my home now. Count me in!" And with that Rebekah chinked her glass with Cara's. "Oh, what was it you wanted to talk about?" Cara suddenly remembered the text that Rebekah had sent her the previous day.

"Oh, er, only this." Rebekah replied dismissively.

"This?" Cara questioned.

"Yes, it was about this contract." Rebekah smiled and gestured Cara back towards the main crowd. Cara shrugged, happy to bask in the glory and feel just a little bit proud of herself.

CHAPTER FIFTEEN

*I*t had been twelve months since Leo had returned from his travels and found out that Cara had left the country. He was still no closer to finding out where she was, or why she'd gone. At first, he'd pestered Vix and Keiran for a forwarding address, or a phone number and all of the emails he'd sent had bounced back. He let the dust settle for a while before going to visit Maggie. Standing outside of her house he felt like a little boy again. Nervously he lifted the knocker, beads of perspiration creeping down his forehead. John answered the door.

"I wondered how long it would take." He said as he stood aside and gestured for Leo to come in. Leo nodded with thanks and with his head hung low, he made his way through to the kitchen where Maggie was sat at the table reading the paper.

"Put the kettle on would you Love?" Maggie peered over her glasses and offered Leo the seat next to her. "It's about time, Mr Dolce." Leo couldn't help but feel he was about to be chastised.

"Tea or coffee?" John busied himself with mugs and tea bags.

"Coffee please, black."

Maggie took a few moments to look at the young man in front of her. Cara had told her that Leo was The One but from there she didn't really know what had happened. She didn't want to press Cara, who had been quite distressed before she'd left, and decided that she would tell her in her own time. In the meantime, Maggie had assumed Leo had been unfaithful, but looking at him in front of her now, sheepish, a distinct lack of sparkle behind his eyes and pining for Cara, she wasn't so sure.

"I can't tell you where she is Leo, you know that, don't you?" she asked. Leo began to cry. "Oh, Love!" Maggie exclaimed, she put her arm around him. "Come on now, why so sad?" She handed him a tissue.

Leo wiped his eyes apologetically. "I miss her so much Maggie, it's like she died! I was so looking forward to seeing her when I got back and without even a message she upped and left. I don't understand!" He choked back more tears. "No-one will tell me what I've done or where she is. All I want to know is that she's safe, that she's happy. Is that too much to ask?" His eyes wide with worry, they pleaded with Maggie.

John placed a mug in front of Leo and went into his adjoining study where he picked up the paper. Maggie rubbed Leo's back and allowed him to calm himself before delving a little deeper. They talked about Leo's travels, about the reason behind him going and how he'd realised within a few days of leaving the UK how much he wanted Cara to be there with him. He swore to Maggie that there had been no other girls, and she believed him. The man she comforted now was a shell of the man she'd known Cara to fall in love with. Maggie felt it would be cruel for him to carry on this way.

"Leo, Love, I can see that you loved Cara very much,"

"Love." Leo interrupted. "I still love her."

"Sorry, I can see you love Cara, but for whatever reason, be that right or wrong, she wants to be on her own for the foreseeable future. What I can tell you is that she is safe and happy. She loves her job and her new place, and I am not sure if I should tell you this or not, but she is still single." A shimmer of hope sprung up behind Leo's eyes. "I also probably shouldn't say this either young man, but she was very much in love with you and you broke her heart when you left."

Shamefully Leo nodded. "I know."

"In a way what you did was incredibly selfish, if you look at it purely from Cara's point of view, but if you look at the bigger picture, you did the right thing."

"Did I?" Leo asked, surprised that Maggie would think that.

"Yes. You fulfilled an obligation to a woman you adored, despite it meaning that you had to leave the other woman you adored behind. You're still young Leo and it was a brave decision. I suspect you have done a lot of growing up in the past couple of years."

"You could say that." Leo replied.

"And although she didn't know it at the time, I think it was the right thing for Cara too."

"Really?" Again, Leo was surprised by Maggie's point of view.

"Yes Love. After losing her parents, Cara was a little distant. She was such a good girl, but I always felt like the love we gave her wasn't ever going to be enough. Then

Harry got his claws in to her and to some extent we lost her. We knew there was nothing we could do about it other than support her in the decisions she made but that didn't stop us suspecting that Harry wasn't the right man. I think that meeting you at work, even before she split with Harry, made her realise that Harry didn't deserve her. You put a spring in her step. She often mentioned you in conversation even before they split up."

"Did she? I, I didn't try and split them up!" Harry was worried that Maggie might think badly of him.

Maggie laughed. "I know that, Leo, but your friendship made her feel valued." Leo thought about what Maggie was saying. Thinking back, he remembered their coffee breaks and the laughs they shared. He loved the way Cara laughed. "When you got together properly it was clear to us that Cara had fallen for you, and I have to be honest and tell you that we had our reservations. We thought it was too soon after Harry. We knew she needed to get Harry out of her system and you seemed to do that for her. We didn't realise how she really felt about you until you left." Leo felt ashamed. How could he have left her? He was kicking himself. "Don't feel bad Leo. You leaving her gave her the chance to re-evaluate her priorities. For once she concentrated on herself and her career. Opportunities opened up for her that probably wouldn't have had she continued to focus all her attention on you. You swore her off men and it had a very positive outcome! She always made too many sacrifices for others and for once she's put herself first."

Leo didn't quite know how to feel about all of this. The woman who had loved him completely no longer wanted a boyfriend because he had made her feel so crap about men! What did that say about him?

"However, looking backwards does no good and that is all in the past. Cara isn't ready to come home yet, and I won't tell you where she is, but you need to make plans, for your own future I mean. You can't know yet whether Cara will be part of those plans but do something for yourself and try and be happy on your own. If you're meant to be together it will happen, somewhen. If life has taught me anything it's that you can't predict it. Sometimes we meet the wrong person at the right time, other times we might the right person at the wrong time, but eventually the right person will come along, at the right time. Maybe you just have to wait for the sand to settle," she winked, "then your time will come."

"I hope you're right." Leo wiped his eyes.

"A word of warning though Leo. If, and it is a big if, she comes back, don't expect her to give everything that she has up for you. You have to be prepared to show her that you deserve to be with her, not the other way around."

Leo finished the remainder of his now-cold coffee. He peered through into the study to see if John had been listening, but he seemed to be snoozing. "Thanks Maggie, thanks for believing me."

"It's not me you have to convince though, is it Leo?"

"No, it's not. I just hope I get the chance to prove it to

Cara. Until then I'll do what you said. I'm going to make a plan for my future. Hopefully one day Cara will be part of it."

Leo stood to leave, hugging Maggie as he did. He left feeling more upbeat. At least he knew that Cara was happy, wherever she was, and that's all he could ask for. What was it Maggie had said? 'Wait for the sand to settle.' And he would. He put the key in the ignition and started the engine. The idea he had been mulling over in his mind for the past few months began to come into focus. He knew what he had to do and couldn't wait to get started.

CHAPTER SIXTEEN

The next eighteen months went well at Moon Shine Events. Cara was now completely fluent in Arabic, French and Italian. Rebekah had encouraged her to learn the extra languages and the business paid for it. Rebekah told Cara that learning these languages would give the her the edge in business and she wasn't wrong. Cara had managed several more events for her prestigious client and his extended family. None as large as the birthday party, but she put no less effort in and she continued to impress. Rebekah had also been keen to show Cara more of the administrative side of the business and now she was pretty much able to run the business while Rebekah had meetings with other clients and when she had to travel abroad, which was happening with increased frequency. Together they recruited new staff and the team had grown by 50%. Each new team member had been scouted by one of the existing members of staff and had been recruited for their skill and efficiency and, perhaps most importantly, their discretion. Everyone within the team was aware that with such high-profile clients, it was key that their employees understood the importance of client confidentiality.

Rebekah had always been very good at incentivising her staff but with Cara in place she found that the office seemed brighter, even more enthusiastic, and positive. Rebekah couldn't be any happier with the way things were being run. Now that she knew she had someone she could really rely upon, Rebekah was able to take more time off to spend with her daughter. Most days she was able to meet Azizah from school and leave Cara to run the office. Launching her company in a male dominated country had been difficult even given her family background. Being half Emirati had certainly smoothed the way for Rebekah, but it wasn't easy. Because of who her parents had been Rebekah had been keen to ensure she was recognised for her own accomplishments and not just those of her father, or just the name of her mother. Being a member of one of the most influential families in the Emirates had its benefits, of course. She had inherited part-ownership of one of the large real-estate firms in Dubai, hence the ability to run an office and own properties within the towers. She was clever enough to know that image was everything and used her family ties to her advantage.

She knew the moment she met Cara that she was the right person. Finding out that they had so much in common and had got on so well was the icing on the cake. She picked up her phone and dialled Cara's number.

"Hi Rebekah! What's up?" Cara asked, surprised to hear from Rebekah on a Friday. Her boss worked the team hard but when there were no events to run she insisted that after working Sunday through to Thursday they have Fridays off. If they ever did meet at the weekend, it tended to be on a Saturday.

"Are you free later?" Rebekah asked. "I just need a

quick chat. If you could pop over for a bit that would be great."

"Of course! I'll be over in ten." Rebekah rang off and Cara stared at the screen. She grabbed her bag, doing her best to shake off the feeling of unease that was fast creeping up on her.

Cara was devastated, there was no other word for it. She'd called round to Rebekah's with a chilled bottle of wine, only to leave it unopened on the dining table. Azizah had heard the Sri Lankan maid, Patma, open the front door and came running through the hall.

"Cici! Come and see my piece of art, it's a landscape!" Azizah had taken to calling Cara this the day after she had met her and the two had struck up an unlikely friendship, akin to that of sisters.

Handing her bag to Patma and taking her shoes off, Cara allowed herself to be pulled through the downstairs reception rooms and into the playroom where Azizah was painting at her easel. Rebekah was sat near the large open doors to the garden, enjoying the breeze. She greeted Rebekah by kissing her on both cheeks and gestured to Azizah.

"Carry on," Rebekah whispered, "it can wait until you're done. She loves having you here."

Cara enjoyed Azizah's company, she was very playful but also had a very mature sense of humour. Rebekah and Cara's relationship extended beyond the office, something that both women were thankful for. Before meeting Cara, Rebekah had been worried about so many things but having Cara in her life had a very calming effect. She still worried about how she'd break the news but knew that it was time she did.

After working with Azizah to create a mini-gallery of masterpieces, Cara asked permission to speak to Rebekah. Reluctantly, the ten-year-old agreed. Rebekah lifted herself out of the chair and directed Cara into the garden with a nod of her head. She called to Patma to bring some tea and the two women sat on the garden loungers facing the kidney shaped pool.

The garden had been lovingly tended to by their gardener, Mr Mohammad who lived in the caretakers flat in the grounds. There were pomegranate trees, lemon and lime trees, and pretty pink and white flowers bordering the beds. The grass was kept meticulously tidy and was watered twice daily via the automatic sprinkler system that rose out of the ground. Azizah's puppy played on the grass, attempting to catch dragonflies. It was idyllic.

Rebekah made small talk with Cara, which seemed odd and a little forced. The panic rose inside. What was she going to say? Patma left the tea on the table between them, Cara smiled at her in thanks, Patma smiled in return, but her eyes were sad. She left the women alone. Cara silently wondered what she had done to get the sack. What she heard next could not have been further from her mind.

Rebekah reached over and took Cara's hand in hers and then placed her other hand on top. She looked Cara in the eye. "My dear Cara. I am dying." Had she heard right? She couldn't have. She shook her head. "No." She protested. Time slowed as she mentally rewound the past two years. There were no signs, were there?

A single tear traced Rebekah's left cheek. This was the first time she'd cried outside the confines of her room. The day they'd met was the day Rebekah had been discharged from hospital. She had been operated on by a specialist doctor friend who lived in Hampshire. Her initial symptoms had begun innocently enough. At first, a light tickle of a cough which Rebekah had put down to a recent sandstorm and the dust in the air that remained. The cough then became more persistent and although Rebekah found it irritating she didn't want to bother a doctor about it. As work became predictably busier when the weather cooled down, Rebekah found she was becoming increasingly fatigued, but there was nothing unusual in that, so she ignored it and tried to catch a bit more than five hours sleep a night. Winter turned into spring and the weather began heating up again and as it did Rebekah had the chance to take Azizah to the beach more often. Rebekah hadn't donned a swimsuit in more than two months but as she wriggled into it one Friday morning she found it hung loosely around the tummy and bottom.

"Ummi, your legs are skinny like mine, look!" Azizah stood next to her mother and compared their legs in the mirror, giggling at their reflections. Rebekah laughed and made a mental note to eat a little more. The cough was still there too but she no longer noticed it. She was still exhausted but told herself she needed to relax a little more and made a mental note to look into hiring another person at work.

That particular day at the beach had been memorable for Rebekah. For the first time in a long while it had been just her and her daughter. They'd built sandcastles, collected shells and jumped waves. As the day wore on Rebekah became short of breath and she noticed an ache in her left shoulder. Sitting in the sand to catch her breath Rebekah watched her eight-year-old daughter as the amber sun lowered in the sky. Azizah became a silhouette, her long dark curls, matted with salt and sand framed her face as she crouched down and concentrated on decorating the fairy princess castle she and her mother had so lovingly crafted. Rebekah marvelled at her daughter's beauty, her looks inherited from her father. He could have easily been mistaken for being Arabic. He spoke the language perfectly and had chestnut coloured skin, black curly hair and the obligatory short beard and moustache sported by every local man of any stature. The fact that Azizah would never know her father stung her heart. Rebekah had loved him, but her marriage had been arranged long before they'd met.

By some cruel twist of face Rebekah had lost her husband in a road accident soon after their wedding day. They'd only been married a short time, but it had been the biggest test in Rebekah's life and finding out she was pregnant had almost destroyed her. The match had been a good one and although her father was western, given his position within the government, Rebekah felt she should obey the local rules and culture of her mother's family and go along with the arrangement. However, she faced the future as a widow. She emerged from the mourning period four months and ten days later with a growing bump and the determination to stand on her own two feet and to create a legacy for her child that was not entirely reliant upon her family name and history. Her emotions dead and buried along with her husband, she never looked back. Meeting Azizah's father had not been part of the plan and it had finished almost as quickly as it had begun. Starting any kind of relationship so soon after losing her husband would have been frowned upon and they agreed to bury any feelings they may once have had and move on. Now, though, she wished he could pay more than just the occasional visit.

"Come Zizi! Time to go, Habibi." Rebekah had called to her daughter who noticed her wince as she pushed herself up and unquestioningly rushed to help her. Rubbing her left shoulder and stifling another cough, Rebekah made a mental note to visit the Doctor when she next had some free time. A month later and Rebekah had still not made that appointment. Increasingly worried, Patma had tried many times to remind her.

"Madam, please, you are too thin, and you still cough. Think of your daughter, you must see a Doctor."

Ascending the stairs Rebekah waved her hand to dismiss Patma but as she did, she felt faint and stumbled the last few steps. She woke a while later wearing an oxygen mask and staring at a white ceiling. After a CT scan and a bronchoscopy, a Consultant joined Rebekah at her bedside and broke the news to her that she had Adenocarcinoma, a primary lung cancer, non-responsive to radiation therapy. He went on to tell her that she would need surgery if she were to survive. The decision then had been an easy one. In that moment she'd been given a second chance and she booked a private operation immediately.

The surgery in the UK had gone well and Rebekah had been sent home. She had been told that with regular check-ups and monitoring, the future looked positive. And it was on her way home that Rebekah had met Cara. Feeling happy about the surgery, Rebekah had no reason to think that the cancer would return, but what she did realise while she was away from her daughter was that she wanted, and needed, to spend more time with her. Meeting Cara had been no coincidence. The universe had gifted Cara to her, of that she was sure. Having her treatment had given her the chance to centre her thoughts and upon meeting Cara she just knew she would be a good person to have in her life. She'd trained Cara and slowly trusted her with more responsibilities and she'd turned out to be the most incredible person Rebekah had ever met. Despite her prognosis being good Rebekah wanted to ensure that if the time came, she had someone she could rely upon to secure her daughter's future, and she found that person in Cara.

The backache had started again six months ago. At first Rebekah had thought it was her new chair at work, but Patma had noticed the weight loss had started again and, although Rebekah tried to hide it, she also noticed the fatigue returning and the shortness of breath. Fearing the worst, Rebekah made an emergency trip to see her Doctor in the UK only to be told that the cancer had spread to the lymph nodes throughout her body and that it wasn't operable. She wasn't certain how long she had left, but in her heart, she knew it wouldn't be long and all she wanted to do was to spend time with Azizah.

Cara listened intently to Rebekah. She had noticed a little weight loss but put that down to Rebekah spending less time at work and more time concentrating on herself and Zizi, stupidly she had though Rebekah was on a diet! She leaned across and hugged the woman who'd invested so much in her.

"Well we'd best make sure the guest suite is made up hadn't we." Cara stated matter-of-factly. There and then she made up her mind that there was no way Rebekah would face this on her own.

"You don't have to, Cara. It won't be easy." Rebekah spoke softly.

"I know I don't have to Rebekah, I want to." Cara replied, reassuringly.

"Thank you." Rebekah whispered. Cara held her friend as she finally let out the pain she'd been hiding for so long.

CHAPTER SEVENTEEN

*A*atif took Cara back to her apartment that evening. Initially she'd asked him to wait but as she stepped out of the Lexus she changed her mind. Rather than grab a few things temporarily, she decided to get everything sorted in one go. "I'll stay here tonight Aatif and pack a couple of cases. I'll call you tomorrow to collect me then, but do you think you could arrange for some movers to come and get the rest of my stuff?"

"Of course, Miss Cara. Just call me when you need me. Have a nice evening."

She waved him off and made her way into the lobby. The staff welcomed her as she made her way across to the elevators. Reaching into her bag for her phone she dropped her keycard on the marble tiled floor. Huffing, she bent down to pick it up, but was beaten to it. Her hand brushed his before she quickly snatched it back.

"Cara-May, we meet again, at last." His Dolcet tones which before had brushed over her this time found themselves a welcome ear.

"Miles Granger." Cara blushed, those emerald green eyes captivating her for a second time. She'd seen him a few times in the lobby or going into the lift but had somehow always managed to avoid him. She had felt an attraction to him, but something told her she needed to stay away.

Miles smiled, his emerald eyes wrinkling at the corners.

His black hair sported more slivers of grey, the unexpected effect this had upon Cara was to light a desire within her that she'd thought had been dead and buried. They stood up in synchronization, not leaving one another's gaze they both reached for the elevator call button. Miles' hand rested upon hers for a moment before he traced his fingers along her arm. Interrupted by the ding of the doors opening, they moved apart to allow two other residents out and stepped in, taking their places. Without speaking Miles' hand hovered over the buttons. Granting him permission with her eyes, he used Cara's keycard to activate the button to the 30th floor.

The elevator shuddered to a halt and Miles led the way to Apartment 3004. He opened the door and stood aside to let Cara enter. She walked into the apartment, putting her handbag on the dining table and stood for a moment, leaning with both hands, looking down and taking a breath. What was wrong with her? Her best friend had told her she was dying and here she was, inviting Miles Granger into her room! She'd been celibate for two years and hadn't acted on any light flirtations, striving to protect her emotions, but seeing Miles today had stirred something in her. Perhaps it was the emotional urge to live in the moment, or the fact that the desire she felt when she met Miles that first time was finally bubbling to the surface?

She didn't know why she was acting to recklessly in a country where relations outside of marriage were illegal, but when Miles began kissing her neck from behind she didn't flinch. Moving her head to one side she allowed him to plant kisses along her neck as his hands explored her body. Expertly, Miles pulled the flimsy dress up and over her head. In turn, Cara unbuttoned his shirt, revealing his tanned torso. She knew she was taking a risk, but she wasn't thinking straight she just needed him, she needed this.

Cara awoke the following morning to find the space in the bed next to her empty and the sound of the kettle boiling in the kitchen. She reached across for the remote on her side of the bed and opened the heavy drapes, the sun shone in, filtered by the fine voiles. She lay on her back and stared at the ceiling. What had happened last night had completely taken her by surprise. She expected to feel guilty but somehow knew that Rebekah would approve, she would tell her to seize the moment. The previous evening's activities had allowed her body to release every bit of tension and emotion that it had been holding. It had been good for her.

Miles appeared at the door. "Breakfast is served. In bed or in the dining room?" He inquired, the service manager side of him not taking a minute's break.

"Bed please." Cara replied. She hadn't had this treatment in a *very* long time, so she decided to make the most of it. Miles reappeared with a tray upon which was a freshly squeezed pink grapefruit juice, a small pot of green tea and a smoked salmon and cream cheese bagel. He put the tray on Cara's lap then leaned forward and kissed her on the lips. "I'm impressed," Cara quipped, "it's almost as if you know my room service orders off by heart!"

"You got me!" Miles smiled, "Perks of the job." He laughed. "I have to get to work though I'm afraid. Perhaps I'll see you later?" He asked hopefully.

"Um, actually I have to move out for a while." Cara replied awkwardly. "Can I call you? It's a long story."

Miles looked a little hurt but quickly replaced the look with a reassuring smile. Cara was relieved, the last thing she needed now was a needy man wanting her attention. "No problem, call me when you can." He kissed her again and left.

She didn't care much for long lie-ins. As soon as she heard the door close, she leapt out of bed. After what Rebekah had told her yesterday she had no business laying around in bed all day. After showering and dressing, she called Aatif to check that he had arranged for a man with a van to collect her belongings. As she roamed around the apartment it struck her how few belongings she actually owned. Mostly it was clothes, shoes, perfumes and photos. Other than that, there wasn't an awful lot to fill the few boxes she'd acquired. Whilst she was busily putting the kettle on, the phone rang.

"Vix! How are you my lovely!" she answered the call, genuinely pleased to hear from her best friend.

"Great thanks Car, you?"

"Oh, you know...busy." Cara replied trying to hide her inner sparkle.

"Oh! Do tell, I can tell by your voice..." Vix instructed. She knew when her best friend was covering for something, she knew it was the hint of a new man. "You didn't?" she giggled, fishing for gossip.

"I might have... but more about that later. I'm sure you didn't call me during breakfast to find out about my sex life." Cara didn't want to give too much away. "So, what's your news? John and Maggs are OK, aren't they?" she asked, suddenly worried that she had been neglecting those at home. She continued to busy herself with her paperwork and packing around the dining table.

"Oh, they're fine Car. But I, actually *we*, have some news...." Vix replied trying, unsuccessfully, to hide her excitement.

"WE?" Cara stopped sorting the papers in front of her on the table and gave the friend her full attention.

"Keiran and I have some news..." Vix was trying her hardest to be sensitive.

"Go on then," Cara instructed, "tell me."

"We're getting married!" Vix screeched excitedly.

Cara was thrilled for her best friend but today of all days really was the worst day to receive this news. She knew this moment was coming but she wanted to be able to shout and scream and feel genuinely excited without thinking about her other best friend living with a death sentence.

"Amazing! Congratulations!" Cara forced. "I am so

happy for you both! When's the big day?"

"Well, that's the other thing...." Vix replied tentatively.

"What *other thing?*" Cara asked suspiciously.

"The, you being an Aunty thing..." Vix replied bashfully.

"You're expecting as well?" She asked quietly. How could this happen? She didn't quite understand her emotions. There was no way in the world she wanted a baby now, or for a while. When she'd been with Harry it had been the natural next step but when that fell apart she pushed the thought of having a family back into the deepest parts of her brain. Leo had made her happy and had made her wonder whether he was the right person to have children with, but his ultimate betrayal had answered that question for her. "Vix, that is wonderful news. Congratulations." She wiped her eyes.

"I know!" screeched Vix, "It's very early days and I wanted to tell you in person, but you being half way around the world kind of put a spanner in the works there." She spent the next half an hour playing along and faking her happiness. She was happy for her friend but there was still a tiny part of her that wished it had been her. When they hung up she scolded herself for her true feelings. How on earth could she sit there feeling jealous when she had more than most people could ever dream of? An endless expense account, a chauffeur, a fully paid for apartment in one of the most exclusive buildings in the world and a career that was currently sky rocketing. A moment later she gave herself a reality check. Yes, she had all of these material things, but she didn't have a man she cared about and having a baby just wasn't going to be on the cards any time soon. She also had a very good friend with terminal cancer who she had to look after.

Her thoughts were interrupted by a knock at the door it was the removal men who'd come to collect her belongings. In the time it took them to sweep up her ten boxes and pack them into the lift she had given herself a swift talking to. There was no room for emotion or worrying about what she didn't have or what might have been. What she currently did have was a wonderful friend who had very little time left. She knew there and then that the part she had to play in life right now was not one of being a lover, mother, wife or partner but that of a good friend to someone who had seen the potential in her and invested more than she could have asked. Cara knew exactly what she needed to do for Rebekah and Azizah and despite being terrified, she put her lipstick on, smiled for the world and closed the door to her apartment.

CHAPTER EIGHTEEN

As promised, Vix and Keiran's invitation arrived a week after Cara had moved into Rebekah's villa. Patma had intercepted the mail and was careful to hand it to Cara in private. Cara sent a congratulatory bunch of flowers and an RSVP saying that she *obviously* would be at the wedding in two months' time. The reality was very different. The three women were living life one *day* at a time. Within a week of moving in, Patma and Cara were pretty much sharing the childcare of Azizah. Aatif was doing the school drop off and collection, Patma was preparing and serving dinner and Cara was doing homework and then putting Azizah to bed ready for Rebekah to read bedtime stories. In between the daily run around Cara would try and ensure Azizah saw her mother as much as possible. Miles had called Cara a couple of times, but she had managed to put him off. She knew she was ready to open up emotionally to someone, but it was more important that she concentrate on Rebekah.

Rebekah's decline had been quicker than any of them could have imagined. She spent most of her time laying in the lounge gazing into the garden through the patio doors. She had a nurse who would administer pain relief visiting the house regularly but beyond that there was no treatment that would make any difference to the state of her health. Azizah would come home from school and run to the lounge for a cuddle and would have to be dragged away to eat. When it was time for bed she begged her mother to read to her and Rebekah obliged for as long as she could get up the stairs. When she could no longer manage, even with help, Rebekah moved into the guest room downstairs and Azizah took to falling asleep alongside her mother before Cara carried her upstairs to bed. Every night would be the same.

"Ummi, tell me a story." Azizah would ask.

"Of course, Zizi, what story would you like?" Rebekah would reply.

"The one about the Queen and the Princess, Ummi, I like that one, it reminds me of us."

A few weeks after Cara had moved in, Rebekah was no longer able to leave her bedroom. Rebekah was honest with her daughter and told her exactly what was going on early one morning.

"Ummi?" Azizah whispered quietly as she knocked Rebekah's door, "Ummi?"

"Shhh Zizi, Mummy's sleeping. We'll come in and see her after school." Cara put her arm around Azizah as she ushered her away from Rebekah's room.

"Zizi." Rebekah called in a raspy voice, "Zizi, Cara! Bring Zizi in, I need to talk to her."

Azizah turned excitedly. Cara, however, had been dreading this moment. Turning back towards Rebekah's bedroom, Azizah pushed open the door and sprung into the room. Sunlight dissipated through the cerise voile curtains bathing the room in a soft pink light. Cara was shocked to see how much Rebekah had deteriorated overnight and knew that the time had come.

"Zizi, come sit with Ummi. We need to talk." Rebekah muttered in a soft voice as she tried to pat the space upon the bed next to her. Azizah approached her mother tentatively but seeing her familiar smile calmed her and she laid upon the bed next to her and cuddled in.

"Ummi, you're all bony!" she exclaimed as Rebekah used all of her energy to lift her arm and place it around her daughter.

Rebekah laughed weakly, "You're right Zizi! I am very bony. But I can still cuddle my best girl."

While Azizah held her Mother's hand, Cara approached the bed and kissed Rebekah's pale cheek. "I love you, Rebekah," she whispered, blinking back tears, "you've taught me so much." She sat gently on the bed.

"Come on now, everything is fine." Rebekah comforted her, her hand grasping Cara's gently. "It is you that I should thank. I invited you out here on a whim and here you are looking after me, after both of us." She smiled as she gestured towards Azizah. "If you learn one thing from me Cara, let it be this. Your life is like the desert. Forever shifting with weather and time. Sometimes the dunes will become so huge that they will seem impossible to climb. Be careful to avoid the rocks hidden beneath the surface." She coughed, her breath growing shorter, her voice weaker. "But keep climbing, and when you reach the top you will be rewarded with the most beautiful view. Settled sand will spread out in front of you, inviting you to run effortlessly towards your dreams. When the time comes, Cara, run. As fast as you can." Cara tried to speak but couldn't for fear of losing control entirely. "You gave me the chance to spend time with my daughter, Cara. Thank you." She closed her eyes.

Cara smiled weakly, she brought her friend's hand to her lips and kissed the paper-thin skin tenderly, as life slipped away it had taken on an iridescent, angelic quality. She checked that Rebekah was comfortable with her daughter by her side and caught her friend smile before leaving the room. She closed the door quietly behind her before sliding to the floor against the wall. Tears streamed down her cheeks. Patma had been waiting outside the room, as she had become accustomed to doing every day, keeping guard like a Beefeater guarding the crown jewels. Seeing Cara collapse she rushed over and held her in her arms, allowing her to sob.

"It's not fair, it's not fair," she cried softly. "Poor Zizi, she'll be all alone."

"No, Miss Cara," Patma whispered, "she has us. She will always have us." For just a moment Patma allowed her mask of composure slip as she too, wept for the child she'd raised.

Half an hour or so passed before they found the strength to do what they knew they had to. Patma called the nurse as Cara knocked the bedroom door and slowly pushed it aside. She saw Zizi laid in her mother's arms, both resting, seemingly asleep. She stroked Azizah's arm.

"Zizi," she whispered, "wake up."

Azizah's eyes remained closed as she whispered back. "I

am awake Cara, but I don't want to open my eyes."

"Why not?" Cara asked softly.

"Because when I open my eyes Ummi will be gone." Cara held her breath. "Ummi told me that it was time for her to leave, but I'm not ready for her to go yet."

"Zizi," she stroked the child's hair away from her cheek as she opened her eyes. "Ummi will always be in here." She took Azizah's hand and placed it on her heart. Azizah nodded, her bright eyes innocently accepting her mother's death.

Cara wiped the tears from her cheeks then, reaching across for Rebekah's wrist, she felt for a pulse. There was none so she turned to Patma and gestured for her to let the nurse in.

"Come Zizi. The nurse needs to come and see Ummi now, she will look after her." She waited for the child to oblige, she didn't want to force her to leave before she was ready.

"You are very lucky Zizi, you know why?" Cara spoke softly.

"Why?" Azizah answered.

"Ummi loved you very much and you were lucky because she was able to tell you. When my Mother and Father left me they couldn't say goodbye, they didn't have time." She wiped away more tears. Azizah put her arms around Cara's shoulders and spoke earnestly.

"I'm sorry Cici, I know your Mummy and Daddy loved you very much too." she kissed Cara's cheek. "Shall we look after each other now?"

Choking back her sadness Cara replied. "Yes, Zizi, we'll look after each other now."

"Are you ready Zizi? You are the lady of the house now. There will be lots of visitors who want to come and pay their respects to Ummi."

The child had impressed Cara with how well she had dealt with her Mother's death. Rebekah had been buried within twelve hours of her passing, as was tradition in a Muslim country when no foul play was suspected. It had been a little alien to Cara yet very peaceful. When they'd returned to the villa Patma went into overdrive and Cara was very grateful for her efficiency. Within a couple of hours, the house began to fill with friends and family. Rebekah had not given much away about her family, but it fast became clear that the funeral would not be a small affair. Cara and Azizah both changed into full Abaya and Shallah, although Cara didn't wear the veil across her face. She had never been able to get used to that, instead she covered just her hair. The two of them greeted each guest and showed them to one of the two large reception rooms. Traditionally men and women would pay their respects to the family separately and as there was no husband to accept the men, the men and women read from the Qur'an and said prayers separately before coming together to share memories of Rebekah with each other and their hosts.

Traditional Arabic food had been delivered by caterers,

and waitresses dressed entirely in black, were moving swiftly and quietly throughout the room with trays and coffee pots. There were many faces who came to pay their respects that Cara recognised, including Mr and Mrs Thawadalia and her husband, and other Emirati ruling families. She was a little surprised to see so many influential families in one room and in a snatched moment took Patma into a side room and picked her brains.

"Patma, is there something I should know here?" she asked candidly.

"What do you mean Madam?" Patma asked innocently.

"Well, I know Cara dealt with lots of these people through the business but an awful lot of them seem very upset. Don't get me wrong, Rebekah was a wonderful person, but I am just a little surprised that business associates would show their emotions so readily."

"Ah." Patma replied.

"Ah? What does that mean?"

"The family." Patma answered.

"Rebekah didn't have any family, at least not that she talked about. Whenever I asked she said that there was no-one left." Cara said, feeling puzzled.

"Yes, she did. They are nearly all family, in some way. Aunts, uncles, cousins, second cousins. There are very few people out there whom she wasn't related to."

Cara's eyes widened as the realisation set in. In her mind she slowly pieced together everything she knew about Rebekah and the business. The office, the clients, her apartment.

"She, she...?" Cara whispered, as her eyes looked towards the door.

Patma laughed. "Yes, Miss Cara, she was very important."

"And you knew? The whole time?" She was surprised, although looking back she realised she hadn't asked.

"Yes, Miss Cara, of course I knew. I have worked for the family for almost fifty years. I was Miss Rebekah's Nanny when she was small."

"FIFTY YEARS!" Cara screeched, "That's not possible Patma, you look so young! I thought you were only in your forties!"

Patma blushed and giggled girlishly. "Thank you, Madam, you are very kind. But I am seventy-two."

Cara was shocked. "And Aatif?" she asked.

"Yes, Madam, Mr Aatif has also worked for the family for many years."

"Right then, now I know what I'm dealing with I'll head back out." Cara raised her eyebrows and returned to the guests.

Upon entering the central hall Cara stopped in her tracks. Coming through the front door was Miles. She didn't know which way to look. Reluctantly she allowed him to approach her.

"Miles?" she smiled self-consciously. Miles returned the smile and held out his arms. Cara awkwardly held out her right hand and shook his. "How can I help? I'm afraid this isn't a great time."

"Oh, er, I've come to pay my respects. I hope that's OK?" he asked, his beautiful eyes bloodshot.

"Oh, yes, of course. I suppose you know her from the hotel, don't you?" she asked feeling suddenly guilty for thinking he was there for her benefit.

"The hotel?" he questioned

"Yes, of the hotel, where the office is." she replied.

Avoiding her gaze, Miles replied, "Hmm yes, something like that. Anyway, where are the men?"

"Oh, they're that way," she pointed to the reception room to her left.

"Thanks, I'll speak to you later then." He smiled, somewhat nervously.

Cara thought his behaviour was a little odd but guessed that people dealt with death in different ways. Moments later, she noticed Miles walking the wrong way. Sighing, she followed him across the hallway. As she turned the corner she stopped in her tracks. What was he doing? She stepped silently behind a pillar. Holding her breath, she peeked carefully to see Miles crouched down on one knee, in front of him was Azizah. Cara let out her breath. She saw him stroke the little girl's cheek which he then kissed gently before hugging her. Cara overheard Azizah.

"Don't cry Bapi, Ummi said we will be OK. She said that we will all miss her but that everything will be OK. When you feel sad, Bapi, come see me. I will make you happy again. We can play like we used to before Ummi got sick."

"I'm not sure that will be possible anymore Zizi. Things will be a bit different now that Ummi is gone. I won't be able to come and see you so much." He sobbed into the child's shoulder as she hugged him tightly. "And my name is Miles," he added quietly, "you must call me Miles."

Shocked, Cara closed her eyes as she tried to figure out what she'd just heard. She'd heard that name before, Bapi, but where? Suddenly from the Majlis came a loud crash as a waiter dropped one of the silver platters. Cara jumped at the noise. Pulling herself together she worried that she might get caught. Brushing her Abaya down with her hands she stepped out from behind the pillar and straight into Miles.

"Ahh!" she jumped.

"Oh, God, sorry." Miles jumped just as much. He tried to not look her in the eye. His cheeks were tear stained. Azizah came bounding around the corner behind him and grabbed Cara around the waist, holding her close. Cara knelt down to Azizah's level and hugged her.

"Are you alright, Zizi? Have you met Miles?" she asked quizzically.

Azizah giggled. "Miles?" she looked up to see Miles lift his finger to his lips. "Oh! Miles! Yes, I've met Miles." She feigned seriousness, then giggled again. Cara cradled Azizah's face in her hands and smiled thinking how innocent she was. Smoothing the child's cheeks with her thumbs, Cara looked up at Miles who was looking down at them. She looked again at Azizah, her emerald eyes sparkling.

Three days later and the initial mourning period for Rebekah was over. Cara couldn't help thinking that the Muslim way of doing things had actually sped-up the grieving process. The household was still sad at Rebekah's passing but they didn't cry for days on end. It seemed that the constant flow of visitors sharing their memories helped everyone to cope with their loss. For much of the time Cara felt her role was to listen, which she found not only therapeutic but also very interesting. It also seemed that in Rebekah's departure Cara was being welcomed into the inner family circle which would be useful given her new status as legal guardian to Azizah.

As the end had drawn near, Rebekah had asked Cara if she would look after Azizah. Without hesitation, Cara agreed. The plan would be for Patma and Aatif to remain in her employment and for Cara to move into the villa and look after Azizah. The discussion had been emotional but factual. The legal paperwork had been written up and transcribed into Arabic, signed by both women and legalised by the court. The remainder of Cara's belongings had been collected from the apartment and delivered to her at the villa, but the apartment remained in her name.

A week after the funeral, Cara had been visited by a senior member of the family who had arrived with a lawyer. It seemed that Rebekah's final wishes had been intercepted by the family and a discussion had ensued as to whether they would be carried out. Cara sat nervously in the lounge as Patma served coffee and dates.

"So, how can I help Mr Kadar?" she addressed the elderly male visitor in Arabic. She was relieved she had decided to dress in her abaya, albeit it one decorated with gold thread along the sleeves. From her dressing-room window she had seen the sky-blue Rolls Royce Phantom pull into the driveway and judged that the traditional dress may be a good option. If Rebekah had taught her anything in the past couple of years' it was to always be prepared for visitors of any kind.

"Miss Cara, the family have discussed the contents of Rebekah's will and it is slightly unusual."

Cara raised her eyebrows in surprise. She couldn't think what might be unusual. She had made the assumption that everything would be left to Azizah. "Unusual?" she asked.

"As you know, Rebekah wished for you to be Azizah's adopted parent, and with no father, the family agree. In the past week every single member of the family has commented on how settled Azizah is with you, here. It is clear to all of us that you have a good relationship with her and we therefore agree that she should stay with you." Cara let out a breath of relief. Mr Kadar continued. "Also as Rebekah's only living heir, and with her father and Rebekah's father deceased, all property and belongings have been left to Azizah."

Cara smiled. "Naturally."

"But, as she is under eighteen, everything is to be left in trust with you until she has completed her university education. You are to ensure that she remains living in this home, and that she is cared for and looked after, respecting our religious beliefs and custom." Cara was shocked. She hadn't thought this far ahead. Effectively this meant that for at least the next twelve years, she and Azizah didn't have to worry about a thing.

"Oh, OK." she replied. "More coffee?" she asked nervously as she poured, regardless. She lifted her cup to her lips.

"And Moon Shine Events, Rebekah's business, she has signed this over to you in its entirety."

Cara almost choked on her coffee. "Come again?!" she remarked, in English.

"Madhaa taquul?" Mr Kadar enquired.

Cara reverted back to Arabic. "I'm sorry, I said pardon?"

Mr Kadar smiled. "I said, the business, you are now the owner and CEO. From what Rebekah told me you are exceptionally competent." Mr Kadar and his Lawyer showed Cara the signed contract.

After absorbing the news, she reviewed and signed what needed signing, including official adoption papers, Mr Kadar made it clear to her that all channels of communications to his family and many businesses would remain open and Cara and Azizah would be welcome anytime.

When the men had gone Cara made her way through to the back garden where Azizah was swimming under Patma's careful supervision. Smiling at the scene in front of her, she stole a moment to take it all in. In the past hour she had become both a parent and a multi-millionaire in one fell swoop. Two years ago, she hadn't known what her future held, she was underpaid, undervalued and under-loved until fate stepped in and she met Rebekah.

She was incredibly thankful for what her dear friend had brought to her life, and she didn't mean the money. Rebekah had shown her a purpose, she'd been a mentor and a mother figure. She'd put her trust in Cara and shown her the value of believing in herself. She had also confirmed for her that a *traditional* family wasn't necessary, but that a family of some sort was still important. The only thing she hadn't shared with Cara was the truth about Azizah. For now, however, this didn't seem important because despite the timing being atrocious, she had a wedding to pack for.

CHAPTER NINETEEN

"Zizi, are you ready?" Cara called up the stairs. "We need to get going sweetie, the plane won't wait if we're late!"

"Coming Cici. I'm so excited! I love England, Ummi took me there when I was four. It snowed! Will it be snowing now?"

Cara laughed at Azizah's quick fire speech. "I hope not Zizi, it's summer time and we are going to a wedding! We don't want to be cold, do we?"

"Ummi said it was always cold in England. I've packed some jumpers, just in case." Azizah was serious as she pulled her wheelie case down the stairs. Aatif rushed up and took the case.

"Thank you Atty!" Azizah chirped, she had pet names for everyone.

Cara turned to Patma. "We'll be back in a week Patma, please make sure you rest. The past few weeks have been exhausting for all of us."

"I am fine Miss Cara. You go, please, go now." Patma hurried Cara and Azizah out of the door, hugging them both before they left. Aatif placed the cases in the back of the Lexus and then opened the rear door for Azizah to climb in. Rushing around to the back of the car, he held open the other door for Cara. Pausing before getting in the back Cara looked at the sprawling villa in front of her. She hadn't had time to call Vix and tell her everything. She'd just have to do in person although she was convinced no-one would believe her.

The plane touched down at London Heathrow late in the afternoon. For this, Cara was thankful. The wedding wasn't for a couple of days, so she had time to get some rest and a chance to tell Vix everything. The flight had been easy. She felt a little embarrassed to say that she had become accustomed to travelling in First Class, but she convinced herself on this occasion that it was OK because Azizah needed to rest. The truth of the matter was that Azizah had been so excited she had spent the seven hours in the air watching films, playing games and making the most of the snack bar.

Cara hadn't wanted to bother anyone with asking for a lift, so she had booked a chauffeur company to meet them at the airport. The moment she signed that piece of paper, Cara knew what her responsibilities were. After losing her mother, Cara just could not bring herself to tell Azizah she would be leaving so soon. Instead she decided she would turn the whole thing into an adventure and take the child with her.

"Where are we going first Cici?" Azizah asked excitedly as she stared out of the back window of the Mercedes.

"Do you remember I told you that when I was growing up some really nice people looked after me?"

"Yes." Replied Azizah, her green eyes wide with excitement.

"Well, I know for a fact that they would love to meet

you. Would that be OK with you?" Cara thought she should tread carefully but she needn't have worried.

"Yes, yes and triple yes! I can't wait. Will I meet Vix too? And will I see her wedding dress?"

Cara laughed, "Absolutely you will!"

Azizah did a mini fist-pump whilst whispering another "Yes" then turned back to the window. An hour and a half later and the car drove up the high street. It wasn't yet dark and as Cara looked out of the window she was reminded of the evening when the rest of her life had begun. Now that she thought about it, she had a lot to thank Harry for. If she hadn't seen him doing the dirty on her then she would never be where she was now. She turned to look at Azizah who was dozing with her head against the window and smiled.

"Take a left and left again please, the house is just up on the right." she whispered to the driver.

As they pulled up outside of Maggie and John's house, Cara took a deep breath. The driver opened her door and she stepped out. Lifting the knocker and letting it fall she wondered how she was going to tell them everything.

Maggie was a little distracted as she opened the front door. "Oh hello Love, come on in..." she smiled and rushed back into the house. Cara didn't move. Just before she reached the kitchen door, Maggs stopped in her tracks. Slowly she turned around. "OH MY GOD!!" She ran back to the front door and threw her arms around Cara, screaming into her neck as she did so. "You're back!" She stood back and held Cara at arms-length.

"Ta da!" Cara did a little curtsey.

"And you seem to have brought someone with you! Hello Love, what's your name?" Azizah had woken up at the sound of the door knocker and climbed out of the car, she now stood on the step behind Cara and was peering around her legs.

"Azizah," she replied confidently, "but you can call me Zizi, all of my family do." She smiled and looked up at Cara.

Maggs held out her hand, "Very nice to meet you Zizi, I'm Maggie but all of my family call me Maggs." Azizah ignored the offer of the hand and pushed past Cara and into Maggie's arms. Maggie was taken by surprise. She looked up at Cara, questioning her with her eyes. Cara smiled, her eyes glistening. Azizah squeezed, Maggie reciprocated. She couldn't help but feel some affection for the little girl, but she did wonder what on earth was going on.

Cara took Azizah into the kitchen where she introduced her to John and made her some hot chocolate. Azizah perched on the bar stool in the kitchen and chattered animatedly with Maggie answering questions about her school and friends in Dubai as Cara stood back and watched. It wasn't too long before the tiredness hit and Cara took Azizah up to her room. Not bothering to unpack anything other than Azizah's pyjamas, Cara and Azizah lay side-by-side on the enormous bed, the two of them worn out by the journey and the excitement of their first trip together.

"Want a cuddle Zizi?" Cara asked. Azizah shuffled across the bed and snuggled into Cara's left side. "I have something I need to tell you." Cara said sensitively. Azizah leant up on her right arm, suddenly scared, her face giving her away. Cara suddenly realised what must be crossing Azizah's mind. "Oh, it's good news, at least *I* think it's good news. I suppose *you* can tell me if you think it's good news too?" Azizah relaxed.

"When Ummi was sick, she asked me to do something for her." Cara started.

"Mmmmm" Azizah replied suspiciously.

"She asked me if I would look after you."

"You are looking after me Cici." Azizah said brightly.

"Yes, but she meant, always." Cara trod carefully, unsure of the reaction she would get.

"Oh that." Azizah commented. "I thought you were going to tell me something really serious!" Cara didn't quite know how to respond. "You're my new mother, aren't you?" she remained on her back.

"I'm your guardian. Ummi will always be your mother, I won't be replacing her."

"But you *want* to look after me, right?" Azizah asked with the slightly American twang all children in Dubai eventually adopt, regardless of their nationality.

"Of course I want to look after you Zizi! You're my partner in crime!" Cara tittered.

"Cool!" Azizah said as she squeezed Cara tightly, her eyes closed tightly, a smile fixed on her face. "Ummi said

192

you'd look after me. I was just checking you wanted to."

Cara was so relieved. She knew there and then that she would give her life for this child and that nothing and no-one would ever come between them.

By the time Cara had seen Azizah off to sleep and headed back downstairs, the lounge was full of women. Peering through a crack in the door, Cara could see that Maggie was hosting a pamper party for Vix and her girlfriends, some of whom Cara recognised, some she didn't. Sneaking past she caught Maggie in the kitchen.

"Maggs." She spoke in a hushed voice.

"Cara! How is the dear little girl, did she get off to sleep OK?" Maggie spoke brightly as she opened the oven door to take out some sausage rolls.

"Shhh." Cara begged. "Do they know?" she whispered. "About Zizi?"

"Not yet!" Maggie whispered back. "Why are we whispering?" she asked.

"Because tonight isn't about me and Zizi, it's about Vix."

"Don't be silly Love. You should tell Vix, well you need to tell me too come to think of it." Maggie smiled.

"Oh, don't worry, I will, but for now let's just make sure Vix has a good time. Agreed?" Cara wasn't ready to tell everyone about Azizah just yet, she wanted to tell her family first and then she'd worry about everyone else.

"Agreed, Love. But you must promise to tell us everything in the morning."

Cara nodded as she grabbed a plate of prawn vol-auvents from the worktop and pushed open the connecting door into the lounge with her foot.

"Anyone hungry?" She asked casually. The room filled with the sound of screams. Vix leapt out of her seat, knocking to one side the lady giving her a pedicure and spilling her champagne across the friend sat next to her.

"Bloody hell Car! I didn't think you were getting here until tomorrow!" She hugged her best mate tightly then looking at the friend she'd thrown her drink over she said, "Oops! Sorry about that, not like me to waste it, especially when I'm only allowed the one! Could you grab Car a drink please?" Her friend smiled and grabbed a clean glass from the table and filled it to the brim with bubbles. Apologising to the beautician as she retook her seat, Vix introduced Cara to her friends in the room who had yet to meet her.

Cara made her way around the room, hugging the friends she hadn't seen or spoken to in two years and politely kissing on both cheeks the new friends Vix had mentioned in their chats. The girls on the sofa shuffled up so that Cara could join them. The chatter started up from where it had left off and Vix leaned over and rested her head on Cara's shoulder. As Cara put her lips to the glass, she smiled, took a sip then rested her head on top of her best friend's.

The next morning, Cara struggled to open her eyes. When she did, she wished she'd not had quite to many glasses of Prosecco! Focussing, she realised Azizah wasn't in bed and initially panicked, but then remembered where she was and relaxed. She knew that Azizah would be sat at the kitchen table eating whatever delicious breakfast Maggie had decided to cook for her. Reaching into her bedside table, left exactly as it had been when she'd flown to Dubai, Cara took out a packet of paracetamol and popped two out of the packet. She gulped them down with the water she'd taken to bed out of habit and pushed herself out from under the duvet.

It was a beautiful July morning, warm but not humid and not a cloud in the sky. It had been a relief to escape the heat of Dubai, and although she thought she hadn't missed home, she realised now as she looked out of the window and into the back garden that she missed how green everything naturally was. There were no irrigation systems clicking on and off and no gardeners cycling along the street towing lawn mowers here. Instead she could hear the hum of people mowing their own lawns and smell the freshly cut grass. She rubbed her eyes as she descended the stairs, stopping briefly to hear familiar giggles coming from the kitchen.

"Cici!" Azizah threw her cutlery down on the table and ran over to hug Cara. Cara ruffled her hair and instinctively kissed her on the head.

"Morning Car, how's your head?" Vix smirked as she made her way over to the door and nudged Cara playfully.

"Fine actually." Cara lied. "I can't be having a hangover when we've got so much to do now can I?"

"You're right, we do have quite a lot on our list, the first of which is shopping for two bridesmaids dresses." Vix replied matter-of-factly.

"Two?" Cara looked confused.

"One for you and one for Zizi of course!" Vix looked at Azizah as she said this.

"Are you sure? You don't mind?" Cara was touched.

"Don't be silly! If you'd have turned up with quads they'd all be welcome. Thankfully for my bank account you've only managed to adopt one child whilst you've been out of the country for a couple of years so yes, I'm sure. Now, get yourself dressed and we'll get going." Vix winked at Azizah as she made her way out of the kitchen and up the stairs.

"How ...?" Cara began, looking at Maggie and Azizah.

"I told them! That's OK isn't it Cici? I told them about Ummi and about how you're looking after me now." Cara blushed.

Maggie pushed the chair back just as John came in from the garden and put his mug on the draining board. She turned and smiled at her husband. "We're very proud of you Car, aren't we John?"

"Very." He replied. Cara could have sworn she saw him tear up. "Your parents would be so proud." And with that he walked over and hugged Cara tightly.

She was taken by surprise, it took her a moment to respond, but when she did she realised she had missed the parental hugs Maggie and John had often given her.

After Cara had showered and changed, Vix drove her

and Azizah into town. Vix had already had her eye on a dress for Cara but now that she saw her she knew it wouldn't be right. Since moving to Dubai Cara had become more tanned, slimmer and more confident. Her entire demeanour had changed, and it occurred to Vix now that Cara had left a girl but had returned a woman. That in itself made her more beautiful.

The friends couldn't talk as openly as they would have done had Azizah not been there but Vix loved the new dynamic. Seeing the interaction between Cara and the girl gave Vix the confirmation she needed. The confirmation of Cara's happiness. Vix missed Cara dearly and although they chatted regularly she could never really get a grip on how she lived her life. They rarely spoke about her personal life, always steering the conversation towards home and what was happening between Vix and Keiran. In part Vix felt guilty for having talked about herself so much but she also couldn't help feeling that some subjects were better left alone after Leo.

"So where do you live now then?" Vix asked.

"With Zizi, in her villa. You must come and visit, it really is beautiful." Cara answered.

"What about your apartment?" Vix asked.

"Oh, I have that too. When you and Keiran come and stay, you can stay there if you like, the location is brilliant."

"Oh, I meant to ask if we could come and stay. Believe it or not we haven't actually booked a honeymoon yet."

"Course you can! Leave it with me. I'll make sure you

have a trip to remember before Keiran junior makes an arrival." Cara made a mental note to book something really special for them for September when the desert heat would subside a little.

"Amazing, thanks Hon. I can't wait to see where you live. Sorry I haven't been out yet."

Vix realised her relationship with Keiran had consumed her. Since her best friend had left she had put all her efforts into their relationship, partly to stop her missing Cara, which she didn't regret, but having heard some of the details of what had been going on with Cara and Rebekah in Dubai she was sad she hadn't been there for her best friend.

They'd found Cara's outfit and shoes pretty quickly, it was Azizah that was proving more difficult to dress. It wasn't that she was difficult or picky, it was actually Cara who was being the choosy one. Sitting in the third and final shop in Southampton, Azizah was packaged off to the changing rooms with a bundle of dresses which the shop assistant insisted she try. In an attempt to make the girl feel grown up, Cara and Vix were asked to remain in the waiting area whilst the staff fussed around her. It gave the friends a chance to properly chat.

"Come on then," Vix whispered, "what's the *real* gossip?"

"There isn't any really." Cara answered, avoiding Vix's gaze.

"Oh, there *so* is. Come on then. What's his name?"

Cara knew Vix wouldn't stop until she'd found out

something. "Miles. Miles Granger." Cara sipped the wine the shop assistant had very generously handed out.

"Oh! Posh! Miles eh, and what does Miles do?"

Cara turned to face her friend. "Miles is nothing special, at least not to me. It's a funny story really. I met him on the plane on the way out."

"Two years ago!" Vix squealed. "How could you have met this man two years ago and not told me?!"

"I only met him two years ago, nothing happened, well, other than him trying to flirt with me on the plane. But after what happened with Leo, I swore off men and thought I had succeeded in giving him the brush off. He played on my mind though. He is gorgeous Vix, there's no denying that. And his eyes...they're the greenest eyes you have ever seen. They're like pure emeralds."

"Cici! How about this one?" Azizah came out of the changing room and twirled in front of them.

"It's OK Zizi, try the next one sweetie." Cara smiled as Azizah turned dramatically and swept herself back to the changing room.

"So, you didn't sleep with him then?" Vix enquired.

"Not then, no. And then work really took off. I was so busy I actually had no time or head space for any kind of relationship."

Vix giggled, "Sod the relationships, didn't you just fancy a shag? Can you honestly say there was no 'Friend with Benefits'?"

"I can honestly say that it didn't cross mind. Well, maybe it crossed my mind a little bit each time I saw him in the lobby."

Vix interrupted, "Excuse me? Each time you saw him in the lobby?"

"Oh, yeah. He works in the hotel where my apartment is, so I saw him quite a lot, but he didn't see me. I knew he was a temptation so every time I saw him and made it very clear that I *hadn't* seen him and made every effort I could to ignore him."

Vix made a face at Cara. "Why on earth would you..."

This time Cara interrupted. "Until last month. Rebekah had just told me she was dying, and I was about to move into her villa to help with Zizi. Perhaps it was because my emotions were running high, I'm not really sure. Anyway, we kind of bumped into one another in the lobby and one thing led to another..." Cara trailed off.

Vix was about to speak when Azizah came running out. "I love this one Vix! Please can I have this one? Please?" She twirled in front of the mirror.

Winking at Cara as she addressed Azizah, Vix said "Zizi, I love it too, but you know what we talked about. You have to try them all, just to make sure." Cara giggled. Azizah rolled her eyes and made her way back to try the next dress.

Vix rapidly fired questions at Cara about what actually happened with Miles. Cara blushed as she gave a few details, Vix listened intently. "Oh my god! It was him, that morning I told you about the wedding wasn't it? Bloody hell Car, you're a bloody sex goddess! I mean look at you now, men can't resist you! They bump into you and the next minute you're at it like nymphomaniacs on the dining room table! Remind me to give it a good scrub before Keiran and I sit down for breakfast." Cara found herself laughing out loud. She'd missed this. "So, what happened next?" Vix asked.

"Well, this is where it gets interesting." Cara replied. "And it is at this juncture that I have to tell you that although the sex was amazing, like mind-blowingly amazing, I don't have any feelings for Miles. The sex was exactly what I needed and made me realise that I need a bit more of it in my life, but apart from that, nada." Cara was doing her best to convince Vix that she wasn't emotionally connected to Miles, that there were complications.

"Go on." Vix was intrigued.

Cara carried on in hushed tones, "He turned up at Rebekah's after the funeral."

Vix pulled a face. "Awkward!" she exclaimed.

"Yeah, a little. I mean, I had a lot to deal with and he wasn't exactly on my mind. However, it soon became clear that it wasn't me he'd come to see. He told me that he had come to offer his condolences for Rebekah, he did see her most days to be honest, given that he worked in the building where our office is situated."

"Makes sense." Vix murmured.

"That's what I thought, until I saw him with Zizi." Cara whispered.

"Zizi? Where does she come into this?" Vix asked, genuinely perplexed.

"Do you remember what I said about his eyes?" Cara asked. As she did so, Azizah appeared in her third dress. The dress was sage green with a cream sash. It was fitted at the top with a long skirt that wasn't overly fussy but was bolstered by a couple of petticoats. The colour sat perfectly against Azizah's chestnut skin and made her eyes pop. Zizi twirled once, twice, three times. She clearly felt as beautiful as she looked.

"Please can I have this one Vix? I love it!" Azizah put her hands in front of her and squeezed them, her eyes pleading with Vix. Suddenly Vix saw it.

"Of course you can darling! It brings out your beautiful emerald eyes." Addressing the shop assistant Vix called out, "We'll take this one please, it's perfect. Thank you."

She turned to Cara. "No!" She remarked. "He isn't?" she asked incredulously.

Cara nodded. "Uh huh. Oh yes. Miles is her father."

"So, what are you going to do?" Vix asked once they'd got home.

Azizah was busy showing Maggie her dress and Vix and Cara were sat in the back garden drinking tea and eating a deliciously light Victoria sponge that Maggie had found time to bake along with organising all the little details for the wedding the next day.

"Nothing. There's nothing I *can* do!" Cara replied.

"What do you mean there's nothing you can do? Miles is Zizi's father, he has a right to see her." Vix argued.

"It's not that easy Vix. Not in Dubai. You have to remember that Rebekah was a married woman. As far as anyone else is aware, Zizi's father died before she was even born. The only reason I worked it out is because Rebekah let slip what her pet name for her own father was. I overheard Zizi call Miles 'Bapi', that's when I put it all together. That and the eyes of course. There's no mistaking the eyes."

"Does Zizi know?" Vix asked cautiously.

"No. She doesn't know. I'm sure of that. To her, Miles is just a friend of Rebekah's who visited now and again. You know Zizi, within five minutes of meeting anyone she has given them a nickname. Perhaps Rebekah suggested the nickname, after her own father. A little secret she wanted to openly keep maybe?"

"And you can't tell anyone? Does anyone else know do you think?"

"No-one can find out. Can you imagine the scandal it would cause if the truth were to come out? It would destroy Rebekah's reputation and that of the family name. Patma must know, but she is like Zizi's grandmother, she won't breathe a word to anyone, not even me. I guess the only issue for me, now that I am her adopted mother, is whether I continue to allow the visits that were obviously taking place."

"Hmm, difficult one." Vix soothed, stroking her delicate bump. "Do you think Miles will still want to visit her?"

"I hope so Vix, but to be honest, not much surprises

me about the way men act now. Our evening together was...breath-taking...but, I don't think I have any romantic feelings for him. Which is a shame because he's amazing in the sack!" Vix giggled and slapped Cara's arm across the table. "I think it simplifies things though. Imagine if I was in love with him and I'd just found out that he was the father of the daughter I'd just adopted...that would just be weird" Cara made a face at Vix as she sipped her tea.

"Or ideal." Vix retorted.

"What do you mean?"

"Think about it." Vix continued. "If you were to get together with a man who clearly likes you, is amazing in the sack, is handsome *and* successful, you could allow Zizi to see her father every day of her life. You would have the perfect family!"

"But what about love, Vix? I don't love him."

"Oh and look where that got you last time! Being in love worked out just perfectly then didn't it!" She chirped sarcastically. "I know it sounds controversial, but isn't that what they do out there anyway? Arranged marriages and all that? See it as a business arrangement maybe."

"It's not quite like that Vix." Cara scolded. "Arranged marriages are considered carefully. Potential in-laws discuss their children and match them based on their personalities. Love matches often happen with the blessing of the families too." She was defensive of the culture she admired and enjoyed being part of.

"Or," Vix carried on "you could tell that man you *really*

love that you'll give him another chance."

"No." Cara replied firmly. "That will never happen. Anyway, I don't love him anymore." Vix raised her eyebrows. "Perhaps you're right. Maybe looking at this thing with Miles as a business arrangement is the way forward."

"I was joking Car! Playing devil's advocate. I didn't mean it!"

"Well maybe you need to be careful about what you suggest, Vix. I know you mean well but I am here for you and Keiran and I want to celebrate the biggest day of your life with you tomorrow without thinking about *him*. Then, when it's all over you can tell me everything. What he's been doing, where he lives, whether he is still with her... all of it. If you must, but be warned, I am not at all interested." Cara leaned across the table and kissed her friend on the cheek. "Now, Champagne?"

"I can't!" Vix pointed at her tiny bump with mock irritation.

"Oh no, but I can!" Cara laughed as she made her way into the kitchen to get a drink.

Peering into the fridge she breathed deeply. She'd done a good job of convincing Vix that she would be OK tomorrow but, in reality, her stomach was churning, her heart pounding. In truth she didn't know how she would react when she saw Leo. Had she been asked two months ago if she was over him, her answer would have been a resounding yes, but when faced with the reality of seeing him in less than 24 hours she wasn't so sure.

CHAPTER TWENTY

*T*he wedding was at 11am so it was lucky that the household had inherited a human alarm clock in Azizah, she was by far the most excited person in the house, if not on earth. By 9am, John had fed everyone and Vix was having her hair and make-up done. Keiran had called to say that he'd collected the flowers, and Azizah was dressed and watching a film whilst trying to keep as still as possible. Everything was running to plan. Taking a couple of glasses of Bucks Fizz from the kitchen worktop, Cara headed upstairs. Handing Vix the non-alcoholic version, Cara raised her glass by way of a toast.

"Here's to your perfect day." She smiled at Vix who was positively glowing. Cara had never seen her look so relaxed and happy. "In three hours' time you'll be Keiran's wife. How does that feel?"

Vix sipped her drink and frowned, thoughtfully. "I can honestly say that I never thought I would be getting married before you. You've always done things first!"

It dawned on Cara that they'd grown up. Here she was having inherited a sizeable villa, a multimillion pound business and a daughter, whilst Vix was dressed in a wedding dress with a baby of her own on the way.

"You're right, but I'm glad you're first this time. You and Keiran are made for one another." For the next hour or so they reminisced about the games they'd played, their childhood friends and teachers that had been universally hated at school. Before they knew it, Cara was zipping up Vix's dress and placing her tiara on her head. Tears stung her eyes as she stood back to admire Vix.

"Car! Don't! If you start, I'll start, and you'll ruin my make up!"

Cara stared at the ceiling. "I'm not, I'm not."

Vix looked up, "What are you looking it?"

"It's a trick... if you feel yourself welling up, look up. It's impossible to cry then." Cara informed her.

"OK so instead of crying, everyone'll think you're admiring the birds or something?!"

Outside a car horn honked. "Come on then, let's get going. You don't want to be late... for the first time in your life!"

Vix threw Cara a look of mock disgust. "As if I'd ever be late! Just the mere suggestion is preposterous." Flouncing across the room Vix pulled open the bedroom door and headed downstairs to a chorus of whoops and cheers from Azizah, John, Maggie and the Chauffeur. Cara looked at herself in the mirror and wiped away a tear. "Come on Car! We're waiting!" Vix called back upstairs.

"Yes, come on Cici, I want to see your dress too!" Azizah shouted.

Cara scolded herself. Deep down, she wished that it was her and Leo. "Coming! Just grabbing my lippy. Go on out to the car, I'm coming right down." She called.

When they got to the church, the congregation were still stood outside, so keen was Vix not to be late. "Shall I do another lap?" the Chauffeur asked as he signalled the

Vicar from the car window.

"What?" Vix suddenly panicked, "He *is* here isn't he? Keiran?"

"Of course he's here you donut, he's just not used to you ever being early! In fact, no-one is! You've taken them all by surprise for once." Cara smirked as she looked out of the back window and watched the Vicar begin to coax the guests into the church with the ushers. She tried to make out the faces in the crowd. As the car swung past the library for the second time, John held Vix's hand tightly and reached across for Cara's. With a daughter's hand in each of his he spoke emotionally.

"Victoria, I want you to know how glad I am to see you so happy. I am so proud of you. When you were born I had no idea what to do, but you helped me figure it out along the way. I probably don't tell you enough, but I do love you." Vix smiled, then stared at the ceiling of the car. John turned his attention to Cara. "Cara, I want to thank you for bringing Zizi into our lives. Your Mum and Dad would be so proud, as Maggs and I are. Thank you for being such a good friend to Victoria, and an even better sister." Cara too found herself looking up. John's eyes followed.

"What *are* you both looking at?" he asked. The girls giggled as they each dabbed under their eyes with a tissue.

"What is it Jiddo? What are you all looking at?" Zizi asked gazing lovingly at John.

Vix, Cara and John all looked at Zizi. "I have no idea Love!" He replied.

"What is it Cici?" Azizah asked innocently.

"Don't cry Car, you'll ruin your make-up!" Vix chided.

"Don't worry, it's happy tears." Cara replied, wiping her face. Looking at Azizah she asked, "Jiddo? Zizi?"

"He's your Daddy, isn't he? Like you're my Mummy now?" she asked innocently.

"Yes, he is Zizi." Cara replied.

"Then he's my Jiddo. I don't know it in English. What is it?"

"Grandpa, Zizi, it's Grandpa."

"Atchoo!" Azizah sneezed then let out a little giggle. The Vicar had just got to the 'You may kiss the bride' bit and the whole congregation let out a snigger. Vix caught Cara's eye before turning back to her new husband. Cara smiled a broad smile at Azizah and then back at the happy couple. Relaxing, she joined the congregation in their applause and, despite having spent the service trying her best not to look over at Leo, she inadvertently looked across at the pews on the other side of the church. She smiled at the happy faces smiling back at her, and then she saw him. He was broader than she remembered, his hair cropped so that it was short on the sides and longer on the top. He was clean shaven and looked, well, handsome. More handsome than she'd remembered. Much more. He met her gaze with a gentle smile. Cara's cheeks pinked, and in a heartbeat, she was back in that bed in Sicily.

Azizah tugged at her hand and gestured for Cara to hand Vix's bouquet back before she walked down the aisle towards her new life. The bride and groom passed by and she and Azizah filed out of the pew. She leaned down to tell her daughter how well behaved she'd been and was caught off guard when she realised Leo had filed out at the same time and now also stood alongside Azizah.

"Hello," he mouthed. Cara smiled uncertainly. Outside, the sun shone, the photographer was busy taking pictures. Cara did her best to steer Azizah away from Leo and into the crowd. She stood where she was told and smiled on cue, all the while her heart was in her throat. The photographer instructed the ushers and bridesmaids to join the bride and groom, and for Vix's sake, Cara did as she was told. Keiran had five ushers and Leo as his best man, so the groom lined them up in a semi-circle and placed the bride, Cara and Azizah in front. Smiling for the camera, Cara felt Leo's breath across her neck. "We need to talk, Car." he whispered in her left ear.

"Later." Cara whispered through pursed lips.

The photos were finally over with and everyone made their way to the reception, five minutes' drive away. With the bride and groom safely in the wedding limousine, Cara and Azizah went with John and Maggie. Cara stared out of the window, contemplating what her next move should be.

"That was very cool, Cici. Will you get married one day? I think you should." Azizah's question took Cara by surprise.

"I don't honestly know Zizi. I'd have to find someone to marry me first!" she remarked, hugging Azizah close to her.

"Are you OK Love?" Maggie asked, peering over Azizah's head.

"Yeah, you know me Maggs. I'll be fine." Cara replied.

"I know you will, Cara, but will you promise me something?"

"OK."

"Give the boy a chance, Love, he might surprise you." Maggie raised her eyebrows as she said this.

"Not you as well!" Cara remarked, sulkily.

"OK, OK. I won't say another word. Just remember how short life can be. You should always give people the chance to explain."

The reception, held in a country manor hotel, went well. Cara was impressed. Having been able to find a cancellation at the last minute, Vix and Keiran had pulled it off. The food was fabulous, the Champagne flowed, the room filled with laughter and the children were entertained. Azizah had made friends easily and fitted right in. Cara became more relaxed with each top up of her glass and was enjoying catching up with friends and family.

When the time came for the speeches, Cara was relieved to be sat on the top table, at the opposite end to Leo. There was no way he could catch her eye as he gave his Best Man's speech and she could maintain her composure. Keiran spoke first, complimenting the beautiful Bride and her entourage as is traditionally expected, then it was John's turn. The room laughed at his wit and dry sense of humour and cried as he talked about his love for his daughter, and his new son-in-law. There was the obligatory sweep stake for the length of the speeches in total and every now and then a heckler would shout for him to hurry up or slow down. Twelve minutes and 39 seconds later John was finished. "To the Bride and Groom." He toasted.

"The Bride and Groom." The room filled with the sound of glasses clinking. "And now, I'll hand over to the Best Man. Leo." John sat down while Leo remained standing.

Cara listened intently as Leo spoke affectionately about his best friend. His words were thoughtful, funny and remarkably touching. Cara tried so hard not to let Leo back into her mind but found it impossible. Hearing the emotion in his voice, Cara couldn't help but turn to look at him.

"...and lastly I'd like to say that I truly believe that Vix is Keiran's perfect match. She is his destiny. She makes him laugh, smile, and makes him a better man." With this statement his kept his eyes on Cara. "I can think of no better woman for him to share his life and start a family with." He turned back to face the room. "So, if you'd like to charge your glasses, ladies and gentlemen, and join me in a toast. To the Bride and Groom." The guests toasted together and Cara took the opportunity to sneak out to the bathroom with Azizah. With the speeches over with she knew she wouldn't be missed as the results of the sweepstake were announced. Cara had bet eleven minutes and nine seconds, so she knew she wasn't winning anything.

Giggling, Azizah and Cara skipped along the corridor hand in hand, back towards the party. The double doors ahead of them opened and in front of them Leo appeared. Cara let go of Azizah's hand and let her skip back through the doors towards the jollity, Azizah smiled at Leo and skipped through the door as he held it aside. Cara didn't move. "Hi." Leo ventured.

"Hi." Cara replied, eager to give nothing away.

"You look beautiful." He commented.

"Thanks." Cara said, looking Leo directly in the eye. "Is there something you wanted?" she asked, determined that he wasn't going to get a grip on her heart before she left to fly home with her daughter.

"I was hoping we could clear the air." He pleaded. "Please." Cara realised that in the past two years she'd grown up. She was no longer the naïve girl Leo had betrayed. She was a mother and she had responsibilities to both herself and Azizah that she had to attend to. Heeding Maggie's words, she answered him sternly.

"OK. Get me a drink and I'll see you out on the terrace." She decided she would give him just a few minutes of her time.

Waiting outside in the warm summer air, the sun setting behind the trees in the distance, Cara listened to the band as they began to play. Through the windows she could see Vix holding Keiran's hand as they worked the room talking to their guests. She was thankful for having found a quiet spot.

"Peace and quiet at last." Leo handed Cara a glass of orange liqueur.

"Solerno? It won't work Leo." She sighed, disappointed that he had tried to use her memory against her.

"What won't work?" he asked, puzzled.

"I'm not going to sleep with you just because you've put a glass of Solerno in my hand."

"Solsera." He muttered.

"What?" Cara asked, somewhat irritated.

"It's called Solsera, not Solerno." He seemed disappointed.

"Sol whatever. I'm not going to sleep with you just because you're trying to recapture a moment that I hold so precious I daren't remember in case my heart breaks all over again." Her voice began to crack. She turned away from him, hiding her true feelings.

"Oh God, sorry. I feel totally busted. I only meant it as a bit of a joke. To break the ice really. Sorry. I had no idea you were still hurting."

Cara took a sip, the warm nectar refreshing her memory as it slipped down her throat and into her stomach, the warmth suffusing through her body. Her mood lifted a little. Perhaps he was telling the truth. "OK. So, tell me Leo, how have you been? What are you doing now? Are you still with her?"

Leo almost spat out his drink. "Wow! You don't hold back, do you?" Cara stared at him, waiting for an answer.

He realised she wasn't going to give him an easy ride. He'd built today up in his head. He knew she would look beautiful but when he saw her he found himself unable to breathe Her hair was pinned into a loose bun at the side of her head, soft curls framed her face and accentuated her cheekbones. Her pearl drop earrings drew his eyes to her neck and the curve that swept down to her shoulders and to the single pearl she wore around her neck. Her skin was sun-kissed, her hair highlighted. Her long lashes and perfect eyebrows emphasized her hazel eyes. She looked more mature, more of a woman. Leo gestured to the table next to them.

"I think we need to sit, don't you?" Cara sat, waiting for an answer to her questions. He pulled out a chair, but Cara remained standing. "First of all, I have missed you. Every day I've thought about you. Every *single* day. I couldn't imagine where you were because no-one would tell me." Cara wanted to believe him. She really did. "When I couldn't, I went back to work. Paul said I could have my job back."

"As in Mr Baker you mean?"

"Yes, that was funny that was. When I went back he seemed so much more relaxed. He told everyone to call him Paul and introduced dress-down Mondays. He

215

thought dress-down Friday's were too predictable and decided that by doing it on a Monday we would all feel more relaxed and would look forward to coming back to work after the weekend."

"Did it work?" Cara laughed a little. The Solsera was doing its job.

"Actually, it did. I've stayed but I've been working on another project too. What about you, Car? What have you been doing?"

"This isn't really about me, is it Leo? We both know it's about you. It always has been." She wanted to know all about it him, every tiny detail, but her self-preservation stopped her. That and her need to know who that mystery woman was. "So, who was she?" She knew she was being ridiculous, immature, but she couldn't stop herself. "Are you still with her, does she, did she make you happy?" "Who?" Cara rolled her eyes at him, "Seriously Cara, does *who* make me happy?" Leo was genuinely perplexed. He didn't know what she was thinking but she was way off track. There was no-one. There had been no-one since he'd left. "I have absolutely no idea who, or what, you are talking about."

"Really? You're just going to deny it are you?" his denial angered Cara. "If you ever had any real feelings for me at all Leonardo Dolce then do me a favour and be honest."

"Seriously Car, you're going to have to tell me what you're going on about because at the moment I think that drink is going to your head." He gestured towards the glass she had poised at her lips.

"Don't be so bloody patronising, and don't' call me Car!" she shouted, "How sodding dare you. I was there Leo, I *saw* you!"

"Where?" It was Leo who was getting frustrated now, he racked his brains but found no memory of anything significant that could make Cara react like this.

Gesticulating wildly, Cara was finally able to express the two years of pent-up frustration she had lived with.

"You're an arsehole Leo. You made me fall in love with you then you disappeared off across the world, telling me *not to wait for you*. Well, how bloody arrogant can you get? How dare you think that I'd sit at home waiting for you. While you swanned around the world, probably shagging everything in sight, I was doing absolutely fine, thank you. I moved on. Then once a month, or less if you were feeling particularly cruel, I'd get a bloody postcard. A postcard that told me nothing other than to boast about which sodding beach you'd been on that week, or which *amazing* sight you'd seen."

She paused for breath and as she did Leo opened his mouth to speak, he reached for her, but Cara pushed him away and continued before he could get a word in.

"Eight months Leo, eight months you were gone! You didn't email, call, even write a proper letter to me. You left me thinking that you didn't care." She was crying now, crying with anger. Her pent-up emotions over Leo, her parents, Rebekah, were spilling out of her uncontrollably. "How you could do that to me. What was it you said? Oh

I remember: *'I'm not asking you to wait, Car. That wouldn't be fair of me. But give me the chance to go, be happy for me and I'll find you again.'* So I told myself I wasn't waiting for you, that I wanted you to be happy, to find what Nonna wanted you to find. Then you email me and tell me you're coming home. I mean, what the hell did you expect me to do?!"

Leo shrugged, feeling ashamed. She was right, everything she said was right. He *had* been selfish. Of course she'd waited! The woman he loved had waited for him. The same way she had waited for her parents to come home the night they died. Cara sat back down and slammed the table in anger. "Yes! I was waiting for you, you arrogant idiot, but you were careful not to tell me *exactly* when you were flying in. I had to find out from Keiran, can you imagine how humiliated I felt? Can you?" She was shaking.

"No." Leo muttered. He hadn't thought about how she'd feel. Not at all.

"So I drove to the airport to pick you up, I couldn't tell you *could I?*" she asked sarcastically, "I had no way of reaching you at such short notice. Anyway, I thought I'd surprise you. I took a punt knowing which terminal you were arriving into and just waited. For. An. Hour." Suddenly the penny dropped. Leo gasped. "Ah, there you go. Understand now do you?" she asked with venom.

Realising what she'd seen, Leo laughed. He couldn't help it. The relief! Cara was furious. She clenched her glass tightly ready to throw the contents in his face.

Realising what she was about to do, Leo held up hands up in surrender.

"No, no, no!" He said quickly to calm her. "You're wrong Car, you're wrong!"

Shouting again, "Wrong? How can I be wrong Leo, I saw you. With...her! My God if only you'd have been that pleased to see me!" Cara threw her drink at him

"Genevieve is my cousin you idiot!" He shouted, swerving, the Solsera spilling over his shoulder as he did so.

Cara's glass smashed on the tiles in front of her. "Your cousin?" She gasped.

"Yes! Genevieve is my cousin." He pulled Cara to him, "I didn't get to say goodbye before I left because she'd been on a modelling job. The day I was coming home she was just leaving to go on another job. When you saw her in the airport she'd come over to say 'Hi' before disappearing again herself for a month."

Cara allowed Leo to hold her. Her slightly blurred memory replayed itself. She remembered the girl, absolutely, she was gorgeous. She also had dark, curly hair and was a similar height to Leo. And they hadn't kissed. They'd hugged. She'd left before she saw anything else. She hid her face against his shoulder. "Oh my God." She whispered feeling foolish. "Oh my God, Leo."

Leo held her tightly, he smoothed her hair. "I didn't want to tell you when I was arriving because I'd been on a plane for twenty-four hours and quite frankly felt pretty disgusting. I was unshaven, a little sweaty, bad breath....

you know, the works. Truly attractive in every way." Cara looked at Leo and began to cry again, but not out of anger, this time out of sorrow, and relief. Sorry for the time she'd wasted not being with Leo and relieved that he hadn't betrayed her like she'd thought. "I was planning on going home to my mother, showering, getting a haircut and some decent clothes and then I was going to ask Keiran and Vix to get you round to their place"

Cara sobbed, angry now with herself, "And what were you going to do then? Tell me how much you had missed me, how much of a mistake you'd made going away and how much you loved me?" She couldn't help herself.

"Maybe." Leo replied as he reached into his pocket. "Maybe I wanted to tell you that I'd realised I'd been inexplicably selfish. That I should've taken you with me. That every sight I saw paled into insignificance without you. But the main reason I wanted you there was to give you this." He got down on one knee and put a box in Cara's hands. Sniffing, she opened it. "If you'd have given me the chance Car I would have asked you to wear this, and to make my life complete."

It was Nonna's ring, yellow gold with a baguette shaped ruby, cushioned on either side by diamonds. She put her hand to her mouth. "I know it's been a while Car, but if you'll give me a chance I'd still like you to wear it. I love you. I've always loved you. I just didn't know how to tell you before." He stood, eager to explain. "The project I told you I was working on? It's almost ready. I've spent the last eighteen months building a distillery in Erice.

Everyone kept saying how amazing our drink was, so I decided that with the rest of Nonna's money I'd make a go of commercialising it. The last few batches we've made have been almost perfect. I'll moving out there next month, temporarily, at least until we're in full production."

Cara looked at the glass she'd thrown on the floor. "Solgio..."

"Solsera. It kind of means evening sun. It reminds me of the time we spent in Sicily."

Cara hadn't expected his life to stand still, but then she hadn't expected any of this. "I, I don't know what to say." She stuttered.

"Say yes, Car, say you'll be with me. I need a professional taster and I think I know who might be perfect for the job." His mouth breaking into a kind smile. Cara saw the hope in Leo's eyes. She could see a future. She could see herself being happy with Leo, being in love again. She wanted it. So badly. Stroking her hair away from her eyes, Leo spoke softly. "It's perfect Car."

Cara shook her head. "No, Leo. It isn't." And with that she pushed her chair away and ran back into bar, leaving Leo alone on the terrace in the dark.

She made her way up to her room and stood with her back against the door. She took a few moments to compose herself before approaching the mirror. Suddenly the door opened behind her. "Can't we talk about this?" Leo begged.

"What's the point Leo?" Cara asked. "You're doing it

again. You're making assumptions about me, about what I am prepared to do for you. You're assuming that all you have to do is show me a ring and tell me you love me and I'll go weak at the knees."

"I've always loved you, Car, and not any old ring, it was Nonna's" Leo interrupted, wounded by her words.

Infuriated, Cara responded. "Grow up Leo. Life isn't a flipping fairytale. I'm not a princess in distress and you're not the prince who is going to bloody well save me. I have a life, a life I love in Dubai and I can't give it up, I won't."

"I'm not asking you to give it up." Leo retorted, irritated at how egotistical he had been to think that Cara would come running. "But you could at least consider the idea?" He added quietly.

"Well it sounded like that to me. I have a house, a job, and a daughter to think about. I can't just up-sticks and leave because you've had a fantasy in your head that you think you can make come true."

"A daughter?" He was confused.

"Yes, the little girl, the extra bridesmaid? She's my adopted daughter, Azizah, and we have a very nice life in Dubai thank you. I cannot, and will not, give that up for any man. Even you, Leo."

Leo backed away from Cara. He'd wondered who the little girl was but had assumed she was one of Vix's cousins. It wasn't that he didn't want children, far from it, it was more that he hadn't contemplated that Cara had moved on so much with her life. She really was a different person to the one he'd left behind. Thinking that there was no way he could compete with the life Cara had made of herself, he turned and opened the door. Turning back to face her, he spoke earnestly. "I'm sorry Car, I should never have assumed anything. I hope you have a happy life. Oh, and Azizah, she's beautiful. I have no doubt that you're a wonderful mother. Congratulations." He smiled sadly and left.

The next morning Cara and Azizah woke early. Cara wrote a note to say goodbye, for now, and crept up the corridor to slip it under the door of the Honeymoon Suite. As she tiptoed back to her room, Azizah taking dolly steps behind her, Vix flung open her door.

"Cara!" Vix rasped. Cara and Azizah stopped in their tracks. Vix closed her own door behind her and followed them into their room. "Not leaving without saying goodbye I hope!" She exclaimed.

"I didn't want to wake you, sorry Vix. Zizi and I have a flight in a few hours' time. There's some business I need to get home for. I'm so sorry." Cara apologised, thanking Patma silently for the text she'd sent during the night. She'd spent much of the night crying and was conscious that even the large amount of make-up she'd applied this morning couldn't hide her bloodshot eyes.

"Don't worry, I know you have a busy life, Car. What's important is that you came to the wedding. We'll be out in a few weeks for the Honeymoon anyway." Vix said diplomatically. "I can't wait to see *you* again either, young lady." she said, squeezing Azizah's hand.

"Aunty V, will you come and play with me, at my house, please?"

"Aunty V, eh? Sure thing Zizi, I can't wait. Love you both." Vix pulled them in and hugged them tightly. "Now, off you go, you don't want to miss that flight." She addressed Cara sternly, "I will be calling you in the next couple of days Madam, OK?"

"Understood." Cara replied.

Leo twisted the ring between his fingers, and stared at the enormous empty bed, which screamed its loneliness back at him. He'd barely slept, all he could think about was Cara and about how stupid he'd been. Why hadn't he told her before he went travelling that he was in love with her? Why had he assumed that fate would bring them back together. He hadn't wanted to admit it, but he had been arrogant, *and* he'd assumed that she'd wait for him. He knew that she'd fallen in love with him, he'd even introduced her to his family, something he hadn't ever even contemplated before. He *had* given her hope. But he'd done it for purely selfish reasons. To keep her hanging on while he pleased himself. Where he'd been so sure before, he no longer had the courage of his convictions. Slipping the ring back into its case and into his pocket along with his keys and wallet, he headed down to breakfast. Whatever had gone on in his personal life, he still had a job to do as best man.

Leo's room was situated in the west wing of the hotel. He'd purposefully booked the second-best room available, in the hope he wouldn't spend the night alone. Walking to the dining room now he felt foolish. He'd imagined doing this walk hand in hand with Cara and announcing their engagement to the bridal party at breakfast. As he reached the door he was greeted by the smiling Maître D'.

"Good Morning Sir, room number please?" Leo smiled back distractedly as he peered into the room, trying to see where she might be sat. "Are you looking for someone Sir? Perhaps I can tell you if they are already here."

"Um, no, it's fine. Room 112."

The Maître D' scanned his list. "Thank you, Mr Dolce, I have here breakfast for two. Will someone be joining you this morning?" Leo smiled awkwardly. The Maître D' understood immediately. "No problem Sir, please." He stepped aside and welcomed Leo into the room.

Keiran spotted him and waved, beckoning him over. Leo shook hands with the groom and kissed the bride. "Good morning Mr and Mrs Taylor. I trust you didn't sleep too well!" He winked at his best mate. Keiran laughed as Vix giggled at his side. "May I say how beautiful your wife looks this morning... and how surprised I am that you are up at this time!" He looked at his watch. 9.30am.

Keiran rolled his eyes "Oh yeah, well, that would have been our early morning alarm, Ca..." Vix kicked Keiran hard under the table. "OW!" Leo felt his shoulders drop.

"She's gone, hasn't she?" He asked sadly.

"Seems that way mate." Keiran answered honestly as he bit into his toast. Vix kicked him again. "OW!" He shouted again. "Why do you keep kicking me!" Vix gave him a thunderous look.

"Keiran I love you with all my heart, but you are so bloody insensitive at times! I'd have thought you'd have learned your lesson by now." She tutted and turned her attention to Leo. "She's gone home Leo, she said she had some urgent business to attend to." She sipped her tea calmly as she looked at the antique clock on the wall. "Although I know she likes to get to the airport way before check-in just in case the flight is overbooked..."

Leo didn't need to hear any more. "Heathrow?" He asked.

"T3." Vix smiled.

Blowing a kiss at Vix he hastily turned away from the table, almost crashing into the waitress behind him. Smiling an apology, he sped out of the room.

He knew his chances were slim. Cara had left a couple of hours before him and was, in all likelihood, already in the departure lounge, but Leo couldn't let this final chance pass. He keyed the destination nimbly into the satnav and put his foot down. The reception had been held in a hotel about an hour's drive from the airport. Keeping his wits about him, Leo drove cautiously, but fast. He knew he had to if he were to catch Cara. As he approached the exit for the M25 his satnav voiced a traffic warning. Thanking the voice, he sped on past the exit

226

and made his way towards Staines where he knew he could navigate the local roads and approach the terminal without having to join the traffic he had been warned about. Crossing his fingers, he looked at his watch.

"I'm sorry about the delay." The driver spoke politely, aware that his failure to listen properly to the traffic warnings ahead had meant his passenger had been sat in his taxi for well over two hours. "I thought we'd be alright on the M25 at this time of day at the weekend, but there's always some idiot not paying attention. Don't worry though, I'll try and get you there on time."

Cara looked at her watch. Initially she hadn't been too worried and had even welcomed the delay. Azizah had fallen asleep and it had given Cara a chance to sit quietly and not answer any awkward questions. They'd left intentionally early, she hadn't wanted to go to breakfast and make polite conversation with anyone and after she'd put Azizah and her life in Dubai first, she didn't want to see Leo either. She was worried she might wobble in her decision.

"Don't worry, we've got half an hour before check-in closes. I always like to get to the airport early just in case the plane is fully booked but I'm sure we'll be OK."

The truth was, travelling first class meant they wouldn't get bumped off the flight, rather they wouldn't get any time to shop. The traffic continued to crawl for the next fifteen minutes, but the taxi driver knew a short cut through the airport terminal traffic and pulled up outside departures with a few minutes to spare.

"Thank you." Azizah said politely as she stepped out of the car. Cara smiled at the driver as she collected up their belongings, paid him and thanked him. She grabbed her daughter's hand and the trolley and headed towards the terminal doors. "Cici, Cici, look!" Azizah was hanging back, pointing across the road, towards the car park. Something had caught her eye.

"Come on Zizi," Cara rushed, "we don't have time to stop, tell me when we're inside." She pulled at Azizah's hand.

Azizah protested. "But..." Before she could say anymore she was pulled against her will towards the building. Trotting to keep up with Cara and the luggage trolley she waved.

Leo pulled into the short stay car park and abandoned his silver VW Golf between two spaces. He knew he risked a parking ticket, but he didn't care. He ran towards the terminal building, in the distance he saw a dark-haired child wave, Azizah? A lorry halted him at the zebra crossing as it rattled by and by the time it had gone, the child had disappeared. The terminal was busy this morning, it was full of families heading away from the UK for a week or two of sunshine where they could forget about the stresses and strains of their daily lives. After almost tripping over a toddler riding on a pull-along case he scoured the departure screens for any clue as to which airline they were travelling with. Seeing the flights bound for Dubai he looked for the check-in desk number. Excellent, he knew where to go but cursed when he realised it was at the opposite end of the departure hall. Avoiding the throngs of people, he walk-ran as quickly as he could, scouring the faces as he went.

Cara thanked the check-in staff profusely. Considering the desk was closing imminently the lady on the desk had worked quickly and efficiently to get them checked-in and on their way. Putting her handbag on her shoulder, she finally relaxed. Holding out her hand for Azizah to take, the two smiled at each other. "Cici?" Azizah asked.

"Yes sweetie?" Cara replied.

"Are you happy to be going home?"

"Of course I am my love. Why do you ask?" Cara was a little surprised by the question.

"It's just that all your family are here, but you have to come and live with me." Azizah replied sadly.

Cara knelt down to speak to Azizah face to face. Holding her by the shoulders, she spoke sincerely. "Zizi, *you* are my family. You always will be. I wouldn't change a thing. From the moment you came into my life, you changed it, for the better. I can't imagine my life without you. I love you Azizah, and as long as you'll have me, I'll be with you." She pulled Azizah close, and closing her eyes, hugged her tightly. She'd never meant anything as much in her life. Azizah hugged her back before quietly saying thank you. "Now, let's go, we've got work to do!"

In the distance, he saw her again. It *was* Azizah! He rushed towards the check-in desks. Composing himself, he slowed to a fast walk. Getting closer, he slowed down. Azizah was looking upset and Cara had knelt down to talk to her. Cara was no longer just Cara, she was a mother comforting her daughter, she was providing warm words and a loving touch. It occurred to him that he was about to make the same mistake. He'd fled to the airport to change Cara's mind, for *his* sake. He suddenly realised that he didn't have the right. How could he possibly unsettle this child again, he had to listen to what Cara had told him last night and that was that she didn't want to be with him.

He hung back and watched. Mulling things over in his head he knew he had to make the right decision. He wanted to be with her, he knew that without a shadow of a doubt, but the circumstances had to be right. She knew how he felt about her, if there was one thing he didn't regret about last night it was that he had told her how he really felt, how he had always felt about her. But, even knowing that, she had decided to leave. He made his decision, they would not be together. Not today. He watched with his heart in his mouth as Cara and Azizah walked briskly towards security. He couldn't help thinking it just wasn't the right time. It hadn't been the right time before and it wasn't today, but he hoped that their paths would cross. For now, he'd have to bury the feelings he had for Cara.

Cara handed their boarding passes to the Stewardess at

the door. Azizah knew that Cara wouldn't want to be
hear what she had to say so she kept quiet and waved one
last time to the figure in the departure hall.

CHAPTER TWENTY-ONE

When they got back to Dubai life took on a new reality for Cara, Azizah, Patma and Aatif. Business continued to pick up and Cara worked hard to juggle work and home life. Patma continued to be the family's rock ensuring that there was routine for Azizah, and Aatif was there for errands and school runs. At times Cara's relationship with Azizah was a little strained as the child got used to life without Rebekah but Cara did what she could to make her feel secure and loved. For the first time ever, she was thankful that she had been exactly where Azizah was and could sympathise with her being orphaned. It was hard though, Cara had to learn how to parent and she had to learn fast. It wasn't the same as visiting now and again and playing games where everything was always happy and jolly. Parenting was challenging and exhausting, she had to learn how to manage the politics with parents and teachers at school as well as with Azizah's extended family, but it was also rewarding.

She no longer lied to herself. Since seeing Leo, her thoughts were once again filled with him and what he'd said. She thought about the life they could have led and the business they could have built together. She spent time reflecting upon her own behaviour and the stupid mistake she'd made that day in the airport, but she refused to accept that what followed was entirely her fault. She considered what her life would have been like if she had waited for Leo to contact her. She occasionally mourned it, but the reality was that life took over. Being with Rebekah and moving to Dubai had changed her. Sometimes Dubai could feel completely materialistic with clients citing money and belongings as the most important things in their lives but Azizah kept Cara grounded and reminded her that life was more valuable. They made a good partnership and when either was feeling sad, the other helped them through.

Vix and Keiran visited for their honeymoon and Cara ensured it was special. She spared no expense when it came to spoiling them with little luxuries and taking them to the most exclusive restaurants but she also made sure they got to experience real-life in Dubai. She took them to the beaches that only the locals knew about and took them to a little restaurant in the fishing harbour overlooking the Persian Gulf where they feasted on local fish and seafood on paper plates. She took them to the Deira and Bur Dubai, the most authentic area in Dubai, and they joined a cultural breakfast where they learnt about Emirati life and customs. Sometimes Cara and Azizah joined them, sometimes they didn't. Cara enjoyed having Vix with her for a couple of weeks and quietly thanked Rebekah for giving her the means by which to entertain her best friend.

For their last evening, the newlyweds joined Cara for dinner at the villa. Patma cooked a delicious Sri Lankan feast which consisted of a range of curries and fresh fish dishes that were aromatically spiced. The friends relaxed and chatted about the holiday.

"It's been fantastic, Car, thank you so much for arranging everything." Vix held her glass of sparkling water up as a toast to her best friend.

"Yes, it really has Cara. Thanks." Keiran joined in, raising his glass in the air.

"You're both very welcome. I'm just glad I could help you celebrate in style." She too picked up her wine and the friends chinked their glasses. "Cheers!" they said simultaneously. "You guys really are the perfect couple, I'm so happy for you." Cara smiled at them.

Vix excused herself, "Excuse me, sixtieth toilet run of the day. I am sure this baby thinks my bladder is a trampoline!" She rubbed her bump affectionately as she got up.

Keiran felt the time was right to gently broach the subject. "It's not too late for you, you know Cara?"

"Too late for what?" Cara asked innocently.

"For you and Leo. He really misses you."

"Does he?" Cara asked a little sadly.

"Yes. You should at least let him have your email address, so he can reach you if he needs to."

"Why would he need to reach me?"

"Well, you never know what the future holds, do you? He knows you're out here, it's not a secret anymore."

"I suppose not."

"How does the land lie with him now anyway?" Keiran asked.

"Well it doesn't really. He's in Sicily building his

distillery business and here I am running mine. I can't really see a future with him. I'm legally bound to staying here for at least the next twelve years and to be honest I don't want to do anything different. I don't want to move. I love it here."

"Hmmm, it's an interesting situation. I guess Leo needs to keep to his obligations as much as you need to keep to yours." Keiran pondered. "Be sure of something though Cara, I was wrong. And for that I can't apologise enough. We've talked about it plenty of times, Leo and I, mostly when he has had a couple of beers and is feeling sorry for himself, when I said he didn't love you when he left... I was wrong."

"I know. I always knew you were wrong, but you made me doubt my gut feelings. Apology accepted though Keiran, thanks."

"I know he's moved back to Erice and I know he doesn't want to make things any harder for you. He understands your commitments and has had to grow up considerably since seeing you. We weren't allowed to talk about you in front of Vix and eventually he stopped trying. He didn't know anything about Zizi and when he realised how much your life had moved on it was a bit of a reality check for him."

"Do you know what Keiran? The time just wasn't right for us. We won't be the only couple to be perfectly matched but not to have met at the right time. The stars didn't align for us and now the time has passed." Cara reflected sadly. "There is an Arabic saying: *In the desert of life the wise travel by caravan, while the fool prefers to travel alone.* Zizi, Aatif and Patma, they are my caravan Keiran. To travel alone and be selfish is not what I want to do. I miss what Leo and I had, but we don't know each other anymore. I love my family, I choose them. Not Leo."

The following day Cara took the morning off work to accompany her friends to the airport. After a tearful goodbye at the terminal Aatif took her back to the office. When they got there, she thanked him and asked him to collect her before picking up Azizah from school. As she made her way into the lobby, Cara caught her reflection in the window and smoothed down her hair which had been caught by a gust of warm wind. She smiled at the doorman who greeted her and held the door open. Crossing the lobby, Cara greeted each of the members of staff by name before reaching the elevators. She pressed the call button before rummaging in her handbag for her phone.

"Which floor Miss Cara?" A familiar voice asked. Looking up, her gaze was met by Miles'. She smiled, feeling unexpectedly pleased to see him. He'd aged since she saw him last, his beard now sporting more white flecks than before, but his smile was warm and welcoming.

"Hi Miles," she smiled, leaning forward to kiss him on either cheek. "It's good to see you. Where have you been?" Totting up in her head, Cara realised she hadn't seen Miles for almost three months. He looked relaxed.

"I decided it was time I took a bit of a break. My Assistant Manager is more than capable, and you know how quiet it gets in the summer. So, I headed off to Switzerland for a little rest and relaxation. One of the perks of having been in the hospitality business for so long is that I have plenty of contacts who are willing to offer me a room at a preferential rate!"

"That sounds amazing! I've always wanted to go. When I was small my parents would take me hiking, mostly in the Lake District and the like, they always said they'd take me to Austria or Switzerland when I was older. I can imagine it was beautiful."

Miles' walkie talkie suddenly crackled into life. "It was, and I'd love to hear what the summer held for you. I need to dash now, but may I take you to dinner?"

Cara didn't hesitate. She had to bite the bullet and move on properly sometime. "That would be really nice. Tomorrow night?"

"Perfect, leave the arrangements to me." He smiled before kissing her again on the cheeks and responding to the call.

Watching him leave, Cara felt a buzz inside. Something she didn't think she would feel again after... Miles definitely had something about him. He was very attractive, although not her normal type, charming, dressed well and worked hard. He was a fair bit older than her, about twenty years she guessed. She already knew he could please her in the bedroom and he was the father of her daughter, although she wanted to forget *that* fact and get to know him properly. If they really did get on, then that would just be the icing on the cake. Maybe she could make it work after all.

CHAPTER TWENTY-TWO

*L*eo adored Christmas in Erice. In England he always felt as though the real meaning had been lost and that materialism had taken over. As a child he remembered his family's annual pilgrimage to visit Nonna and Nonno where they would arrive in time for the Christmas Eve feast. Travelling from the airport they would pass bonfires lit as part of the tradition of the Night of the *Luminari* to keep the baby Jesus warm. It was always a race to get to his Grandparents' house before midnight but whatever time they arrived they would be met by an enormous table surrounded by friends and relatives, each of whom had provided a gargantuan plate of food which formed part of the feast fit for a village. The noise and the smells remained imprinted on his brain and after missing the past three Christmases when he'd remained in England, he couldn't wait to re-join the tradition.

He'd decided to relocate permanently after what had happened at the wedding and had moved into his Grandparents' house. Maria still lived there as housekeeper, but Leo did his best to significantly reduce her workload. She did, however, continue to cook, something Leo was thankful for. It was fair to say that since moving to Erice he had developed something of a pasta belly! He did his best to take a daily run, if he didn't he knew he would be twice the size!

Leo and his team had perfected Solsera's recipe and

the drink was now in full production. In the new year Leo would be ramping up his promotion efforts and would be offering exclusive rights to high-end hotels and restaurants, starting with Europe and the Middle-East. He knew where Cara stood and told himself that he'd send a member of his sales team to Dubai, should any opportunities arise there. He told himself that it would be strictly business all the time knowing he didn't want to break their link completely. This Christmas Eve, however, he wasn't going to think about work. He looked at his watch, he had about an hour before guests would arrive. The vast table was presented beautifully, as usual, and bottles of Solsera and Spumante sat chilling, waiting to be drunk.

"Come, my darling boy." Leo's mother reached around her son's waist and reached up to kiss him on the cheek. "Time for the fire to be lit!" Leo put his arm around her shoulder and, feeling happier than he had in a long time, grabbed his coat before heading out into the street.

The night air was cool and crisp, Leo and his parents had joined the throng of villagers climbing their way to the Piazza San Domenica where the bonfire was already burning brightly. From their vantage point high up in the hills, the sky burned amber with the glow of smaller bonfires all around. The atmosphere was exactly as he had remembered it to be and he glowed from within. Leo's parents exchanged a glance, Eleonore was relieved, Leo was beginning to relax.

Leo had arranged with the Mayor for drinks to be handed out to everyone sharing the celebration. The tradition was for a glass of fizz so, in an attempt to update the tradition, Leo had created the 'Solserini' a mix of the gorgeous Solsera orange liqueur and Prosecco, the cost of which would be covered by Leo's company. He had to admit that it was a stroke of genius by his Marketing Manager, Floriana. He had known her since they were little, they'd played together as children each summer when he visited until their bodies had outgrown their childhood shells and he had become awkward and embarrassed. He had started the business pretty much single-handedly, but as it had grown, and the distillery had reached production stage he realised he not only needed staff to create the drink, he also needed someone to promote it.

His ideal was to employ all local people and for the local economy to benefit. He had advertised but he had failed to find anyone with the skills and experience he needed, until he had met Floriana's parents at Uncle Giovani's one evening. Floriana's mother had thrown her arms around Leo and smothered him with kisses, telling him that she longed for her Flo to return home and that her job in London was exactly the same position Leo was looking to fill. Initially Leo had been reluctant to feel positive, but inside his stomach churned with excitement. A local girl, whom he knew, currently working as a Marketing Manager for a large drinks distributor, looking for something exciting to get her teeth into. He told himself she could be the perfect candidate.

He hadn't wanted to sound too keen when he'd spoken to Floriana on the phone, but she sounded as excited as he did. When they finally met, Leo knew she was perfect for the job and although she was hesitant to return to the island at first, he hoped that when she stepped off the plane, any concerns would melt away. Waiting for her at the airport, Leo fidgeted with nerves. He was twelve years old again, sitting on the wall opposite Nonna's, waiting for the prettiest girl in the street to walk by. When Floriana finally arrived, Leo remembered why he felt that way. She was beautiful. Her long, mahogany hair tumbled across her shoulders, a slight wave giving it a spring as she walked. She wore black trousers and a tight black t-shirt, cut in a v at the front, heeled wedge peep-toes that extended her petite legs and a white casual waterfall fronted jacket. She certainly knew how to dress in a way that flattered her tiny figure, yet gave her the air of a confident, professional woman. When their eyes met, that twelve-year-old began to sweat!

"Ciao, Il mio piccolo Leo!" She embraced Leo and kissed him on both cheeks.

"Hey! Less of the little!" Leo laughed, reciprocating the warm greeting. He reminded himself to remain professional and that Floriana was here to work for *him*. Clearing his throat, he straightened his shoulders and offered to take Floriana's bag, which she graciously accepted.

That had been three months ago and from what he

could tell, she was happy working for him. She had worked hard from the beginning. Her knowledge of the drinks industry was vast, and she came up with new and unique ideas for promotions on a daily basis. As time progressed, Leo felt no less awkward in Floriana's presence, he just tried his hardest to cover it up. As he approached the drinks booth positioned in the main square, he saw her holding a tray of Solserini cocktails. Eleonore noticed a sparkle in her son's eye.

"Ciao Floriana! You look beautiful this evening." Eleonore kissed Floriana on both cheeks who thanked her boss's mother and offered her a drink. "Thank you my dear, Tony, come, these two have business to discuss." Leo's father, oblivious to the exchange took a glass and allowed himself to be pulled into the crowd.

"Floriana, the booth looks fabulous, you've done a great job. Thank you." Leo took in the atmosphere as he took a glass for himself.

"Thanks Leo. It wasn't hard persuading the staff to help tonight. They owe so much to you, you know?"

Leo looked surprised. "Really?" he asked.

"Yes! Just look at them! They're so happy to be here, in their hometown, producing a drink they love, and being paid for it. With the lack of jobs in winter, many of them knew they'd have to leave and find work elsewhere, but you've changed that. With the new distillery, they can stay all year long, forge careers. You've done so much for the whole town, you've given them a future!" Floriana couldn't hide her gratitude.

Setting up in Erice had been a gamble, Leo had known that, and he couldn't have been sure that the drink would be so successful, but with Floriana on board they had opportunities appearing out of nowhere it seemed. They were a good team.

"Come Floriana, tell the others to take a break. Everyone has a drink, anyone else who doesn't can help themselves. It is important that we celebrate too." Floriana signalled to the staff who each took a glass for themselves and made their way over to the bonfire. Leo held out his arm to Floriana and she slipped her hand through. Leo held up his glass and Floriana held up hers. "To our future!" Leo smiled. They chinked their glasses. "Our future!" Floriana repeated.

CHAPTER TWENTY-THREE

*M*arch. The perfect month in Dubai Cara thought. The February chill had ebbed away, and the days were pleasantly warm. She could run in the morning and not need a shower before she began, sit on the beach and enjoy a picnic without the oppressive heat that would be upon them in a matter of weeks. It was Friday. Her day off. She lay in bed watching the curtains flitter in the breeze as the early morning sun shone through. Miles always opened the windows as soon as he got up. She turned to see him enter the room with a tray in his hands. It was also her birthday

"Good morning beautiful." He smiled. He was a kind and considerate man. Without fail he made her breakfast in bed on a Friday morning.

"Thank you, Miles." Cara sat up and let him slide the tray onto her lap. There was something different about the tray this morning. Along with her usual pancakes and fresh fruit, there sat a red rose, two Champagne flutes filled with orange juice and a small black box wrapped with red ribbon. "Oh, this looks fancy! It must be my birthday or something!" she laughed.

Miles climbed onto the right-hand side of the bed next to her. He picked up the box. "Cara," Cara opened her mouth to speak, she felt the panic rise inside of her. She knew what was coming. Her stomach flipped, she felt nauseous. Miles hushed her. "Cara. I want you to know that you, and Azizah, mean the world to me. Every day I wake up happy and look forward to what the day will bring. I can't imagine my life without you both in it. Cara, will you please do me the honour of becoming my wife?"

What could she say? For once she was speechless. This was perfect. The setting, the weather, breakfast in bed. But he wasn't Leo. She had wanted all of this, but she wanted it with Leo. She took a breath. "Miles, I..."

"Cici!" They were interrupted by a squeal at the bedroom door. "Tell me you said yes!" Azizah ran into the bedroom, she hopped from one foot to the other at the foot of the bed.

Cara fought back tears. She couldn't do it to her. She looked at Miles, he sat beside her, his eyes filled with hope. He had opened the box and an enormous diamond solitaire stared back at her. It wasn't the ruby she'd always hoped for, her heart sank. "Miles, I... Yes, of course my answer is Yes."

He took the ring from the box, Cara held out her hand and Miles slid the ring onto her ring finger. Azizah danced around the room. Moving the tray onto her bedside table, Cara leaned over and hugged Miles. One solitary tear traced its way down her cheek. Quietly she wiped it away. Miles reached for the glasses and handed Cara one. "Thank you." He smiled. They held their glasses by way of cheers and each took a sip.

"Oh!" Cara exclaimed, it wasn't orange juice. The drink fizzed in her mouth. She took another sip. "This is nice!" She looked at the glass, held it up to the light. She recognised the taste.

"Mmmm, isn't it?" Miles replied. "It's a new cocktail that's doing the rounds, something a bit different to a Bucks Fizz, something a bit special. He raised his eyebrows.

"What's in it?" Asked Cara tentatively despite already knowing the answer.

"It's a new liqueur called Solsera, mixed with Prosecco. One of our new bar tenders mixed it for me. I've got a meeting with the rep for the company tonight actually."

Cara almost choked. The rep, for Solsera, here! That could only mean one thing. She steadied herself before asking, as casually as she could. "Oh really? What's his name?"

Miles took another sip before closing his eyes as he tried to remember. Cara's heart pounded. "Um..." Miles headed for the door "Ah, that's it!" He called out as he ran down the stairs. "Someone Dolce."

Cara sat in front of her computer screen, she was using the latest video conferencing technology and had paid for Vix and Keiran to have it at home too. She was raring herself up for calling Vix when she was beaten to it.

"Hello." She answered with a plastic smile. In front of her a newborn baby's face filled the screen. "OH MY GOD!" she screamed "YOU DID IT!" She burst into tears. Tears of joy, tears of sorrow, all at once.

"Aunty Cara, this is Charlotte. Charlotte, say hello to your Aunty Cara." Vix pulled the baby away from the camera and settled her back into her arms. "Happy Birthday Car! I hope you like your present." Vix beamed, Keiran sat beside her positively glowing.

"She's beautiful." Cara sniffed. "Perfect." She reached for a tissue but couldn't stem the flow of tears.

"Hey! Stop it!" Vix sniffed back, "You've got me started now!" Vix cry-laughed.

"Tell me the details then, what time, weight, drugs... the lot." Cara sniffed. As Vix relayed the minutiae of the birth, Cara tried to compose herself, but it only reminded her of what she could have had with Leo. No matter how hard she tried to, she just couldn't forget him. She hadn't planned on saying yes to Miles. She still loved Leo. What she had with Miles was fine, but it wasn't the earth shattering love she knew she should feel for the person she was going to marry. But when Azizah came into the room, full of expectation, she knew she couldn't let her down. She hadn't heard anything from Leo, but why would she? She'd told him to leave her alone! She was silly to think anything would ever happen with him.

"... and you would not believe how sore my nipples are! I know it's the best thing for her, but God does it sting... Look!" Vix held the baby out for Keiran to take and whipped out a breast, in all it's enormous, veiny glory for Cara to see.

"Agh! Too much information Vix!" Cara laughed and raised her hands to shield her eyes as she laughed through her tears.

"Hang on a minute!" Vix pushed her voluminous bosom back inside her top and leaned in to take a closer look at the screen in front of her.

"What?" Cara laughed, peeping out from behind her fingers. "What on earth are you going to show me next?!"

"What the hell is that on your hand?!"

Remembering her own news, Cara looked at the ring on her hand. "Oh, yes. That."

"That! What kind of answer is that?!" Vix asked. Despite her own news, she still knew Cara better than anyone and sensed all was not right.

"Miles proposed." Cara replied, forcing a smile.

"Congratulations?" Vix ventured. At this, Cara's face crumpled, she hid her face in her hands again. "Oh Car! They're happy tears, right?" Cara sniffed. She couldn't bring herself to tell Vix the truth, so instead she nodded.

Cara was due to meet Miles after his meeting and although she'd tried not to think about it for the entire day, she just couldn't let the opportunity pass. She *had* to see Leo. She took Azizah for a mother-daughter manicure and pedicure in an attempt to calm herself down, but mostly to assuage the guilt she felt. She spent longer than usual choosing the right dress, making sure her hair was perfect, applying her make-up, all the time telling herself that it was for Miles, to celebrate their engagement.

Dinner was booked for 8.30pm and they were

planning to stay at Cara's apartment in the hotel that evening. Patma had insisted that she care for Azizah, despite it being her day off. The meeting was being held in the Lounge bar, where Miles met most of his business associates. As she made her way through the lobby, Cara knew that Miles and Leo would be sat inconspicuously in one of the booths. Upon reaching the entrance she stopped. Her palms were clammy and her heart thumped inside her chest.

"Miss Cara! It's so good to see you!" Annie, the receptionist who had welcomed Cara on her very first day in the city held out her arms and rushed in Cara's direction. The women embraced.

"Annie! Hi! I haven't seen you for a while, has Miles been overworking you?" She joked. The women made small talk for a few minutes, it calmed Cara down. The women parted with the promise of catching up properly and Cara headed into the Lounge. She scanned the room which buzzed with the light hum of conversation. Many of the tables were occupied, mostly with couples enjoying a pre-dinner drink but Cara couldn't see him. Approaching the bar, Cara addressed the bar tender who greeted her with a warm smile and a perfectly mixed Gin and tonic, dressed with muddled strawberries and lime, her favourite. Cara noticed a lone woman sitting at the other end of the bar and, knowing how awkward women can feel alone in a bar, strolled over. Cheerily she asked if the seat next to the woman was taken.

"Not yet." She replied warmly, a hint of an Italian

accent, and gestured for Cara to sit down.

Holding out her hand Cara introduced herself, "Cara, pleased to meet you."

The woman shook Cara's hand in return, "Floriana." She returned.

"I hope you don't mind me sitting with you, I'm just not keen on sitting in bars alone." Cara said light-heartedly.

"Ah no, thank you, it's a relief actually, I feel the same way!" Floriana laughed. "I am meeting someone but I'm a little early. I always like to be prepared, you know?"

"Ah, yes I know that feeling. Thankfully I no longer have to worry about it." Cara fiddled with the diamond on her ring finger and forced a smile.

"Oh, what a beautiful ring, very similar to mine actually, look!" Floriana held out her left hand for Cara to see, her right hand resting on her stomach. Cara glanced politely as she sipped her G&T. "When will you marry?" Floriana asked earnestly.

"I'm not sure, this only happened this morning." Cara replied, "We're meeting here before we go out to celebrate." Her engagement felt very business-like. Proposal in the morning followed by a celebratory meal booked by Miles' PA in the evening, slotted in after another meeting. Cara pondered how Floriana looked so pleased to be someone's wife, so excited. "How about you?"

"Oh, I am not waiting for my husband, I am here to meet a client."

"I see! I'm sorry, I thought you were here on a date." Cara laughed at the misunderstanding. "What business are you in?" she asked innocently.

"Drinks! Well, more specifically, one drink in particular. I'm here to speak to the hotel manager about stocking it."

Cara found herself concentrating on Floriana 's lips. In slow motion she watched her mouth move as the words filled the bar around her. Her stomach flipped. She heard the words leave her own mouth before realising she'd said them. "Solsera? You're here about Solsera?" Floriana looked delighted. She brushed her perfectly lustrous long hair away from her face, Cara noticed her unblemished skin and sharp cheek bones. Beautiful.

"Here you are! I'm so sorry I'm late." Miles' dulcet tones rumbled behind Cara. "And you've met my beautiful fiancée already I see." Miles leant over Cara's shoulder to kiss her on the cheek before reaching out his hand to Floriana and introduced himself. "Miles Granger, it's a pleasure to finally meet you." Cara felt sick.

Floriana held out her hand. "Floriana Dolce at your service Mr Granger."

"To us!" Miles held his Champagne flute in the air.

Cara obliged, zombie-like. She plastered a smile on her face and went through the motions pleasing not only Miles, but also the staff in the restaurant who knew them both. She cooed excitedly when a celebratory cake arrived adorned in sparklers and the staff hip-hip-hoorayed them. She looked every part the overjoyed fiancée and politely flashed her engagement ring whenever she was asked. Cara could tell that Miles was congratulating himself internally. She knew he loved her, but she also knew that he wasn't *in love* with her. He always did such a great job of painting a public face, of showing how it *should* be. His perfect life, with Cara and his daughter. They were both living a lie but for a good reason, the difference was that Miles didn't know that Cara knew his secret. He was as much putting on a show for Cara as he was for the rest of the world to see.

What choice did she have? What choice did either of them have? There was no way Cara could be with Leo now, even if she wanted to. And she wanted to. The day's events had confirmed that for her. It was as though all the misunderstandings and emotions had come to a climax in her head. Perverse. That's what it was. All the time she'd had to be with Leo and she decided not to. She'd kicked herself so hard inside as each minute ticked by that her heart was battered and bruised. She only had herself to blame for the situation she'd created. When she'd accepted Miles' proposal, she thought secretly that she still had the option of meeting up with Leo. But not now. Everything was different now. Now that Leo was married.

The moment she'd heard Floriana's surname, Cara hoped and wished that it wasn't true, but she couldn't deny the evidence sitting right in front of her. She was angry that Leo hadn't attended the meeting himself, even to say hello, but she knew why he hadn't. She'd rejected him so spectacularly, why on earth would he chase her anymore? Every time she slept with Miles, she thought about Leo, every time they kissed, she felt Leo's lips. The memory of him just couldn't be erased. She had to find peace with the decision she'd made and move on.

As it turned out, Floriana was genuinely pleasant. Cara wanted to hate her, but she couldn't. She was a couple of years older than Cara but looked younger. Her professional career to date was impressive and she had a major stake in the distillery. She and Leo had only recently married but had known each other since childhood. Floriana hadn't said much more than that as she had professionally steered the conversation back to business, but Cara was surprised that in the 8 months since he'd proposed to her, Leo had married someone else. She asked herself why he might do such a thing. He'd supposedly spent three years pining for Cara yet after she'd turned him down just once, he had married a childhood sweetheart after just a couple of months. Again, Cara's heart sunk. She knew it was irrational, but she couldn't help but feel betrayed.

"So, we should probably set a date, don't you think?" Miles' comment nudged Cara back to reality, her thoughts temporarily shelved.

"We should." She whispered. Clearing her throat, she took out her phone and consulted her calendar. "Do you have a date in mind?" She asked.

Miles looked surprised. "Oh! Er, well I suppose the first question we need to answer is, where will we get married?"

Cara switched to work-mode. "Easy, the Maldives." She rapidly fired information at Miles. "We can't *legally* marry there but we both need a holiday and we can do the legal bit here, or wherever you want really. You must admit, we could do with a holiday and it's lovely in April. A month is plenty of time to make the arrangements. I assume you want a Christian wedding? I'll have to check with Azizah's family that they are happy with that, but I can't see it being a problem. At least once we've had the ceremony you can officially move in."

Miles didn't know what to say. He hadn't expected Cara to want to move so quickly. "I guess you put your day off to good use! That all sounds lovely to me but wouldn't you prefer a bit longer to think about what you'd like? I guess I assumed you'd want a big wedding, like Vix's."

"Why would I want something like that? I can't think of anything worse! Being the centre of attention in front of all those people? No thanks." She lied. She wanted to scream that of course she wanted a big wedding. She wanted the works. She wanted to show everyone she knew how happy she was to marry the love of her life. But Miles wasn't the love of her life, so it wasn't what she wanted. Not with him.

The month passed quickly. Cara continued the pretence of being the excited bride-to-be in public. Behind her office door she treated the event as she did any other, her client in this case was Miles and she did her utmost to ensure he would be impressed. With money no object she was able to book the most luxurious resort, Soneva Fushi Resort and Spa, where her connections allowed her to book the villas she needed to accommodate herself and Miles, Patma and Azizah, Aatif, Maggs and John, Miles' parents and Vix, Keiran and baby Charlotte at a favourable rate. She called her client turned friend, Aiya Thawadalia and asked if she could take up her husband's offer of the use of their private jet. She was more than happy to oblige. She shopped for her wedding dress alone and with efficiency, choosing a backless pale beige silk dress with string straps and a simple white flower for her hair. It was only when she took Azizah shopping for a bridesmaid dress that her emotions showed. Azizah was fast becoming a tall, striking beauty like her mother had been, and as she grew, the resemblance to her father became stronger too, her emerald eyes shone brightly behind her long, dark eyelashes.

"What would you like me to wear Cici?" Azizah asked as the stood in the boutique bridal showroom, slowly flicking her way through rails.

The question took Cara by surprise, she looked up from her phone. "Well, whatever you like I guess."

"Well, surely you have an idea of what I should wear, you know, like Aunty V did. Do you have a specific colour that you'd prefer?" For the first time, Azizah was losing her patience with Cara, who quickly realised her lack of enthusiasm for the wedding was not being as well hidden as she had thought.

"I'm sorry Zizi, I've had a lot on at work. Let's see." She put her phone in her bag and held Azizah by the shoulders, fussing around her as though she were a dressmaker. She smoothed her long dark hair and stared into her eyes before pushing her around into a twirl. Azizah giggled. "I would say that Madamoiselle would suit any colour but in particular a baby blue might be nice, or perhaps a nice golden chiffon which will complement both her hair and eyes." She danced exaggeratedly over towards the rails and ran her hands along the silk, satin and chiffon bridesmaid dresses, stopping at the end in a pronounced curtsey.

Azizah rolled her eyes. "Do you *have* to be so embarrassing?" she hid her pinking cheeks from the assistants who were peering from the other end of the shop. Cara picked out a satin dress with a large underskirt. Azizah wrinkled her nose and shook her head. Cara returned to the rail and picked out another similarly poofy number. Azizah shook her head, more defiantly this time.

"Well, what do *you* want to wear then?" Cara asked, her hands on her hips.

Aziziah approached the rail. She was only eleven, but her body was already showing the early signs of womanhood. Evidently, she had already scanned the rails and chosen a dress she'd had her eye on. Reaching for the hanger, Azizah pulled out a long, simple peach satin dress with a cream chiffon overlay that covered her shoulders. Gently tapered at the waist, the bodice was lightly embroidered with cream beads and a peach satin belt tied in a long bow at the back. Azizah held it up hopefully, her eyes pleading with Cara to allow her to wear it.

Cara nodded. "It's beautiful. Very grown up. Try it on." As Azizah sashayed towards the changing rooms, Cara's smile faded. If only she could feel the same anticipation for her wedding day.

The sales assistant who had helped Azizah change pulled aside the curtain to the dressing room and stood back, a large grin spread across her face. Shyly Azizah took a few steps towards Cara. Her emotions took Cara by surprise.

"Zizi! You look stunning!" Azizah swished the chiffon overlay, a reminder that she was still on the cusp of childhood. "That's definitely the one. Ummi would be so proud of you." Cara wiped the tears that stained her cheeks.

Azizah reached out and Cara pulled her close. "She would be proud of you too, Cici."

PART THREE
2017

CHAPTER TWENTY-FOUR

*I*t was the evening before Azizah's twenty-first birthday party and Cara was more nervous than before any other event she'd organised. She so desperately wanted it to go well for Azizah, not only because her friends would be there, but because it was an important event for the Arabic family. It was an opportunity for Azizah, should she want it, to be introduced to a suitor. Azizah was typically stoic about the option. Thus far she hadn't met anyone she liked enough to date and so she couldn't rule out the option of her family choosing for her, but she also had a keen business head on her shoulders and was keen to join Moon Shine Events. Traditionally if she were to marry, there would be the expectation of continuing the family line sooner rather than later. The Carter-Granger Clan, Cara, Miles and Azizah, socialised with the family every few months and they were keen for Azizah to respect their traditions.

Azizah had requested that Miles and Cara take her out for dinner, which they were happy to arrange. It was something they often did when they were first married but as Azizah had grown up and become more independent, Miles are Cara threw themselves into their work whilst Azizah studied hard. Tonight, Miles had booked the private dining room at 'Atmosphere' for the meal, on the 122nd floor of the Burj Khalifa, it was the highest venue in Dubai. Bookings were almost impossible but for Miles a table would be available anywhere. He had kept the venue for the evening a secret.

"Bapi!" Azizah exclaimed as Aatif drove up to the entrance of the hotel. "How did you...?"

Miles grinned at Azizah, relieved at her excitement. "I thought you might like to try it here, I know how much you love seafood. You know you could have brought a friend with you."

"No, I wanted this evening to be just about us. Thank you though." She reached across the back seat to hold Cara's hand.

Cara, who had been mentally checking off her to-do list for the following day was nudged into the present. "That's nice Zizi. Very considerate of you." She smiled, suspecting there was more to this evening than she'd originally thought.

Aatif opened the rear door of the Mercedes and wished the family a lovely evening before promising to meet them later. Miles held out either arm and Cara and Azizah took one each. As the doors to the elevator opened on to the 122nd floor, the aroma of freshly cooked scallops and garlic wafted toward them. The chefs cooked in an open kitchen and the restaurant was buzzing with the chatter of excited clientele who were watching four chefs as they flambéed the house special dish in time to music. Jané, the most respected Maître D' in Dubai, welcomed the family with open arms and led them to the private dining where they had the best view of the Dubai fountains. Darren, the celebrated UK chef who'd been headhunted for the restaurant was waiting for them with a bottle of Champagne in his hands.

"Miss Azizah. Many happy returns for your birthday!"

"Thank you, Darren!" She hugged the chef. "Thank you Bapi, this is amazing!"

Despite her privileged upbringing Azizah was genuinely appreciative. The death of her mother had taught her to never take anything for granted and every day she was thankful for her family.

Cara reached affectionately for Miles' hand. "Miles, it really is gorgeous. Thank you."

Miles smiled and withdrew his hand from her touch. "There's no need to thank me. It's a pleasure to be able to bring my two special ladies to a place like this." He nodded in thanks at the sommelier as he pulled out Azizah's chair for her to sit down. "I think it's time we toasted our young lady, don't you Cara?"

"Absolutely!" Cara replied. They each took a Champagne flute. "To our wonderful daughter who has grown into a kind, thoughtful, modest, hard-working woman. Not only are we proud of you but we know Rebekah would be immensely proud of you too." Her eyes sparkled at the thought of her friend. "All we wish for you now is for you to make the right choices in life, find fulfilment. Do what makes you happy first, then see where life leads you." The family chinked glasses and each took a sip.

"I wish you'd done the same." Azizah commented quietly as she put her glass back on the table.

"Sorry?" Cara and Miles replied in unison.

"I wish you had put yourself first Cici. I wish you were happy."

"But I am happy Zizi!" Cara choked.

"No, you're not. Not really. You look happy, but inside you're sad."

"What on earth makes you say that?" Cara met Azizah's glaze but couldn't bring herself to look at Miles.

"I see it in your eyes." Cara's heart pounded. Miles sat silently, watching. "You're cheerful, that's true. You're upbeat too. But I know deep down you've never been truly happy." Cara tried to smile, to put Azizah's concern at ease, but she couldn't. After all these years she had been found out. "You've always put me first..."

"Of course I have! That's a mother's job Zizi." She spoke quietly but with feeling. "Just because I have put you first, it doesn't mean I haven't been happy! Everything you have achieved, everything we have achieved together, as a family. If I had never met Rebekah, I would never have had any of this. Rebekah gave me a chance to carve a career of my own, before that I just had a *job*. She introduced me to responsibility, she trusted me. I don't know what she saw in me, but whatever it was, it was enough to trust me with her daughter. Can you imagine? She fixed me Zizi, you fixed me, you gave my life real purpose Zizi. The day we lost her not only changed your life, it changed mine too." She reached for Azizah's arm and squeezed it affectionately.

"I know what you have done for me, Cici. Really, I do.

I couldn't have asked for a better person to look after me. Especially after you married my Father."

An audible gasp filled the air. Miles and Cara exchanged glances. "How...?" Miles began.

Azizah chuckled. "I've always known, silly." A smile spread across her face. Cara lowered her head.

"Then why didn't you say anything before now?" Miles asked incredulously. He couldn't quite believe what he was hearing. "Cara?"

Cara nodded. "I knew." She said quietly. She looked at Azizah. "But I wasn't sure if Zizi did."

"The clue's in the name!" Azizah rolled her eyes at them both. "It's what Ummi called my Grandpa. She told me when I was four. Oh, and did these not give it away?" She fluttered her eyelashes dramatically.

The atmosphere around the table changed, eased. The worst kept secret in their family, finally revealed. Cara eyed Miles cautiously. "How?" He asked, she too gestured at her eyes and shrugged. Miles let out a snort and before long all three of them were chuckling. "All this time...." Once their mirth calmed, Miles reached for Cara's hand and asked, "Did you only agree to marry me because of Zizi?"

Cara had always dreaded being asked this question. Had she been asked a few years ago, in fact even an hour ago, she would have denied it, but she felt that now the truth was out in the open, Miles deserved an honest answer. "It wasn't the only reason Miles, but I can't lie to you anymore. Zizi was the main reason I agreed to marry you, but I want you to know that I don't regret a moment of our marriage. When Rebekah was ill, I made a promise that I would look after Zizi and given that I fell in love with her the moment I met her, it wasn't a hard promise to keep. I had already been living in Dubai for a couple of years by then and had an established career at Moon Shine events. I was happy. Rebekah's illness put my life in perspective. Having a child in my life made me grow up. When I was a child and my parents died, I was sad, but Maggs, John and Vix made sure I still had a family. When I saw you and Zizi together at the funeral, I was pretty certain you were her father. We got on, I liked you, you liked me, we enjoyed each other's company. We were compatible in many ways," she blushed lightly, "I didn't see the harm in trying to make a go of things. That's not wrong is it?"

"It's wrong when you sacrifice your own happiness." Azizah interjected.

"I didn't sacrifice my own happiness at all Zizi! I've been perfectly happy, I promise. We've had a great time, haven't we Miles?"

"What about Leo?" Azizah asked carefully. "Why didn't you marry him?"

This took Cara by surprise, she was certain Azizah didn't know anything about the proposal. "What do you mean? How do you know about Leo?" She looked at Miles, worried, she'd never told him about Leo despite the fact the hotel had a long-standing contract with The Solsera Beverages Company.

"Leo?" Miles asked, puzzled. "As in Leo Dolce?"

Azizah turned her attention to her father. "Yes, as in Leo Dolce. He was the man who broke Cici's heart before she moved to Dubai." Cara opened her mouth to protest. Miles raised his eyebrows, unsure how to react. Azizah continued. "After Ummi died we went to Aunty V's wedding, Leo was there. I was only young, but I remember that he kept looking at Cici, I could tell he was sweet on her. The morning after the wedding we left early, Cici said she had some business she had to fly back for. I was surprised because we were supposed to be meeting everyone for breakfast but all of a sudden we had to sneak out of the hotel and not tell anyone we were leaving."

"You don't understand." Cara protested quietly. "You don't know what happened."

"He proposed to you, I saw him, on one knee. At the reception, outside on the terrace."

"I couldn't have married him, Zizi. It would never have worked."

Azizah smiled at Cara. "You could have made it work, Cici. You should have. He even followed you to the airport! I didn't really understand at the time but over the years, I've put together the pieces of the puzzle. I found this a couple of years ago."

She passed Miles a greetings card that Leo had sent to Cara, it was dated the summer after Miles and Cara had got married. It was a postcard from the Erice. It said simply: *Perdonami, cara mia. When the sands are smooth we'll meet again. LD x.*

"What does it mean?" Miles asked

"Forgive me." Cara replied quietly.

"Vix filled in the gaps for me. We have a verse in the Qur'an: 'Ina ma'al usri Yusra.' It means 'With difficulty comes ease.' All this time Cici, you've been sifting sand, removing the rocks, but now, there is nothing in your way. The sands are smooth now Cici. You must find Leo Dolce."

Miles knew only of Leo by name. After Floriana had the baby, Solsera employed a new rep was employed to deal with overseas contracts and Floriana worked from Sicily. Leo had never ventured to Dubai as far as they knew.

"I understand." Miles commented calmly. "I understand why you agreed to marry me, but I feel dreadful that I've stolen something you can't ever regain."

"Hang on a minute!" Cara interjected. "You've never stolen anything from me. Anything I gave to you both, I gave willingly. My energy, my time, my love!" Tears filled her eyes again. "Just because I loved Leo, once, doesn't mean he was the right man for me. At lot happened between us but the reality was that we fell in love at the wrong time, we were too young. We both had lives to live, and lessons to learn. Leo learnt his when he gave me up to chase his dreams. I didn't stop him because I loved him. If I had stopped him going travelling he would never have forgiven me, I would never have forgiven myself."

"So why didn't you get back together when he

returned?" Miles asked, genuinely interested. He had always known he was second best for Cara, he just didn't know who to.

"There was a bit of a misunderstanding. It was my fault. It was down, to some extent, to my immaturity. By the time I realised what I'd done, it was too late. I wasn't prepared to give up my life in Dubai and my new daughter. The need to be with her was far greater than the need to be with Leo. Nobody could understand what Zizi was going through better than I, there was no way I was taking away the stability she needed." Azizah wiped a tear from her cheek. "I'd finally become a woman, a mother. Leo had romantic visions of me giving up my hopes and dreams and moving to Sicily to complete this perfect fairytale he had concocted in his head. The drink, the business, the romantic proposal at my best friend's wedding...none of these things were what *I* wanted. How could Leo possibly know *what* I wanted? We hadn't seen each other for a couple of years and by the time we met again at Vix's wedding, I was a different person. He had broken my heart once and I didn't have the strength for it to happen again. The pull of the known was too much. That's why we left early the next day, Zizi. I couldn't change the path we had already begun to tread together. I loved you more." She turned to Miles. "And you Miles. I've loved you. You weren't my first love, but you've been the person I chose to spend the past eleven years with. I think we've done OK, haven't we?"

Miles nodded. He knew this day would come. He'd

tried to deny it, but he and Cara had become more like best friends and were great business partners. Their love life had slowed but when they did spend time together it was nice to have the familiarity, the comfort of knowing she'd still be there the next morning. Miles owed Cara so much. She had taken an incredible risk marrying the illegitimate father of her adopted daughter. If the family had known the truth they would have both been cut off. In marrying Miles, Cara had not only ensured Azizah and her father had a relationship, but she also ensured Azizah remained respected within the family. In addition, her independent financial future would be secure because Cara had built the business up and it now had branches worldwide. He knew the only thing he could do now was what she had done for Leo all those years ago. He had to set her free.

"So, what happens now?" He asked, his eyes searching Cara 's for an answer.

"I really don't know. Zizi? What do you think should happen now?" Cara asked, genuinely perplexed.

Azizah was stumped. "I, I, well I'm not really sure..." she stuttered. "I guess I wanted to give you the opportunity to be free. To follow your heart for once, instead of worrying so much about ours."

"OK. I suppose that's food for thought." Cara smiled. "But can I ask a favour?"

"I suppose." Azizah felt a little embarrassed. She knew that with everything out in the open, nothing could ever be the same and she didn't know what to do next. This was the bit she hadn't thought about.

"Can we just carry on as we are, for now at least? Everything we've talked about tonight, there were truths I hadn't thought needed to be shared. Yes, I had a past, but so did your father. It doesn't mean that either of us has been wanting to change anything. What matters now, and tomorrow is your birthday and your party. We both want to make sure it's one you'll never forget. OK?" Her eyes pleaded with Azizah.

Yes, she missed Leo every day of her life. Deep inside she craved to be near him, to hear his voice, but she'd learnt not to give in. She'd learnt to live with the status quo. She wasn't unhappy by any means. Miles and she had an understanding. Their relationship worked because they both knew what they had to lose if the truth came out. They both loved Azizah more than anything else and would maintain the equilibrium they had come to live by. She wasn't sure what tonight meant for the rest of their lives, but what she knew was that she needed to see her daughter come of age before any other chapters could begin in her life.

"And besides, I *really* want the oysters, I hear they're amazing here!"

CHAPTER TWENTY-FIVE

$\mathcal{A}$ few days after the party, Miles and Cara avoided the conversation they knew they would need to have. Azizah had started the ball rolling but she could no longer be involved in the discussions concerning their relationship. When they did finally discuss things, they agreed that nothing really needed to change. Over time they had become the best of friends and they wanted it to stay that way. They were business partners too, very successful ones, so it was imperative things didn't become awkward. Their priority was still Azizah and her future, that would never change.

Life continued, uninterrupted, the seasons changed from hot to warm, to pleasantly cool in February. Cara and Miles still shared their lives and a bed, although more out of comfort than lust. Azizah joined Moon Shine and showed an immediate aptitude for handing client relationships, a skill she inherited from Rebekah. Many of the clients even requested they work with Azizah for the very reason that they remembered her mother so fondly. The status quo was restored, and everyone was content.

"Cara! I can't believe you've talked me into this!" Vix exclaimed. She was sat in an enormous bubble bath that resembled a small swimming pool, in the penthouse suite of The Mayfair Hotel in London with her best friend, sipping champagne.

"You deserve it Vix," Cara commented as she took a sip from her glass, "after three kids you deserve a whole month in this place."

"It's just so...so, decadent!" Vix gasped. Cara was used to staying in hotels like this but she knew that Vix never had much time away from the children, so she thought it was important she showed her how much she valued her friend.

"You're right, it is decadent, that's the perfect word, and you're totally worth it. We've got a couple of the hotel spa therapists coming up to the room in a bit to pamper you, then we've got a table booked at a nice little place I know near Covent Garden. It's not every day you turn thirty-five you know!" She raised her glass and winked at her friend.

The afternoon was as relaxing as Cara could make it for Vix, so relaxing that after her massage, she'd stayed asleep on her bed and not woken up. Cara helped herself to another bottle of Champagne and then some luxury chocolates from the mini-bar. She passed some time looking at Facebook before checking-in:

*Cara-May is with **Victoria Taylor** at **Mayfair Hotel.***
Two hours later, fully dressed and made-up, Cara sent a text to Miles telling him all was well before posting again:

Cara May: Sat watching my best-friend sleep. It seems I may have helped her to relax a little too well! Seems a shame to wake her! Looks like I'll be heading out on my own tonight after all.

Cara giggled as Vix let out a satisfied, sleepy, snort. She found a plush blanket and pulled it over her friend, ensuring she didn't wake her. She crept out of the room and quietly closed the door. A taxi to the restaurant would take around ten minutes but Cara decided to walk as it was such a pleasant May evening and would only take her 20 minutes on foot.

She made her way along Piccadilly and through Leicester Square, absorbing herself in the sights and sounds around her. She had so many happy memories of London. Whenever she visited, she liked to wander, smug in the knowledge that she was not a tourist like everyone else. With Miles' knowledge they'd visited many hidden culinary wonders dotted around the world, but she loved Clos Maggiore because she'd found that herself one day with Azizah. It was her secret. She wanted to share it with Vix, and she would, just not today.

She checked her watch. She still had an hour before her table would be ready, so she left the restaurant behind her and carried on into Covent Garden itself. She passed the crowds, merry from their afternoon drinking in the sun as they made their way to theatres and restaurants, shopping bags in hand. She smiled as a group of lads in their twenties wolf-whistled their appreciation at her - it *had* been a while. She passed the Royal Opera House on her left and then onto Russell Street on the other side of Covent Garden. She knew where she was going but had no idea why she chose to go there now, it was almost as if she had no control over where her legs were carrying her.

When she reached the bar on Catherine Street, a smile spread across her face. "Hello Nell." She muttered, "Nice to meet you at last!"

Nell of Old Drury was a traditional London boozer, hidden but in plain sight. She'd been intrigued to visit it because Leo used to go on about it being one of his favourite Uni haunts. She pushed open the large wooden door and headed toward the bar, her intention was to find a little table by the window and watch the world go by. Smiling at the barman, he nodded in her direction signalling that he would take her order next. While she waited, she reached into her bag for her purse.

"It's been so long." Came the voice in her ear. Cara closed her eyes and felt his kisses touch her neck first, then her cheek, his hands rested around her waist.

"How did you know?" Cara asked quietly. She opened her eyes as he moved alongside her at the bar.

"Solserini and a pint please mate." Leo requested from the barman before turning his attention back to Cara. "Well, I saw you were in the area and I wondered. I know I used to talk about Nell all the time and I just got this feeling." He smiled gratefully at Cara.

"It seems that *feeling* was spot on then!" She said as she pulled him close and kissed him.

It had been so long but there it was. The electricity sparked inside them both, Cara felt as though a thunderbolt had struck her. His smell, his taste, they were new but so familiar. His lips, oh how she'd missed those lips.

"Sorry guys, we don't do rooms!" The barman chirped cheekily as he put their drinks in front of them.

The couple pulled away, both blushing slightly. Leo paid and, taking her hand in his, led her to a table near the window. He slipped his arm around the back of the chair and Cara let it rest on her shoulder.

"How are you?" They chorused together. Cara giggled, blushing more. She felt like that twenty-one-year-old again. Leo began again. "I've missed you Cara. How have you been?"

"I missed you too Leo, but I've been good, thank you." She stared into his eyes.

Leo touched her cheek with his free hand. "You haven't changed." Again, his lips searched for hers. They sat, their mouths barely touching, feeling each other's breath. Lightly, Leo traced her cheek with his thumb. She sighed, lost to him, she let him kiss her, this time with no interruption.

Over the next hour the two of them made small talk when all they really wanted was to kiss and not come up for air. Then Cara's phone rang. It was the restaurant letting her know that her table was available.

"Thank you, I'm just around the corner, I won't be a moment." She pulled the phone from her ear and stood up. "Shall we?" she asked as she pulled on her jacket.

Leo looked puzzled. Cara tutted and turned toward the door. Quickly, Leo too jumped up, grabbing his jacket. They walked together silently, hand in hand. When they reached the restaurant, Cara asked Leo to wait.

She went inside briefly before returning and grabbing Leo's arm.

"Where are we going?" Leo asked, puzzled.

"To hail a cab." She smiled, a mischievous look in her eye. Leo's expression was one of disbelief. "Oh, don't be such a prude." She laughed. "We're both grown-ups!"

When they reached the hotel, Cara approached the desk while Leo held back, and tried to look inconspicuous.

"Good evening Mrs Carter-Granger, what can we do for you?"

Cara explained that as Vix had fallen asleep earlier in the evening and needed her rest, she would need an alternative room for herself so as not to disturb her. The clerk smiled, remaining the sole of discretion and handed her another keycard. Cara knew that if Vix awoke, she would call, so, guilt free, she gestured for Leo to follow her. Upon reaching the room, he virtually pushed her inside. Barely waiting for the doors to close, their bodies pushed against one another. One hand on her waist, the other holding Cara's hand above her head, Leo traced her lips with his tongue. Cara's body weakened. In all that time, nothing had changed at all.

Cara had set her alarm for 6am, she was convinced that Vix wouldn't be awake before seven at the earliest. "Leaving so soon?" Leo pulled Cara to him and kissed her.

"I'm not leaving but I do need to pop back to my room.

Vix will worry if she wakes and I'm not there. I'll be back, don't worry. I've arranged a little surprise for Vix. Can you stay for a while?" She pleaded with her eyes. She didn't want Leo to leave just yet.

"Yes, I can stay. I've waited fourteen years for this. You'll actually have trouble getting rid of me! I might need to order some breakfast though. I've got a bit of an appetite. Can't imagine why!" He winked naughtily, Cara blushed.

She kissed him on the lips before grabbing a robe and putting on a pair of hotel slippers. She grabbed her handbag and key for the penthouse and made her way towards the door. For a moment she stopped. The thought went through her mind that Leo might not be there when she returned. Leo read her mind.

"I said I'll be here." He reassured her. She knew for sure this time, he was telling her the truth.

Cara was thankful that the penthouse suite had its own elevator. It was early on a Sunday morning, but she still wasn't keen on being seen in her dressing gown heading back to her own room. Quietly she opened the door, thankful that it was situated some way from the master bedroom where she had left Vix the previous evening. She placed her handbag carefully on the hall table and her shoes on the fawn carpet underneath. Tiptoeing, she crept through the lounge and towards her own bedroom, stopping momentarily to listen for any movement coming from Vix's room.

She hung her dressing gown on the back of the

bathroom door and turned the shower on. She stood for a moment in front of the mirror and looked at her reflection. For thirty-five she still felt pretty good. She kept herself in shape. She kept her hair long and no longer needed to use highlights because the sun kept it naturally sun-kissed. She looked at her ring finger. On paper she was still a married woman, she wanted to feel elated about seeing Leo again, but she felt disappointed in herself, disgusted and guilty.

She had never had any intention of cheating on Miles, although she must have wanted it to happen, deep down. She would never have stayed in the pub had she not. Regardless of the fact that she and Miles weren't romantically involved, she still loved him. He was her best friend, the father of her daughter. She respected him and didn't want to hurt him. When he found out he would assure her he didn't mind, but she knew, in truth, that he would be upset. Her reflection blurred in front of her as the steam from the shower filled the room.

She stood for some time in the shower, allowing the boiling water to wash across her body, she let her mind empty, if only for ten minutes. She was jolted back to reality by a knocking. "Car! Can I come in?" Vix peeked her head around the door.

"Since when did you ask?" Cara laughed. Vix pushed the door open and Cara turned the shower off. "Pass me a towel would you, hon?" Vix did as she was asked.

"God, you're fit!" Vix commented, tutting. "Look at your boobs, they're so bloody perky. Not like my saggy old pillows. That's what having three kids sucking them dry does to you!" Cara wrapped the towel around herself. "And you've got no stretchmarks. God, I am so bloody jealous of that." She opened her own robe and pulled at the loose skin around her stomach.

"Forget the skin, what about those pants! God Vix, how old are they exactly?"

"Shut up! These are my comfy pants."

"Yeah well, your comfy pants no longer have a place in your life! Especially for what I've got planned for you."

"And what have you got planned for me exactly?"

"Well, in approximately three hours you'll have a handsome man knock on that door and he may well be expecting some action."

"Gary Barlow? You've arranged for Gary Barlow to come and give me a good seeing to? Bloody hell, Car, I know you've got a few bob, but I thought he was happily married!" Vix raised her eyebrows and tied the belt of the dressing gown around her waist.

"Funny." Cara smirked. "Keiran will be here in a bit. Your Mum and Dad are having the kids and you guys have got another night here, together. However, there is no way I am letting him see you in those when you've got the chance to be together without the kids around."

"What do you suggest I do, then? I can't exactly borrow any of yours, I'd only get one leg in!"

"Gross! I wouldn't let you borrow my knickers anyway! Follow me." Cara made her way into her bedroom and pulled a small case out of the wardrobe. She put it onto the bed and gestured to Vix to unzip it.

Vix put her hand on the top. "Wait. You haven't smuggled a load of drugs in the room have you? Is the plan to get Keiran so off his face that he can't see straight and he'll shag me anyway."

Cara rolled her eyes and grabbed Vix by the shoulders. She looked her friend in the eyes and spoke firmly. "Listen. I know that you and Keiran have been struggling lately, but you are perfect for one another. You are beautiful Victoria. You have grown three beautiful young people inside of you. Every part of your body shows how much you love them and Keiran. Don't be embarrassed, be proud! Keiran adores you, all he wants to do is spend some time with you and show you how much he loves you." Vix smiled weakly as a tear fell on her left cheek. "Now open the bloody case will you!" Cara demanded, her voice cracking slightly.

Vix unzipped the case. Inside it was packed with beautiful clothes. On the top was underwear. Not cheap, tacky looking sexy underwear, but proper, silk and lace sets that would make her feel a million dollars. She pulled out four of the sets and laid them on the bed. Then she ran her hands over the next few items. There was a pretty fifties style navy dress, adorned with plump red cherries, a red cardigan with three quarter-length sleeves and a pair of bright red fifties style heels. There was a new bottle of her favourite scent and a new make-up bag, full to the brim with Estee Lauder make up, perfectly colour matched.

"Wow Car! This is amazing! Where did you get it all?"

"Not me, Vix. Keiran. It mostly Keiran. I would love to take the credit, especially for that stunning dress, but alas I cannot. I chose the underwear, and the shoes, naturally, but Keiran paid for it all."

"I'm gobsmacked! How did he know? I've been after that sort of dress for a while, but I don't normally have anywhere to wear it."

"Well you do now. You've got a couple's session booked in the spa, then you'll be left alone for a while before heading out for dinner tonight. I figured you might like to go where we would have gone last night." She winked at Vix.

"God! Sorry Car! I so didn't mean to flunk out on you like that! I must have been exhausted. Well, I am exhausted, permanently, but I didn't think I'd sleep solidly for thirteen hours! I'm so sorry, you must have been bored silly sat in here on your own!"

"Nah, I popped out for a drink then came back for an early night. I knew you needed the rest. Don't worry about it. Anyway, you'd best get showered and dressed. My hairstylist will be here in a bit to give you a re-style. It's time you got rid of that Mum 'Do'!" She smoothed Vix's hair. "No offense but I think it's been a while?"

"You're not wrong there, Car! I don't get to pee by myself let alone find the time to get my hair done!" She hugged her friend. "Thank you so much. You don't know what this means."

Cara was well aware what this meant for her friends.

She knew she wouldn't be able to save her relationship, not now, but at least she could help theirs.

"Oh, and there's one last thing." Cara opened the bedside table and took out a small package wrapped in a soft black fabric pouch. She handed it to Vix. "The one thing I couldn't trust Keiran to get you." She quipped.

Vix put her hand inside the pouch and pulled out a beautiful leather Marni clutch bag. She put the bag to her nose and sniffed. "Thank you, Cara, it's gorgeous. Totally me...before kids anyway!"

Cara laughed. "Just because you've had children, it doesn't mean you can't have a nice handbag!"

"No, but I can't fit in nappies, wet wipes, Anywayup-cups, spare children's knickers and a change of clothes, can I?"

"Yeah, you're right." Cara sighed, then reached under the bed and produced a similar handbag, three times the size with a shoulder strap. "I guess that one will have to be for date nights and *this* one you can use every day."

"I can't accept that!" Vix squealed.

"Actually, you can. And you will. Remember when you bought me that beautiful red dress for my 21st?" She asked. Vix squinted, trying to recall the memory. "Well, to you it might not seem that important but to me it meant everything. I had seen that dress everywhere, it was *the* dress of the season. You knew there was no way in the world that I could have afforded it and despite the price, you got it for me. And when I put it on, I felt so special. When I saw Harry that night, it actually didn't matter. I think that dress made me feel in control, you know? In a way it changed my life!"

"Well, bloody hell. I bought you a dress that changed your life. If I'd have known I was capable of that I would have started some sort of niche business. 'Life Changing Dresses R Us.'" Vix held up her hands as though framing a shop sign.

"Hmm, think you may have needed a better business name than that to be fair." Cara laughed. "Anyway, it was time for me to return the favour, so you will accept it."

Vix grabbed the bag excitedly off the bed and ran back to the master bedroom calling behind her: "Fair enough, then I might as well fill it up now and get rid of my crappy mum-rucksack thing."

Cara collected up the new clothes and bag and placed them carefully back into the case. She zipped it up and wheeled it through to Vix before returning to her own room and packing up her own belongings. By the time Vix had showered, Cara was dressed and ready to let Vix get on with her day. She hugged her best friend who was still in her dressing gown and told her to enjoy herself. Vix blew her a kiss and practically skipped back to her room. Cara opened the door to her suite to find a massive bouquet of flowers in front of her.

"Keiran! Thanks! You shouldn't have!"

"I didn't!" He moved the flowers to one side so that he could see Cara's face. "I was about to knock, I was expecting Vix to answer."

"Well you're at least an hour early. Your wife has only just showered and isn't even dressed yet."

"Excellent! Then my timing is perfect." He grinned cheekily. Cara laughed. "And I think it's about time you headed back to your other room isn't it?" He whispered, his eyes darting into the room, ensuring Vix hadn't heard him.

"How did you...." Keiran winked and tapped his nose. "Did Leo call you?" She whispered back.

"No, my darling Cara, I called Leo. How else do you think he knew you'd be in London?"

"Why would you do that?" Cara asked.

"Because it's about time you two sorted out your differences. From what I can tell, I think things went quite well didn't they?" Cara blushed. "I'll take that as a yes then. Now, off you go, it's time you thought about yourself, even if it's just for the rest of the day." He held the flowers in his right hand and hugged Cara closely with his left. "He's longed for this as much as you have. Just don't screw it up this time." He pecked her on the cheek before practically pushing her out of the door way.

Cara took a deep breath before opening the hotel room door. She closed her eyes and hoped he would still be there. She stepped inside and opened her eyes. The bed was empty, the covers rumpled. Her heart sunk, her head dropped. Not again. She turned to leave, she couldn't do this again.

"Cara? Is that you?" Came his voice from the bathroom. Cara's heart leapt. "I won't be a moment, I'm just making myself beautiful!"

A smile spread across her face. Cara wheeled her case in to the room and placed it next to the dressing table. Nervously she checked her reflection in the mirror. Would he still feel the same about her in the cold light of day? She smoothed her hair and rubbed her bottom lip with her forefinger.

"You took ages! I was starting to think you weren't coming back."

Cara took in every inch of his muscled torso, still slightly damp from his steamy shower. Her eyes travelled down to where his towel sat around his waist.

"I was just making sure Vix was ready for her husband's arrival." She mumbled quietly. She stepped towards Leo, her eyes travelling back up to meet his. She reached across and hooked a finger in the top of his towel, tugging slightly so that it came loose. "But I think right now, my time might be better spent here. Don't you?" She removed her hand and Leo's towel dropped to the floor. "I hope you left plenty of hot water for me." She smirked.

"You look like you've already showered." Leo grinned.

"Hmm, well I'm feeling especially dirty this morning." She pulled her dress over her head and began to undo her bra. "I think I might need some help lathering up the soap." Leo stood watching her, he couldn't quite believe his luck. He'd finally found her again. After all this time, they were back together. She was even more beautiful than he had remembered her. Her hair longer, her body more lithe than before, not that it mattered to him. It was Cara he loved, not the way she looked.

"Well? Any volunteers out there?" she purred from the bathroom. Leo didn't need to be asked again. Raising his eyes to the sky he whispered a 'Thank you', before closing the bathroom door behind him.

CHAPTER TWENTY-SIX

Cara had another week in the UK. She spent the Sunday and Monday with Leo in London. They took the opportunity to date and get to know each other again. They walked through Hyde Park, sitting often to talk without interruption. Cara told Leo everything, about her life in Dubai, about Miles and about the conversation she'd had on the eve of Azizah's twenty-first birthday. Leo listened intently to every word. He wanted to hear every detail of what Cara's life had been like without him.

Soon it was Leo's turn. He explained how he and Floriana had known each other as children and how they'd got together one Christmas Eve. What had started as a bit of a fling had become much more serious when a few weeks later Floriana had discovered she was pregnant. He explained that after Cara had made her feelings clear to him, he felt he had to do the right thing. Being a good Catholic boy, he promised Floriana he would look after her and the baby. Business was going well, and it seemed the best option at the time. They married quickly in a small village wedding, before signs of the pregnancy started to show.

"You must have loved Floriana to have married her though Leo?" Cara questioned, not really wanting to hear the answer.

"I had known real love, Car, like Nonna did, and I didn't think I'd find it again, not like I had with you anyway. I decided that I could be happy with Flo. That we could build a life together and have a family."

"I liked Floriana when I met her. In fact, the day I met her was the day that Miles had proposed to me. When I realised she was your wife, I knew my chance with you had finally flown."

"But you told me you didn't want to be with me Car! I didn't realise there was still a chance!" Leo couldn't hide his disbelief and his disappointment.

"I know. I'm so sorry Leo. I should have given us more of a chance, but I guess I was frightened."

"Frightened? What of? I wanted to give you the world, but you wouldn't let me." He sounded exasperated.

"That's just it, Leo. I didn't want you to give me the world. I was frightened that I'd give up everything I had worked for - my career, Azizah, my life in Dubai - and then you'd break my heart again."

"But I never would have."

"I know that now, Leo, but I couldn't take the risk. I also couldn't do that to Zizi. No-one can know what it's like to be an orphan. She needed me, more than you did. You also seem to have forgotten something."

"Floriana?"

"Floriana. And your son."

"I haven't forgotten either of them. Flo and I are still married, at least on paper, but we separated three years ago. Flo wanted another child but it never happened. Eventually it broke us. They still live near to the distillery, I see my son, Enzo, most days. You'd like him. He's a real charmer." He smiled.

"Like his father then!" Cara raised an eyebrow. "You and Floriana still get on?"

"Yes. We've some honest conversations in the past couple of years. It came to a natural end eventually. We both agreed that if we had really been in love with each other, we'd have made it through the tough times. We weren't strong enough to hold it all together. And it wasn't good for Enzo, seeing us both so unhappy. It's better the way it is now, for all of us." Leo smiled, but his eyes betrayed him. Behind the smile he was still sad about the way his marriage had ended. He looked deeply, seriously at her. "What about you, Car? Didn't you want any more children?"

Cara wanted to brush this question away, pretend it hadn't been asked but she knew she had to be honest with Leo this time. She didn't want there to be any more misunderstandings, half-truths or miscommunication.

"Honestly? Of course. I would've loved to have had more children. Zizi is wonderful, having her in my life has made me realise a lot about life, about myself and what I am capable of. She taught me not to stress the little things in life because every minute we have is a privilege. Whenever I've been asked before I've said no, but do you know what?" Her eyes welled up, she looked down at her hands as they lay folded in her lap, "I can't help thinking what could have been. I've never felt a new life growing inside of me, the first kick, the anticipation of knowing if it's a girl or boy." Leo put his arm around her shoulders to comfort her. "I married Miles because it was the right thing to do. I fancied him and convinced myself that I could make it work, that I'd love him eventually. But the truth is, he wasn't you, and no matter how much I wanted a child, I didn't want it to be with just anyone. Miles never asked if I wanted another child. I think deep down, he knew."

Leo was shocked. At one time he'd felt the same way but when Floriana had become pregnant he pushed any concerns he had to one side and focussed on the baby. He figured he could make it work.

"Maybe you were right though! I mean, just look at Flo and me. We have a beautiful child together, but he must split his time between both of us. I knew after the first night that Flo and I wouldn't work but she fell pregnant that first time and we didn't really have a choice."

"You tried to make it work Leo, that's what counts. A lesser man would've walked away and not even tried."

Leo shrugged. "I suppose. Anyway, it's not too late for you, Car, you know that."

Cara let out a laugh. "Ha! I'm 35 Leo! And I'm hardly going to have a baby with Miles now, am I! No, it's too late for me now." She looked away, let the words sink in.

"No Car. It's not." He stroked her cheek.

"Yes, Leo, it is. I can't have a baby now."

"Why not?" Leo asked

Cara found herself back where she'd been at 21, trying to decipher what Leo really meant. "What do you mean, why not? Because my marriage is pretty much over and done with, and I'm hardly a catch now am I. Plus, I am the less favourable side of thirty. Did you know that my fertility has apparently plummeted? My chances of getting pregnant are now only 20% per month."

"I didn't mean with Miles." Leo murmured.

"Pardon?" Cara was becoming irritated. Leo clearly had no idea what it was like for a woman over 30. She'd thought about having a baby, naturally. For a couple of years, she thought about nothing else, but she'd had to fight not to give into her maternal urges. She hoped the feelings would pass. She told herself it wouldn't be fair on Zizi, or that she was too busy at work but in the back of her mind she knew they weren't the real reasons. "You honestly have no idea what goes on in my head, do you Leo? But then why would you?" She wriggled away from the arm around her shoulder and folded her arms. She watched a toddler chase a pigeon and giggle as it escaped his grasp.

"I think I know more than you think I do Car." He spoke urgently, he didn't want to lose her again. "We can start again, properly. And you know the reason Flo and I didn't work out? Because she wasn't you. I'm sure she didn't fall pregnant because it just wasn't meant to be. The first time was a fluke, a wonderful fluke you understand, but it was still a massive shock to both of us. We weren't prepared. We didn't really know each other well enough to get married, and by the time we had got to know each other we realised we didn't really like each other very much!" He shrugged, Cara smiled and turned her body to face him again. "But don't you see, we have another chance. A chance to do things properly."

He hadn't planned this, but it felt right. As Cara remained seated on the park bench, Leo knelt in front of her. He took both of her hands. "Cara. I've spent the past fourteen years regretting that I ever left you. Every day of my life I have wondered what you were doing, if you were happy. The day Flo told me she was expecting, I cried. She thought they were tears of joy, but they were tears of regret that I wasn't having a child with you. On our wedding day, I couldn't bear to look at her walking down the aisle for fear of acknowledging the truth, that she wasn't you."

Cara stared at Leo. The children around her fell silent, as did the birds and the mothers chattering as they walked with their buggies. She saw and heard only him.

"Nonna was right when she told me I'd know when I'd found the right woman, I was just too much of a coward to accept my feelings for you. I knew that first night. Sleeping with you in my bed, it felt right, we were the perfect fit. If I'd known how much I'd miss you, how much my heart would ache for you every time I woke without you beside me, or each time one of my aunts told me how much they'd loved you, I'd have never let you go." He took a deep breath. "Cara, it's not too late for us. We still have the rest of our lives, hey if Nonna is anything to go by I'm only just a third of the way through mine, really it's just been a warm up!" He smirked as he reached out and stroked her hair. "I want to wake up with you, Car, I want to take you home and tell all the old women that I've found you again, I want to make you dinner then run you a bath with candles." Cara tilted her head in appreciation. Leo became more animated "Cara, I want to see you walk down the aisle, I want to be able to say you're my wife. And if we're lucky, I want to have children with you."

"Easy tiger! Just the one, I think more than that might be pushing our luck!" Cara beamed.

Leo couldn't quite believe what he was hearing. "So?"

"So, what?" Cara replied.

"So, you'll marry me?"

"Well, I guess it depends on the quality of the proposal." She teased.

"Cara-May. I have loved you since our first night together. I have thought of no-one else. You consume my thoughts. I can think of nothing better than you agreeing to spend the rest of your life with me. Please, would you consider becoming my wife?"

"On one condition." Cara answered.

"Anything."

"That you're always honest with me and that I don't have to ever try and guess what you're thinking."

"You won't have to Car. I'm telling you now that I love you. I can't live without you and I want to be with you."

"In that case I say yes!" Cara pulled Leo to his feet before pulling him close and kissing him. 5110 days' worth of missing each other overtook them both. The passion they'd missed, the love, the lust. They both knew, this was it. At last they were one.

"I still have the ring. Nonna's ring, your ring." Leo admitted.

"I know." Cara confessed.

"How?" He asked.

"Because you never gave it to Floriana."

"How do you know that?"

"When I met Floriana in Dubai, I saw her engagement ring. It was just like mine." She held out her hand.

"Only smaller!" Leo laughed.

"Hey! Size isn't everything." Cara quipped.

"Two weeks. I need two weeks." Leo and Cara found themselves at Heathrow again. He departing to Sicily, she back to Dubai. "I owe it to Miles."

"It's OK. I understand." Leo put Cara's mind at rest. She didn't want to leave him again, but she had to. In theory she was married to one man and engaged to another. It was a situation she needed to rectify. "And I need to divorce my wife! I'll wait for you."

"I know you will, and I will come."

Cara had spent a lot of time considering her options. She could remain in Dubai and commute to Sicily every couple of weeks, maintaining her position in Moon Shine Events or she could step back and officially pass the business onto Azizah. She wasn't sure how things would work out just yet, but she knew she had to deal with one thing at a time. Reaching for each other, they embraced and kissed, neither wanting to part but finally safe in the knowledge that they'd soon be back together.

"I love you Leonardo Dolce."

"And I love you Cara-May Carter-Granger." Leo passed Cara her case. "Oh, I almost forgot!"

He reached inside his jacket and took out a small navy box, she didn't need to open the box to know what was inside. She removed her diamond solitaire and wedding band and placed them safely in a zipped pocket inside her handbag. She held out her left hand. His hands shaking slightly, Leo opened the box and took out Nonna's ruby and diamond ring before sliding it onto her finger.

Tears welled in his eyes. "Nonna was wrong, Car." She raised her eyebrows. "I *had* known real love but living without you just wasn't enough. I tried to enjoy my life, but something was missing. I felt our first kiss every day and eventually I guess I felt that fate needed a helping hand."

"Thank you for not giving up on me, Leo"

"I never gave up on *us*, Car. I told you once that the time would be right for us, and that time is now."

"Then we'd best make the most of it."

They embraced, imprinting themselves on each other's lips as travellers hustled around them. The final call came for Cara's flight and she joined the throng around her with their carry-on cases and duty-free bags. As her passport was checked, she looked back and waved to Leo through the glass separation. The light she felt inside radiated throughout her body. She remembered it now, this was the love she'd missed. For once, it felt good to say goodbye for she knew she had the life *she* had chosen stretching out in front of her.

THE END

ACKNOWLEDGEMENTS

I would like to stay a huge thank you to my very patient and understanding husband, Mike, thank you for your love and patience, you know that without our move to Dubai this book would never have been started. I would also like to thank my friends at home and in Dubai who have encouraged me or helped me by critiquing the book in its various guises, particularly Cathy, Tracy, Stacey, Abbie, Jules, Tony, Jo, Nicky, Christy, Shana, Becky, Jane, Kelly Anna and Ruth.

Thank you to my Mum and Dad, who have never done anything but encourage and support me in my varying endeavours, and my siblings, Lil and Andrew. Also, to the British Mums in Dubai who have supported me with their encouraging words and helped with finalising the title.

Immense gratitude to my very talented friend, Jodi Davies who provided my beautiful cover image, you are more talented than you care to admit. Also, to my lovely model, Lexie, and to Bryan Vint for producing the book cover.

And to Aimee, Casper, Gabi and Alice, you are the reason this book began, but more importantly, why I needed to finish it. I love you.

About the Author

Caroline Meech graduated from London Metropolitan University in Modern History and worked in Marketing before having a family and focussing on supporting children in both Primary and Secondary Education. *Sifting Sand* is her first novel, inspired by her time living as an expat in the UAE. When she isn't writing Caroline can be found working as a Life Coach.

Facebook: @carolinemeechauthor

Printed in Poland
by Amazon Fulfillment
Poland Sp. z o.o., Wrocław

54459108R00176